THE TORN CASSOCK

Sligo Active Retirement Writers

STORIES, POEMS AND OTHER WRITINGS FROM
SLIGO ACTIVE RETIREMENT WRITERS GROUP

THE TORN CASSOCK

First published October 2005

By Sligo Active Retirement Writers
Circular Road, Sligo

Editor: Bernie Doyle
Front Cover: Bernie Gilbride

The writers wish to acknowledge with gratitude, the encouragement and monetary assistance received in the production of this book from Sligo County Council and Sligo Vocational Educational Committee.

SLIGO - LEITRIM
artseducation
PROGRAMME

Printed in Ireland by Clódóirí Lurgan Teo. 091-593251

FOREWORD

In this our fifth publication we leave our past behind, having already recorded our most poignant recollections of former years. Time to move on in our writings; time to try our hand at fiction. This came about because our members often use imagination instead of memory in our weekly writings. We found these imaginings fascinating and one day someone suggested the idea of a book of our own stories – a break with our tradition. So the idea was born,

This new idea was exciting and our best storywriters agreed to contribute their work. The less imaginative spent many hours, and even days, wracking their brains for any sign of imagination and were amazed at the outcome! The result is this story book.

Writing it has been an eye-opener for us all. We sincerely hope that it will cause you to keep your eyes open long after bedtime – suspense being the incentive to keep you awake.

Our Group wishes to acknowledge with gratitude the encouragement and financial contributions of our sponsors: Sligo County Council and Sligo Vocational Education Committee, which have helped to make this publication possible.

My sincerest thanks to our writers for their help, dedication, understanding and sheer hard work; and to their families for their patience when writing took precedence over other matters.

Our thanks to Dermot Healy from whose invaluable workshops we have greatly benefited.

To Martin Gormally a special thanks for his guidance, knowledge, expertise and understanding, so readily available at all times.

We hope you will enjoy every story, poem and article as much as we have enjoyed the challenge of putting together our first story book.

Bernadette Gilbride
October 2005

Contents

The Bent Copper

Nineteen twenty-eight was a good year for hay. High midsummer temperatures following on a wet and windy month of May resulted in heavy swards ready for cutting in July. Marty had manured his meadow field in spring and he looked forward to a bountiful return of hay to feed his livestock for the winter. Living alone in his neatly thatched farmhouse since his wife had departed this life, he had become accustomed to carrying out most farm tasks without having to call on Corley, his nearest neighbour, for help.

'Any self-respecting man should be able to look after himself,' he was wont to say when he gathered with acquaintances for an 'after Mass' drink on Sunday. It was the Lord's Day, a day on which only essential tasks like watering the donkey or milking the cow were undertaken. There was no law against taking a drink; Marty was aware of this latitude and 'however, at any rate', (his customary prefix to every statement), he took full advantage of it.

In The Squawking Magpie where he met other men of like mind, he was wont to hold forth in deep discussion on matters national and local, proclaiming his views on philosophical and political allegiances, without fear or favour. A raconteur of great ability, he told many stories, mostly about his many escapades and experiences when he returned home late at night following visits to the local hostelry. There wasn't a story of ghost or goblin in all of the district that anyone could mention but Marty was able to add his own version:

'I remember one night I went astray,' he told them, 'when I took the short cut on my way home from Clooneen. For the life of me I couldn't understand what happened; I knew that path like the back of my hand but somehow I found myself in the middle of a bog, following what I thought was the light from Hourican's window. The more I walked, the farther away the light appeared. I stood for a minute trying to figure out where I was; the light stopped too. I was confused. Looking in every

1

direction, I couldn't see another light anywhere. I began to realise I was lost; I shouted, hoping someone would hear me, but all that came to me was an echo of my own voice. What was I to do? Would I sit on a stack of turf and wait for daylight? The neighbours would have a great laugh at me if they knew. It was a cold night; I missed the comfort of my own bed and I knew my wife would be concerned when I didn't arrive home. However, at any rate, I hit on a plan. I had heard stories about the *foidín mearbh* leading people around and around at night. There was only one way to get away from it – I took off my jacket and turned it inside out - as soon as I did the light disappeared and I was able to see where I went wrong. I had crossed the path that led towards the fairy fort. By leading me astray the fairies made sure I wasn't going to intrude on their nightly activities. However, at any rate, I got back on the right path and I arrived home before daybreak; nobody was any the wiser. That's my story now. I'll have another one for the next night at any rate.'

On the afternoon of Friday, the tenth of July, Marty looked with pride at his crop of grass standing ready for cutting. He surveyed the skyline to the west, studied the cloud formation and saw the swallows soaring high. Satisfied that there was a prospect of dry weather ahead, he returned to the barn and took from the rafters the long-bladed scythe that had been stowed away in safety since the previous harvest. The blade was clean and rust free – it had been rubbed with grease before being put away. Taking hold of a hammer he tightened the wedges that held the blade in position at the heel of the long crooked shaft and he repositioned the short stubby doirneens to his satisfaction. 'That Corley fellow could never set a scythe properly,' he muttered to himself. Taking the long sharpening stone from its perch underneath the thatch, he applied it directly but gently to the curved blade, finishing with a flourish on both sides of the point. There was only one correct way to sharpen a scythe; he tested it gingerly with the thumb of his right hand. Back in the field he took a swipe or two at growth on the head ridge to make sure that all was in order. Tomorrow would be the day for action.

Saturday morning before the sun had risen above the eastern horizon, Marty pulled the front door after him and with a can of water from the well, into which he had thrown a fistful of oatmeal, he headed for the field. Stripping to his undershirt, he tied a band of grass below the knee on each trouser leg and slipped the long sharpening stone into his hip pocket. Making the sign of the Cross, he started to mow. Taking long studied steps, his body swayed to left and right in rhythm with each stroke of the scythe as it swished gracefully through the grass, cutting a swathe three feet wide and piling it in a continuous row to his left. Before the sun had reached its zenith he had already covered three strips of the long fort field. Stopping momentarily to refresh his thirst from the can of white drink, he looked with a sense of fulfilment on what he had already accomplished.

'On a day like this, the only time to start work is in the cool of the morning,' he mused, 'Corley never begins his work until the day is half over.'

Pausing only long enough to return to the house for a mug of tea and a boiled egg, Marty forged ahead until, by six in the evening, the last of the grass had succumbed to his scythe.

'That's it for today,' he said. 'Tomorrow is a day for rest and, if the weather holds, by Monday those swathes will be ready for shaking out to wilt. I'll ask Corley to give me a hand later in the week when the hay is ready for gathering, although the man couldn't build a straight cock if he tried.'

Picking his weary steps, the scythe on his shoulder, he headed for home. Boiling a pot of water, he washed and shaved, ate a hearty meal of bacon and eggs and reclined in the fireside chair to read the weekly newspaper. By ten o'clock he was already nodding; it was time for bed. He laid out his best suit, his white shirt and starched stiff collar, and polished his boots in preparation for the morning.

Sunday Mass over, Marty felt he owed himself a little relaxation after yesterday's labour. The cool back room of The Piper's Reel was a blessed retreat from the burning July sun. There he met with a number of his boozing comrades who, like himself, had come in for a quick drink before heading to their respective homes for the midday meal. Conversation became animated – nobody appeared in any hurry to break up the party. Before they realised, the six o'clock Angelus bell roused them from their revelry. Finishing their drinks quickly, all crossed their foreheads, reached for their headgear and beat a hasty retreat – most of them, including Corley, would have some explaining to do. Marty didn't have to apologise to anybody; bidding farewell to his companions he set out merrily on the return journey. The cooler evening air refreshed his brow when he removed his collar but he still sweated profusely as he rotated from one side of the road to the other. Sitting for a while on the verge, he tried to recollect how many drinks he had consumed. Memory eluded him.

'I must be careful not to let myself go that far in future. Did everybody stand rounds?' he wondered. 'Have I paid more than my share?'

He searched his pockets – he had no money left from the three clean pound notes he started out with.

'Surely I couldn't have spent it all! Where has my loose change gone? Did I leave it behind on the counter? It's too late to go back and find out.' Struggling to remain upright, he finally made it home where, without undressing, he rolled into bed and fell into a sonorous sleep from which he was awakened by the postman's knock on Monday morning.

'My poor head,' he muttered as, bleary eyed he opened the front door to take in a letter.

'Feeling not so good, this morning?' the postman commented. It wasn't the first time he had found Marty in this state.

'It'll be a right good day for hay,' he added laughingly as he departed on his rounds.

'The hay,' Marty recalled. 'I must shake it out so that it can be drying in the sun. How on earth will I be able to work with this pain in my head? I must have a cure before I can even think of starting. There's only one thing to do; I'll head for town and get a hair of the dog that bit me.'

Wasn't there a snag? He had no money. Maybe he would find a few shillings around the house! He searched the dresser, turned out every jug and mug, pulled out drawers and rummaged through knives, forks and spoons – not a sign of a coin anywhere. If only he could lay hands on a half-crown he would get by on that; however, not a solitary silver coin could he find. In one drawer, a copper coin appeared among a collection of rusty nails and screws. It was a penny, blackened from age and lack of use, and it was bent almost double from having been subjected to abuse by somebody in the past. With the hammer he flattened it on the flagged kitchen floor. It would have to do.

Harnessing the donkey under the neat trap that he used for special outings, he gathered the reins and set out at a trot, thankful that he had access to wheeled transport. The grinding of iron shod rims on the rough road surface sent pain shooting into the depth of his brain but the prospect of a 'cure' kept him buoyant. He was well known to publicans in the town; most of them would willingly allow him a drink 'on the slate' but that was not Marty's way of going:

'I have never gone into debt to buy drink; I must think of another way.' Having secured the donkey to a ring in the yard of The Suckling Pig, he made his way first to the tobacconist's shop where he normally bought his supply of uncut plug. Clay pipes cost a halfpenny each; with his solitary penny he bought two. He returned to the pub and entered the public bar. On this Monday morning only two other customers that he didn't recognise, were present. Johnny, the young barman, was busy washing glasses and wiping down the counter after the previous night's drinking. With the clay pipe firmly grasped between his teeth Marty approached him.

'Johnny, *a grá*, I'm after buying a new pipe. Would you ever throw a drop of whiskey into the bowl to season it before I fill it for a smoke?' Johnny was only too happy to honour the traditional practice. He reached for a bottle of Jameson and proceeded to pour some into the bowl of the pipe. As he poured, Marty sucked hard at the liquid as it flowed through the stem.

'Begorra, Marty,' the barman said laughingly, 'that pipe of yours has an enormous thirst.' Marty didn't appear to hear.

'I have to do a little errand,' he remarked, 'however, at any rate, I'll be back in a little while,' as he disappeared out the door.

There were fourteen other public houses in the town. Marty, well known in all of them, repeated the performance at each one in turn, using the second clay pipe when it could be seen that the first one had already been seasoned. An hour later he was on his way home, feeling great relief and silently laughing at how he had slaked his thirst for free.

'Thank Heaven for that bent copper,' he mused. 'Only for it, this wouldn't be my hay day.'

Martin Gormally

The Captain

So far it had been a good summer. Six-foot Dermot O'Hara leaned on the wooden fence looking with satisfaction at the ripening field of barley, basking in the warm July sun. Yet he was uneasy as he reviewed the events of six months ago. Unconsciously his mind drifting back to a bleak January evening when his two cousins, Donal and Cathal, from over the border called to see him. It was a surprise to see them because they rarely called. Usually they met on family occasions like weddings, funerals or sometimes christenings. The purpose of their visit was not social. They began by explaining that their expert in explosives had broken his arm in an accident, and the Movement needed a replacement for an urgent mission. Dermot was aghast.

'The solution to the problem will only come through peaceful means – not through physical force and needless deaths,' he told them. Donal and Cathal replied that the Movement needed to carry out this operation to restore morale and to show that they were still a force to be reckoned with. They assured him that there need be no loss of life and appealed to his sense of nationalism to help out this one time only.

They both knew that after graduating as a civil engineer six years ago, Dermot had worked for three years in a Quarry Mining business where he had gained a reputation as an explosives expert. Subsequently he had set up his Consultancy business three years ago, when he inherited the two hundred acre farm from his uncle. Against his better judgement he agreed. The target was three large munitions trucks parked in the compound of a base in Belfast. He was to travel to Monaghan town on Thursday where he would be briefed and meet his three assistants, who would be known as Number One, Number Two and Number Three. He would be known to them as 'The Captain'. Another team would have taken care of the sentries. The explosion was to take place at midnight on Sunday and a timing device was to be used. From the maps and measurements his cousins had with them Dermot was able to calculate what he needed. Before they left the maps and data were burned by his cousins.

The whole operation went like clockwork. A relieved Dermot was back in his house when a newsflash at 12.30 am on the TV announced that there was a massive explosion By one o'clock some pictures were transmitted showing the devastation. He was relieved to hear that there was no loss of life. The following morning he was even more relieved to hear that the four sentries had been found in a van parked in a remote area. Dermot was not interested in the huge furore his mission had caused. As usual he went to eleven o'clock mass that morning.

Joe O'Hara had left the farm to Dermot because, from the age of twelve onwards, Dermot spent a lot of his spare time and holidays helping out. Even when he went to university in Galway he kept up this practice and a strong bond developed between uncle and nephew. The home farm of two hundred and fifty acres was run by his brother, Tom, assisting their parents. It was about ten miles from Dermot's land. About fifty acres was given to barley and the other one hundred and fifty acres was given to cattle rearing. Dermot operated his Consultancy business from his house, as it was only five miles from Sligo.

Going over events that July evening, Dermot thought that one particular person on that mission, Number One, had been a woman. 'A particularly capable person with nerves of steel,' he murmured. He thought her image floated up in front of him – slim, dark-haired, attractive, about five foot eight, sallow complexion. There had been an intense look in her dark brown eyes all through the mission. The image faded. He shrugged and went down the lane to look at the cattle, many of whom were standing in a fenced off portion of a small lane at the bottom of the farm, cooling themselves.

September rolled on. The barley had been saved and sold. The fenced cattle were sold in October. These would be replaced by a fresh batch in the spring. Between the farm and the Consultancy he had had a good year. It was not a case of 'all work and no play' for Dermot had listed golf, leisure centre, tennis and fishing as his favourite hobbies. Not too keen on housekeeping, he still managed to look after himself and keep the house neat and tidy. He went home on the tenth of

November for his thirty-first birthday as his mother tried to mark family birthdays with a party. Afterwards he and his father went for a short stroll. They had always been close. Dermot told him what had been bothering him. As usual Tom Senior uttered a few wise words.

'We have all done things that we regret later on. We cannot undo them so it is best to bury them and resolve not to repeat them.' There was no censure in his voice; no approval or disapproval of Dermot's actions. It eased his mind.

'No more looking back,' his father cautioned.

A week later he was jolted by a visit from Number One, now introduced as Mary McKinney from Belfast. She turned out to be the daughter of the Company Leader.

'I expect that you will hear in the news that "the Captain" was behind the large explosion in January and that an all-out effort is being made to apprehend him. Unfortunately there was a mole in the organisation – Number Three to you – but he was under the impression that you came from another cell in Belfast, so the search will be made there. You have my assurance that your name does not appear in our records.'

Dermot absorbed this information for a few minutes and then shrugged: 'No point in my getting upset about it then, is there?' He asked. She was surprised at his cool response.

'I wish I could get to know you better – but it is not to be! One boyfriend is enough!' He smiled, feeling disappointment. The evening was closing in. She finished the light meal he had given her. Then he walked her to her car. She handed him a slip of paper with her mobile number on it saying:

'In case any problems arise from what I have told you and you need to talk to us.' Dermot nodded.

Just then Jessica Logan appeared on horseback. Mary took off at speed. Dermot knew Jessica from the Tennis Club and waved a cheery hand to her. She dismounted. He invited her in.

'I came over to ask you if you had seen a stray pony,' she asked.

'Yes. He is in the paddock at the back of the house – arrived here about three hours ago.'

There was relief in her voice as she explained that the pony was her younger sister's favourite. He offered to bring the pony over in the morning, an offer that Jessica gratefully accepted. The Logans lived about two miles away. Jessica was the oldest of the four children who lived on the family farm with their parents. She was a paediatrician in Sligo General Hospital. Dermot found her very attractive and had often wondered why she had not been snapped up by now. Over a cup of tea she asked him if he would partner her on the following Sunday in a Winter League Doubles match,

'But maybe your girlfriend might not like it.'

'My girlfriend,' he repeated and laughed. 'The young woman you saw is a friend of my cousins and just paid a social call. Of course I will be delighted to partner you.' Jessica smiled at her mistake. Then to her surprise Dermot murmured,

'In fact I would like to start dating you.' She blushed. Teasing him she replied,

'It took you long enough to ask me out – I was beginning to think you weren't interested and I was getting tired of waiting.'

'How about having a meal after the match?'

'I am looking forward to it already.'

They won their match. Dermot felt it was a good start. The restaurant lived up to his expectations. Everything went very smoothly. They laughed over their last glass of wine. Their eyes met and locked. Dermot was smiling.

'To think you were right under my nose all this time!'

'It can happen,' Jessica whispered.

Sunday was a bright, crisp November day. After lunch he picked her up and they walked the beach at Rosses Point, well wrapped up. They talked about their work and their interests.

'I remember when you used to come to your Uncle Joe's farm over the years,' she told him.

'I am sure I would have remembered you if I had met you! And I mean that as a compliment.' Jessica smiled.

'You have a great way with words, Mr O'Hara. You must have broken a lot of hearts.' It made him laugh. 'Hundreds,' he joked. They continued seeing each other regularly after that. The New Year came and with it came a bombshell for Dermot, dropped by Jessica.

'Father mentioned that old Mrs Lynch was selling the thirty acres adjoining your land.' Dermot stopped.

'First I heard of it.' He was surprised.

'Will you buy it?' she asked.

'It would suit me fine – it is good farming land.'

'I suppose the Dalys will be after it too.' Jessica did not like the Dalys.

'We'll see.' There was a determined note in his voice.

James and Michael Daly were two bachelor brothers, who had originally inherited the family farm of fifty acres. They had discovered a large gravel pit on the land, which made them rich and well able to buy any bits of land that came on the market. Over a period of twenty years they had accumulated three hundred acres, but were still hungry for more. Both were in their fifties – loud and boorish. It was said that they bullied anyone who might stand in their way at an auction. A week before the auction they appeared at Dermot's farm indicating that they had heard that he was interested in buying the land. Dermot stood his ground, telling them that it would suit him to buy it. They became angry and left him in no doubt that he would be making a big mistake. A coldness came into his voice,

'We will see who is making the mistake.' And he left them.

'Two bullies, they need to be taught a lesson,' he muttered. He had hatched a plan. Mary McKinney was surprised to get his call, explaining his situation and suggesting a certain course of action.

'No problem, glad to return the favour.' She sounded cheerful. The following Monday night, around ten o'clock, the Dalys were having their supper when they were disturbed by a loud knock on the door. James answered it. Four burly men, dressed in black leather jackets, brushed past him. The last one caught him roughly by the arm and marched him into the kitchen. The two bullies were petrified.

'We hear you want to buy more land.' The leader spoke in a harsh voice. Michael nodded; he was too frightened to talk.

'We also hear that you are giving "The Captain" some grief over it.' Silence – the brothers were shocked, unable to speak. The big man glared at them, visibly angry.

'If you are foolish enough to pursue the matter, or utter a word about our visit, you will certainly join the ranks of "The Disappeared".' They both nodded in desperation. The four men got up and evaporated into the darkness. An hour later the two Dalys were still glued to their seats, resolving never to mention 'The Captain' again.

The auction room was full of curious neighbours, who all seemed to know that Dermot had a visit from the Dalys. They expected drama and were not disappointed. There was no sign of the two brothers and Dermot bought the land at a reasonable price. There was further drama after Mass on Sunday, when the two brothers shook 'Mr O'Hara's' hand vigorously, congratulating him and wishing him the best of luck. Dermot played the game and thanked them. It was a mystery to all and they put it down to divine intervention. Jessica was as perplexed as anybody else but did not pry. He appreciated that, as he had no intention of divulging what he had done to anyone, even Jessica.

Spring was a busy time for Dermot, but he didn't drop his courtship of Jessica, whom he now knew was the woman he loved. On the twelfth of July they had a meal out to celebrate her twenty-eighth birthday. She mentioned that there was a wedding invitation from Hilary Burke, a friend of theirs from the Tennis Club. Dermot seized the opportunity.

'I suppose we should return the invitation.' A shocked silence. Jessica stared at him, almost inaudibly whispering,

'What did you say?'

Dermot repeated what he had said, at the same time producing a small square box, saying,

'Jessica, will you please marry me?'

In answer she leaned over the table and kissed him. She whispered,

'The sooner the better, Mr O'Hara.'

[Extract from work-in-progress]

John Deasy

Uphill for Pleasure

A tour of Kathmandu, the Swayan Buthnanth Stupa and Bodnanth acclimatised us to the altitude and gave us a good introduction to the beautiful country of Nepal. We were thirteen, aged from twenty-six to sixty-five, and had travelled from Ireland, England, Columbia and New Zealand. Our trek in the Annapurna region, was to start from Pokhara which was reached by a nine-hour bus journey along corkscrew roads among the Himalayan foothills.

We were glad to have a night's rest before we started our first day's trek up 6000 steps (each 12 -15 inches high) to Maihabatti for lunch. We had a Sherpa Sirdar (leader) Bhim, and his assistant Bejhardiah and eight porters to carry our bags. A little boy appeared at one of the stopping places for porters. He and his little brother had two large saucepans of water in which were stuck bottles of minerals. He told us he was fourteen years, although he looked like ten, and was going to school. 'When I grow up,' he said, 'I am going to be a business man, run tours. Already I speak English, French, Italian, German and Japanese'. And he rattled off a few words of greeting in each language. He told us that he needed money for school books and I parted with my first contribution towards education in Nepal.

A few of us had a mild form of altitude sickness with symptoms of breathlessness and weakness of the leg muscles. So we proceeded at a slower pace and stayed for our first night at Nandanda instead of Birethanthi. Our hostess at the tea house had not expected us but she cooked a variety of meals for us. Meanwhile we sheltered, by dim candlelight, in the open-ended dining area as the rain teemed down and the thunder rolled. Darkness falls at 6 pm and it often felt like an 11 pm bedtime when, in fact, the time only 9 pm. The sleeping accommodation was in a long low building separated into wooden cubicles, two beds to each cubicle. We slept on wooden bunks in sleeping bags.

On the morrow word had reached Bhim that there was a landslide at Lumle. We made our way down to a tea house on the main road to await transport to take us past the landslide. Heavy rain made us pick our steps carefully. Soon a lorry stopped on the roadway, packed to capacity in the back. Rows of smiling faces beamed out at us. We were expected to climb up and join the others on the roof under a tarpaulin. Four people climbed up while Bejhardiah negotiated with the driver to allow me into the cab. I clambered up to the cab, put one foot into the gearbox space past two men and a child, and slowly hauled the other leg in. The cab also contained two men to the left of the driver, a girl to his right with two women seated behind the driver. I stood in this space for an hour as we drove close to the edge of the road, meeting other trucks, herds of sheep and trains of mules and ponies. I could see clear down to the foot of a two-hundred-foot ravine.

Our schedule having been interrupted we went up to the ridge at Khare and ascended to Changrecot which rewarded us with some spectacular views of hills and streams with outcrops of flowers and shrubs on the way. Our descent to Birethanti for lunch led us to our first suspension bridge into the lovely flower-decked village along the Gandraki river. A group crossing the suspension bridge was dicey enough. Then a silly young man jumped onto the bridge setting the whole structure wobbling, and nearly threw us all into the river. The ascent to Lambale was more gradual and after a gentle climb we came to Tirkedunga where we stayed for the night.

Tirkedunga is famous for its local brew 'chang', which we tried and found very fiery to taste. So we stuck to the small bottles of Russian rum that were on sale everywhere. The booze-up led to a concert performed by the porters who sang and danced while we joined in the chorus and tried their vigorous. rhythmic style of dancing. Next morning we had the usual 7 am start. The weather had cleared and the sun blazed down fiercely from a blue sky as we toiled up the steep hill towards Ulleri with lunch at Hille on the way. I made my usual stop for water at the next tea house. We could hear a radio playing in the house but no one came out to serve us. Bejhardiah went over to the doorway and spoke to the woman inside. They had a brief conversation. Then he turned to me, nodded and said 'We go'. Further up the trail I asked him what the woman had said. Poor Bejhardiah looked uncomfortable and said:

'Oh, don't mind her. Take no notice. She is a very cross woman'.
'Why', I asked, 'what did she say?' She said:
'Great fun in Tirkedunga last night. All dance, all sing. Nobody comes here. Don't bother now'. It seems our sounds of revelry must have travelled up the valley.

So far the clouds had obscured the mountains although we were now 9000 feet up. The last part of our upward journey was a fairly long haul up to Gorepani where we were to stay for two nights. As I had been having altitude sickness, the Sirdar decided that Bejhardiah and I should do the last leg in two stages, with a stopover at Nuathanti. A large notice in English proclaimed that a tea house was run by an ex-Gurkha soldier, and there we stayed.

'I served for fourteen years with the British army', our landlord informed us. 'Saw service in India, Malaysia and Borneo. Then I set up this tea house. My son has also served fourteen years with the Gurkha regiment. I know what British like – clean house, everything English style.' He showed us upstairs – four large concrete steps up to the eight-foot high first floor. There we saw the results of his Gurkha training. All was arranged in barrack style, two beds to each of three rooms. On the large landing were three palliasses for the Sherpas, arranged with military precision. I asked Bejhardiah where he would be sleeping, and he pointed to the centre palliasse outside my door. I felt like a character in a Somerset Maugham story.

Later I asked a young girl where the toilet was. She brought me to her mother who took me by the hand, led me across the street, up the usual two-foot steps and along a garden path until we rounded a corner. Here she pointed onward and left me. I continued along the river bank expecting to see the usual concrete hut. No hut. At last it dawned on me that it was simply the nearest bush. When I came back the landlord whispered to me that I need not go so far away if I had to go in the night!

Dinner, cooked on an open, blazing, wood fire, was shared with two men by the light of a Tilley lamp. This was a vast improvement on the average dim candlelight. Both Tom, the Australian, and Jack, the Englishman, were travelling on their own without guides or porters. We spent a pleasant evening exchanging travel stories and retired early. Trees and shrubs abound at 9000 feet. Rice, potatoes, vegetables such as carrots, parsnips, cabbage and onions, wheat, oats and barley had all made their appearance on the cleverly terraced hillsides on our journey. On our way the next morning I asked Bejhardiah what animals we might see on our way. 'Bears', he said, and added when he saw my face, 'but no bears today!'. A long series of steps and the appearance of good quality tea houses augured well for Gorepani. Our tea house was at the top of the town and boasted a garden with tables and chairs at which members of our group were seated reading or writing. As yet we had not seen the mountains. Some of the younger people went up to the viewing platform for the Annapurna range on Poon Hill, but all was hidden by the clouds.

At 5.30 am next morning Bejhardiah pushed in the door and shook me. 'Wake up, get up and come and see the mountains', he cried. In the cold pre-dawn I gazed up, up up into the sky at the cold, white, arrogant Himal that is Annapurna IV. My first reaction was that the peak is so high up in spite of the fact that I was myself standing at 12,000 feet. My next thought, and this remained constant at every subsequent viewing of the peaks, was of the comparative insignificance of the human being. This, the youngest and highest mountain range, has been here for so much longer than us, and looks with as much cold indifference on us as we would look on a tiny midge on a summer's evening. The long fingers of the sunrise changed the colours of the snow from pale yellow to deep golden, to orange and finally back to white. The clouds gradually rolled away revealing Annapurna II, Manaslu, Lamjing and finally Machapuchara (the fish-tailed mountain) – the most dramatic peak appeared. Further to the west, Hunchuli, Annapurna South and Mount Dualagari were spread before us. It was the moment we had all been waiting for, the high point of the trip.

Everybody was so happy that morning. We had achieved our goal and besides we thought it would be downhill all the way from now on. As was our custom Bejhardiah and I set out an hour before the others. We were still climbing!. 'Just to the top of the hill', said Bejhardiah as he pointed to Poon Hill down on our left. We trudged through woods and then green fields to the sixth 'top of the hill'. The peaks were still visible and we admired them as we trekked along the Deorali Pass and descended to Banthati for lunch. Lunch was always a pleasant affair with plenty of laughter and exchanges of views.

Downhill to Gandrung whose streets are paved with stones and has an air of prosperity. There are flowers and waterfalls in abundance on this side of the hills. Across the valley at night the lights of the twin Gurung village, Landrung, shine bravely. It is the pride and jewel of the Annapurna region. In between lies the Modi Kola to which we descended next day and found evidence of a suspension bridge and a private power supply washed away. On this part of the trek we had some exciting stream crossings on single planks and stepping stones. But the Modi is crossed by a worn suspension bridge. Traffic is heavy on this trail. This is also leech country – a colourless insect at first, gradually turning to dark red as it sucks your blood. I had found a toilet spot for myself when Bejhardiah's head popped round the bush, crying 'Leeches', and there they were all over the grass. One had stuck on his leg and turned dark red.

The climb to Landrung is quite steep although the day's trek was short - about four hours. I lay on the bed for an hour and heard a musical instrument being blown at regular intervals going up the hill. Looking through the window I saw a funeral procession passing behind the houses in the village. In single file, the musician was followed by three monks in saffron robes. The pall-bearers carried the corpse in a square throne-like chair to which it was lashed in an upright sitting position. They moved rapidly up into the hills, and from every house a man hurried out and joined them. The corpse is usually cremated on a pile of wood and the relatives and friends remain until all is consumed. The village men had not returned at bedtime. Landrung is a pretty village, with stone-paved streets and lots of flowers round the houses and electricity. Sadly the electricity proved disappointing to say the least. It only meant the light derived from a 25 or 40 watt bulb.

Our trek was now mostly downhill with pleasant wooded areas and wonderful plants and shrubs many of which are supplied here in garden centres. But in Nepal they grow much higher and much more vigorously. We continued to negotiate planks, stepping stones and suspension bridges and the further downhill we went the better I felt in the lower altitudes. We spent our last night on the trail in Luinborg. Next morning the rains of the night had cleared to a glorious sunny morning. An hour's journey down steep steps brought us to the metalled road again and we walked about two miles to the bus stop. A local bus brought us down by the old Tibetan refugee camp to Pokhara, where we had beds, baths and European toilets. It was strange to see the travel shops advertising buses to India and Tibet. By then I think everyone had had enough trekking having walked 90 miles in the mountains in ten days.

Back in Kathmandu we took a flight through the Himalaya in a small plane. At close range on a clear day, flying over their grey rocks, gorges and rivers near the snow-capped summits is an unforgettable experience. The biggest surprise is Everest, which I had seen in schoolbooks as a triangular peak towering over the other mountains. In fact it is flanked by Lotse and Nuptse which are only 300 to 400 feet lower than Everest. So it is hard to distinguish them. I would love to go back again, if only to Kathmandu.

Bernie Doyle

Sally

'I don't really want to go Dad. Please don't make me. You know well there is nothing much to do there and nobody to talk to but Grandma.' 'Sally, just what do you mean. You usually love going to your Grandma's and it will be only for the next few weeks. Mum and I are going to see Margaret's new baby, our first grandchild. We will be in Sydney for her christening next week, as arranged. You know Margaret is expecting us. Poor Aunt Mags will be hospitalised for at least two weeks, having broken her leg, and cannot possibly come to stay with you while we are away. Before you ask there is no way you are staying here by yourself, even if two of your friends are willing to join you. I am locking the house and you, young lady, are going to Leitrim.'

She knew she was losing the battle on all fronts. Her Dad had all arrangements made, and nothing she could say would change his mind. Tickets bought, passports, visas, everything was ready.

Now Sally loved her Grandma but it was so quiet there, out in the country, not even in the town, but miles from anywhere. She raced upstairs and throwing herself on the bed, texted Marie the bad news knowing that in five minutes all her friends would hear what had happened. Usually she loved going to Leitrim but the gang were going hill walking in Kerry and she had been really looking forward to that.

Nothing for it, she started to pack. Discarding her party gear, not much social life with Grandma beyond perhaps a trip to the cinema. All she would need there were jeans and tops, the odd blouse, her swimwear and, of course, raingear. As it was July, the harvest would be on its way and perhaps she might help on the farm next door. That was always good fun. Thinking about it, she had not been down for a summer holiday for a couple of years. Now she might as well make the best of it, catch up on her reading and enjoy country life.

Connolly Station was buzzing with people. Queues at all the ticket windows. She took her place noting the variety of travellers around her: Indian, African, Asian, Eastern European. Having found a seat on the train she opened her paper but glancing at the headlines, decided the people around her were much more interesting. She became aware of someone watching her and was surprised when a girl, two seats away called.

'Hello Sally, don't you remember me, Denise. I met you in Tullaghan at your Grandma's house three years ago. Remember the day you came to help with the hay. We had great fun that evening at the hop in Grange hall, but remember you turned on your ankle and were unable to come.'

'Of course I remember you Denise', Sally   replied.

She had been so disappointed at the time. Brian, one of the lads helping with the hay, had even suggested he would be watching for her that evening at the dance. 1t flashed across her mind that maybe he might still be around. Her spirits lifted as Denise came to sit with her and began to fill her in on all the news down the country.

'I've just completed my second year at Galway University.

'What are you doing?'

'I am doing Arts and hope to be a teacher. What are you doing?'

'Me. Oh I am doing Science. Just finished first year in UCD. How come you were in Dublin?'

'I am working in Dublin for the summer, as a waitress in the Montrose Hotel, staying with Aunt Phil, off Morehampton Road. I just love it there. It's my first time staying in Dublin and I am only beginning to get to know my way around.'

'I will be looking for a summer job when I come back from Leitrim. I will meet you then and introduce you to my friends. We will show you around the city. I was supposed to be going on a walking trip to Kerry with the gang and was so disappointed having to cancel it now.'

'Don't worry about that, my brother John will include you in his next walk. It's lovely hill or mountain walking on Benbulben, just as good if not better than Kerry.'

Sally did not like to ask if Brian was still around but hoped he was. She had kind of fallen a bit for him but he might even be in America now, for all she knew. Chatting with Denise, Sally never found the journey and as they drew into Carrick-on-Shannon, Denise suggested that Sally ring her Grandma and save her coming to Sligo to collect her. Her Dad was collecting her and there was lots of room for Sally too. Mobiles are great and when Sally rang her Grandma she was delighted the Barrys would bring her down with them.

At the station Denise's Dad was indeed waiting and soon they were on their way. Sally loved the run towards Bundoran, especially the view from Munninane Hill, the whole country seemed to be spread out before her - Grange village, Classiebawn Castle sitting out on its promontory to the left with Donegal Bay and mountains behind. To the right majestic Benbulben.with lovely old Munninane Church almost at its foot. Through Grange, past Cliffoney a few miles and the first left turn, down the laneway with its fuchsia hedges, today in full bloom, her Dad's home came into view.

As they turned the car on its wide street, Sally's Grandma was at the door with her arms outstretched and, with a feeling of being home, Sally jumped out to embrace her. Saying goodbye to Denise, and thanking her Dad, Sally collected her luggage. Denise promised to call for her next morning to take her swimming at the new leisure centre at the Beach Hotel, Mullaghmore or, in the sea weather permitting. Already the holiday was looking good and with a light heart Sally waved them goodbye.

As agreed Denise called and as it was a glorious day Sally enjoyed the first morning of her holiday swimming in Mullaghmore in the sea. It was the first of many outings with Denise and before she knew it a week had passed. During the following week John told her he would be going hill walking the following Sunday and invited her along. Denise was coming too and some of the young people from around, many of whom Sally had already met.

On the Sunday morning to her delight Sally saw Brian in the group. She just watched while the others greeted each other, a little afraid he might not even remember her and suddenly too shy to approach him. However she need not have worried. As soon as he saw her, he came over with his hand outstretched and again she felt a warm glow as she had three years before.

'Good to see you again, Sally. You are coming with us today?'

'Lovely to meet you again too, Brian, and yes I am coming.'

They began their walk with John taking the lead. Up through Cliffoney, across the Ballintrillick road and straight on to the bog road. Soon they came to the river. The road wound uphill along by the river which gurgled and splashed its way downhill to the sea, with bog land on either side. The roadway narrowed as they tramped to the foot of the mountain and began the slow climb up the lower reaches of Benbulben. As they climbed the sea seemed to come right in under them and the view was magnificent, with Inishmurray Island almost at their feet.

They stopped for a light lunch, enjoyed the craic and the rivalry, everyone talking and telling stories. Sally sat entranced. Hill walking in Leitrim was indeed every bit as good as it would have been in Kerry especially with Brian in the group. As they progressed up the mountain path the more seasoned walkers began to draw ahead. Soon Sally and Brian were bringing up the rear and were inclined to dawdle. Coming on a large flat rock they sat for a few minutes to admire the panoramic scene at their feet. With Brian's arm around her Sally was in no hurry to proceed. The stillness and quiet of the place on that beautiful afternoon made them speak in whispers in case they might disturb the *karma* of the area. Lost in their own thoughts they were contented to sit side by side knowing they would suffer the jibes of the rest of the gang when they returned, having conquered much higher paths and even perhaps reached the summit. Happy in each other's company, feeling the attraction for each other, that they had first experienced while haymaking, three years ago, they felt that for them this was a magic place. With Brian's arm casually resting on her shoulder Sally was enchanted.

A faint whimper reached them. At first they thought they had imagined it; again they heard something some distance away. Brian was on his feet at once calling back and trying to detect the source of the sound. He climbed on top of the rock and then on to another a short distance away, on to another in the direction of the sound. The whimper was closer. He kept calling, trying to locate the dog from which the whimpers were coming. Just then the dog answered with a feeble bark and, looking down, he saw a ledge behind an outcrop of heather. He realised there was a man lying on the ledge some twenty or more feet down with a dog beside him. As there was no movement from the man he feared he might be dead. The dog was beside him with its head across the man's chest. While trying to reassure and comfort the dog Brian turned to Sally who had followed him.

'I rang Denise on my mobile,' she said. 'She has alerted John and he and the others are on their way down to us. Thank God I had my mobile with me. Help is coming.' She was clearly visible on the high rock and in no time John joined them. He had brought ropes in his knapsack with him, as he always did, just in case anything went wrong. He proceeded to organise himself to go down by rope to the ledge to see what he could do as they waited for help. He had already rung his father, and the mountain rescue team. John and Brian decided to climb down, the others holding the rope, which they had secured firmly around a large rock. After many slips and rope tugs they reached the ledge. Inching their way along the ledge they were relieved to find the man alive. They tried to assess the extent of his injuries and those of the dog. The dog's paw was caught under a heavy stone and it appeared to be crushed. He whimpered when they touched him. The man was only semi-conscious and moaning. Fearing he was suffering from hypothermia, they covered him with their jackets. Soon the rescue team arrived with stretchers and blankets. Lowering the stretcher to the ledge John and Brian succeeded in easing the man and dog, whom they had freed, on to the stretcher. A big cheer went up as it was lifted to the top closely followed by Brian and John. By then a helicopter had arrived and the stretcher was winched up and brought to nearby Sligo Hospital, where a medical crew was waiting. All made for home, glad that their hill walking had a happy ending and thanking God they had decided to go on the mountain that day.

Next morning Brian and John went to the hospital and were glad to see the man propped up in bed recovering. He had spent the night on the ledge. The dog, while trying to free itself, lay as close as possible and by its warmth helped to keep him alive. Luckily it had been dry and he had not tried to move, as there was a sheer drop of hundreds of feet from that ledge. He had suffered some broken ribs and a broken collarbone. His leg was badly lacerated, but that was all. He was indeed lucky to be alive. Though still groggy, he realised that the dog, which had followed him from the village, had saved his life with its whimpers, and the heat from its body during the night, had helped keep him warm. He had been able to give his name: Alfredo Orbansi from near Riva, Lake Garda, Northern 1taly and have his family informed of his accident. On hearing all this when they came home, Sally could only marvel at the bravery of Brian and John, their presence of mind and competence in a time of emergency. As they had sat around the fire the night before, they had realised that one false move could have spelt disaster for all concerned.

Sally learned that Brian was a third year engineering student at Galway University and would be coming to Dublin when he qualified, in a year's time. He was already making sure she would be waiting for him. He was arranging to visit her over the summer and the following term. She still had two week's holiday left and they made plans to spend as much of this time as possible together. John, who ran his father's farm, and was a lifelong friend of Brian's, would be glad of their help if needed with the harvesting. Sally thought of how she had hated coming to Leitrim but now she was in no hurry to go back to the city.

Sally was anxious about the dog, which was a stray, and at present was a patient in the Vet's clinic having his paw treated. Everybody's pet, he was lapping up all the attention. She kept wondering if perhaps her Grandma might find a place for him with her or knew of a good home for him. He really was a nice little fellow though still little more than a puppy. In the end it was John who gave him a home. As he was part collie he should be easily trained to gather sheep or even bring home the cows for milking. Sally was overjoyed knowing he would be well looked after. Alfredo was determined he would keep him in dog food for the rest of his life.

Two weeks later she and Brian went again to visit Alfredo in hospital. Well on the road to recovery he told them a lot about his home at the foot of the Italian Alps, where he was well used to mountaineering.

'That evening I was to climb Benbulben with my friend who was travelling with me. Unfortunately he received news of an emergency at his home and he was forced to cancel the rest of his holiday. However I decided to do the climb alone. As I started the climb the dog joined me and I was glad of his company. As I stood admiring the view near a thick clump of heather I slipped and fell and the dog fell with me. I was lucky that the narrow ledge broke my fall and that rock that trapped the dog's paw must have hit me too. I could not move and must have passed out as everything was very hazy until I woke up in hospital.' Alfredo invited them to his home for a long holiday at the end of the summer, promising to show them the Alps with their snow-capped peaks, vineyards on their lower slopes, beautiful gardens at their feet and to take them sailing on Lake Garda.

It was a happy Sally who met her parents at Dublin Airport and having listened to their stories of Megan, their first granddaughter, and heard all about Margaret's new home they were suitably impressed at Sally's own adventure while holidaying with her Grandma.

Over the following year Brian came to Dublin as often as possible, accompanying Sally to college events, concerts and dances. He became a regular visitor to her home in Rathfarnham. Sally enjoyed all the attention and his company but was secretly getting a little tired of it all. She could not understand herself but felt restless and discontented even in Brian's company. She sometimes wished that he were not coming. So she was not at all unhappy when the intervals between his visits began to stretch. She suspected there was a girl in Galway, of whom he often spoke admiringly. She would be glad to be free again, as she was not eager to settle down yet. When she had obtained her degree she wanted to see the world. Having visited Alfredo in Italy with John and Brian last autumn she had fallen a little in love with that historic country. She hoped to work in Italy and see its famous places at her leisure not just as a tourist. Her degree in Science would surely open doors and she felt her Italian was improving since joining a language class in the city.

Her father was her biggest problem now. She was afraid he might not agree to all this. One day she arranged to meet Denise, who was teaching in Galway and was up for a meeting in the city. She discussed her plans and worries with her and Denise decided to throw in her lot with Sally. She would take a sabbatical year and together they would tour. Sally knew this would satisfy her Dad, knowing that as long as she had a reliable friend with her he would be happy to let her go. So, with a good degree under her belt they set out on their travels.

Italy first, and after spending two weeks with Alfredo and his family, who took them wind surfing and sailing on Lake Garda and climbing the lower reaches of his beloved Alps they moved on to Venice. Finding work there in a shoe factory they explored the city, its canals, and waterways, bridges, magnificent cathedrals and palaces at their leisure, loving every minute. They thoroughly enjoyed the amorous Italians, who brought them in their gondolas on the many canals and even sang to them in best Venetian fashion. When they were ready, having feasted their eyes on its magnificence for long enough, it was on to Florence for them.

Florence with its bridges, art galleries, jewellery shops, some gleaming like Aladdin's caves on one of the bridges, and famous leather works producing the softest, most beautiful leatherwear, delighted them. Here they worked as chambermaids and longed for extra money to buy some of the lovely crafted goods they saw all around in shops, boutiques and even on stalls in the marketplace, for themselves or their families back home. Again the feeling of centuries of elegant living everywhere around them, the magnificent buildings, the sense of history filled them with awe and they were glad to have made the decision to travel and see for themselves a little of this beautiful country. Everywhere they met with friendliness and had no problem finding jobs or being understood, even with their so correct phrasing, The Italians loved to hear them try their language, encouraging them in every way and Sally was glad she had joined the Italian class back in Dublin. She intended keeping it up when she returned and looked forward to telling them some of the funny incidents when she had first tried to communicate.

As they left for their next port of call, Assisi, they vowed to return when they were more affluent – maybe when they had captured the millionaire husbands still dreamed of, hazy figures of the future. At Assisi they realised it would take them a lifetime to see even a fraction of the country and having visited the old church of St Francis, built into a hillside, and attended Mass in the more modern church directly on top of the original and with autumn now fast approaching they decided to leave Italy and Europe and head south for Australia. But first they simply had to visit Rome. Who could travel in Italy without visiting Rome?

They bought books with histories of the Roman Empire to add to their school knowledge. Some books depicted it as it is today with overlays of the artist's impressions of what it had been 2000 years ago. Armed with these they set out to see it for themselves. First they visited the Roman Forum. Here they walked miles through the ruined remains but seeing in their mind's eye some of the historic events enacted therein. They thought of Caesar and his friend, Brutus, and as they stood on what were to them the steps where Brutus stabbed Caesar a shiver ran down their spines. History was changed by that foul deed. Who could tell what might have been the outcome had Caesar lived. Looking at the impressions of how it once was and closing their eyes they experienced the magnificence of this once columned, paved elegant shopping centre. With its many temples and basilicas used as business centres, what must it have looked like with its white marble-faced walls, its statues, parks and fountains? They climbed the Palatine Hill with the imposing ruins of the palace of Caesar, walked the gardens attached and looked down on the stadium of Domitius made familiar by the chariot races in the film *Ben Hur*. It took them two weeks to see the important buildings: the Colosseum, Pantheon, considered a miracle of engineering, now the burial place of the Italian Kings. By this time they both felt they were suffering from cultural and historical indigestion. Deciding they could absorb no more they determined to head for Australia which they were longing to see, especially Sally, who was in constant touch with her sister, Margaret.

Margaret met them with little Megan at Sydney Airport and what a re-union that was! It had been nearly four years since the sisters met and their delight in each other brought tears to Denise's eyes. They were staying with Margaret and that night Sally and Margaret talked late into the night catching up on all the family news. Denise left them to it pleading tiredness. After a few days when they were well rested and had played with Megan to their heart's content Margaret took them sightseeing in the city. Sydney was a complete contrast to Italy. Here was a modern fast-moving city – vibrant, with young people everywhere, out-going, friendly with no reserve. Life was for living every moment. In the evenings and on weekends the beaches were packed, especially the famous Bondi beach, with energetic golden-tanned teenagers surfing, swimming, sail boarding: the very air seemed to energise them all.

With Margaret, Ian her husband, and Megan a demanding toddler, all meals were outside in the garden, it being an extension of the living room, The swimming pool also a part of the house, gave them a lifestyle Denise and Sally just loved.

They had found work as waitresses and were looking forward to Christmas Day on Bondi beach. This would be a completely different Christmas dinner in bright sunshine, 30º hot. Christmas on the beach, with salads and icecream, the menu was as far removed from home as one could imagine. Turkey they did enjoy but that was all of the usual Christmas fare out there. Nevertheless a pang of nostalgia touched them when the mobile phone rang late that night to wish them a Merry Christmas and to enquire if Santa had found them?

Staying with Margaret was a bonus. It was so much like home and gave them added freedom. They in turn babysat Megan allowing Margaret and Ian to socialise much more with their friends, so it worked both ways. They met and fell in love with and out of love with some of the gorgeous tanned lads – like themselves just finished College or starting out on chosen careers, who worked hard and played hard. But when it was time to move on they did so with hearts intact and fancy free – the millionaire husbands still shadowy figures of the future. Margaret teased them about their jobs, reminding them of all their hard study to attain degrees now lying idle. With spring coming to Europe, America beckoned and Sally's older sister, Sheila, was to be their next port of call. Sheila was a dress designer in New York – the Big Apple and with her own apartment she drew them like a magnet. It was with real regret they said goodbye to Margaret, Ian and Megan, who came with them to Sydney Airport to see them on their way.

They arrived in America in time to see the cherry blossom festoon Washington in all its glory. Having seen all the tourist places, including the White House, Arlington Cemetery and the museums they moved to New York. What an eye opener! Staying with Sheila, in her apartment just off Times Square they got a real feeling for the city that never sleeps. A very different city this, with its towering skyscrapers, never ending traffic and constant noise, it hummed with life twenty-four hours a day. Awake at the crack of dawn they went everywhere: museums, art galleries, concerts and of course, fashion shows with Sheila. Backstage at those shows was hustle and bustle as the beautiful models were dressed in the elegant designs, exhibiting them on the catwalks. The photo calls, the checking, the patrons, famous stars of the theatre world and the designer world. They enjoyed the partying when the shows were over and the inevitable post-mortems as they waited for the early morning papers, where critics with a line or two could make or break a collection. Often, in the past, they had fancied themselves as models, but after a few shows, they were glad they had never tried it as a career. Sally wondered how Sheila could live with that kind of tension every day. But Sheila loved the challenge and the excitement of success when one of her designs was acclaimed.

By this time they were beginning to tire of travel: they had had enough. In fact they were holidayed out, travelled out. Home beckoned and saying good-bye to Sheila who came home often, they arranged their flight, this time to Dublin.

Dublin airport and familiar faces were so welcome. As their parents came into view behind the barriers, to their amazement tears pricked their eyes as a strange delight spread through them. They, who could not get away fast enough, were actually glad to be back in Dublin surrounded by loving families. It took a few days to get used to home again, to tell the tales of their travels and their many jobs in the different countries. Working as waitresses in cafes and hotels, working in crêches, nursing homes, teaching, chambermaids, and shop assistants. They had done the lot.

Sally went to visit her Grandma. Calling to Denise's home, she met John, who teased her about her travels and wanted to know if she had helped rescue anyone since. Ben, now a fully-fledged collie dog, welcomed her too. She was glad to see him looking so well. John, with Ben his faithful shadow, was going to check his sheep on the mountain and invited her to come. She accepted, enjoying the walk. This turned out to be the first of many such walks. Soon whenever she visited her Grandma, a walk with John became the norm. He was always interested in her doings. Whenever he came to Dublin on business he would call to her home in Rathfarnham, as Brian had once done. They would enjoy an evening out and a meal or perhaps a concert. Sally found him great company with a wry sense of humour that she enjoyed.

Sally had found herself a very interesting job in research and was busy getting back in touch with her friends and making new friends at work. For a few months she found this satisfying, but there was something lacking in her life and she just could not put her finger on it. She met, and went out with many men in her activities as she was a member of many clubs, loved golfing, swimming and had recently joined a gym. In spite of this and the busy life she was living she found herself often thinking of John, the way he teased her and the fun they had whenever they were together.

After one of his now frequent visits she realised she was falling in love with John and while he was most attentive and kind whenever he was with her, he never showed any emotional attraction for her always giving her a quick hug and laughingly going on his way. She feared he only thought of her as Denise's best friend and Brian's ex-girlfriend. She wondered how she might get him to see her for herself.

Some months later when Brian announced his engagement to an American girl, John called her at work, inviting her out to lunch. Sitting on a bench in Stephen's Green he expressed his anxiety that she might be upset at Brian's engagement. Sally laughed, assuring him she had long ago outgrown that romance. It was as much her fault as Brian's that it had ended. She admitted she had not been ready for a lifetime commitment at that time. She had already sent Brian and his fiancee, her warmest congratulations and good wishes. Brian, her first boyfriend, would always be a little bit special but that was all. John, whose arm had been resting along the back of the seat, turned her towards him and looking into her eyes could not believe what he was hearing.

'Oh my darling, since you came home, I thought it would be of your engagement to Brian I would hear. You must know how much you mean to me. Oh darling, I have loved you since that first day on the mountain, but I could not cut in on Brian, one of my best friends and had to be content with seeing you as often as possible making sure you did not guess my secret. Thinking you had had only a lover's tiff and would be together again when you had sorted things out'. Her face lighting up, Sally admitted how dear he had become to her and how she had gradually come to love him. Putting her arms around his neck, their lips met in their first real kiss.

'Marry me soon my darling, we have wasted so much time.' With a radiant smile Sally replied, 'Yes, oh yes, please.'

On her wedding day, as she walked down the aisle, a radiant bride on her father's arm Sally blessed the day Aunt Mags had slipped and broken her leg, but was happy to see her smiling a big happy smile all dressed up in her wedding finery. Making sure to catch Sally's eye as she went up the aisle, she gave a very definite wink as if to say 'I had a lot to do with this wedding'.

When John stepped out into the aisle she thought her heart would burst with love and pride. He too gave a knowing wink with laughter in his eyes. Taking her hand in his, he drew her towards the altar and she knew that that would be the way they would face the world, hand in hand, secure in their love for each other. A mature love, giving them the strength to care for and support each other, whatever the future might bring.

[Extract from work-in-progress]

Bernie Gilbride

The Torn Cassock

'What a waste of a handsome man,' Mary said to Bernie on the way home from Mass. She was commenting on their new curate's first appearance in church.

'I hope he doesn't go the way of his predecessor!' responded Bernie. She was alluding to the scandal of Father Oliver Stokes who had fallen for the lure of the flesh and disappeared with Mary Long, the young wife of a local publican.

'Twas too fond of a sup, he was, and she put the "come hither" on him,' continued Mary. They were not the only members of the fair sex who found Father Mark pleasing to the eye, but kept it to themselves. Instead of the usual Sunday sermon, Father Mark decided to sate their natural curiosity by giving a brief outline of his background. He grew up in the parish of Milltown, which was about twenty miles from this parish. His parents were both teachers, as was his older brother, Tom. His only sister, Nell, was a nurse in Sligo General Hospital. Tom was teaching in Dublin; he was married with two young children. Nell, who was younger than him, was living in Sligo – as yet 'another unclaimed treasure.' (The unmarried in the congregation took pleasant note of his definition of their status). After attending the local national school, he proceeded to secondary school in Summerhill Diocesan College, Sligo. 'Now I remember him,' said Dan O'Rourke, a fanatical GAA supporter in the congregation.

'Sure wasn't he an outstanding minor footballer in the college and county – Mark Somers,' he murmured to himself. 'I often wondered what became of him.'

The subject of Dan's thoughts continued to whet their curiosity. After Summerhill, he felt he had a vocation, but decided to take a year on the outside to test his vocation and worked in the local Co-op Store.

'Pity I wasn't around then – I would have tested it for him,' whispered the irrepressible Bernie to Mary, earlier on. He lived the normal life of any eighteen-year-old and when the year was up he entered Maynooth Seminary and was ordained at the age of twenty-four. The following two years were spent doing a doctorate in Divinity and the six years prior to coming to this parish were spent teaching Maths and French to Leaving Cert students in Summerhill College. So there they had it – his new parishioners at least had some outline of his background and something to talk about until the novelty of his presence in the parish had worn off.

Two weeks earlier, Mark had been summoned to the Bishop's house. Bishop Brown was an urbane, genial man, respected and liked by his clergy and flock, with whom he kept in close touch. Mark was not surprised to learn that the Bishop was aware of his desire to move from teaching to parochial work. The clerical grapevine worked well, he thought.

'I have always thought of you as an academic person,' began the Bishop, 'But it appears you would prefer to toil in the vineyard,' he continued. 'Very well: I wish you to take up duty as curate in Rathmore in two week's time,' said the Bishop.

'Rathmore! Isn't that the parish ...?' 'Yes, yes,' interrupted the Bishop, not wanting to discuss the acute embarrassment concerning Father Oliver Stokes. He continued:

'Canon Mullen is getting on in years, and the fall of his former curate has affected him deeply, so I want you to give him as much support as you can and restore the parish's confidence in its clergy.'

'Of course I will,' responded Mark.

Their meeting turned social.

'I hear that you are still playing some football,' the Bishop smiled – he knew that in earlier years, Father Mark could be quite fiery on the field. Mark reddened.

'I have learned to count to ten.' The Bishop laughed.

'Maturity comes with age. I was no angel myself on the field.'

Mark was aware of the stories concerning Leo Brown in his football days. They both laughed. Mark thanked the Bishop for the posting. At sixty years old, Bishop Leo had learned to be cautious in his speech, but unexpectedly he said as they parted at the hall door.

'I predict that you will have a great future in Mother Church.'

Mark was dumbfounded – the bishop was never known to voice his feelings to his clergy. He could only manage a 'thank you' and bade goodbye. Rathmore occupied his thoughts as he strode back to his flat at the College.

'A town with a population of about one thousand, two hundred,' his memory told him. A well laid-out town with the River Mór running through, a good football pitch, was his obviously biased memory. He spoke to himself, 'It is about twenty miles from my home parish – good footballers.' It was strange how his football days seemed to dominate his knowledge of Rathmore.

The next two weeks saw him busy in tidying up loose ends prior to his departure. As it was holiday time, he did not have to say goodbye to his students and most of his colleagues were away; time enough for that later on. The local Mercy nuns gave him a beautifully embroidered tablecloth; he had said Mass for them during his four-year sojourn in the College. Finally, the two weeks were up and he headed for Rathmore, ready to 'toil in the vineyard,' as the Bishop had put it. It was a beautiful Saturday evening in August. As he drove he could get the scents of the countryside and hear the music of its avian population. It brought him back to his roots and his father saying, 'the savage loves his native shore!' He was more convinced now that his wish to move to a country parish in preference to an academic life was the right one: he was returning to his roots.

He was surprised to find his mother and sister, Nell, at the bungalow at the end of the town, with dusters and cleaning materials in the car. Typical of his mother and sister – didn't they know he could fend for himself at this stage?

'Never mind. They only mean well,' he whispered to himself, glad to see two familiar faces. He carried in his belongings, while his mother and sister busied themselves around the house. It was a warm comfortable bungalow with three bedrooms, bathroom, living-room/office, kitchen and utility room. There was a good-sized garden at the rear (neglected), and also an overgrown front garden with a lawn and a garage at the side. He could see that there was plenty to be done, both inside and outside – he looked forward to the challenge. Around seven o'clock that evening they sat down. Looking around, Father Mark could see the women's expertise with brushes and dusters and when he saw the fruits of their labour, he was very pleased that they had turned up. They had a light tea and Mark's mother had stocked up the larder and fridge with all his favourite foods – if she didn't know his likes and dislikes in the food line, who would? About an hour later his mother and Nell left for home. He was lucky to have such a thoughtful mother and sister. No doubt his father would turn up to help in the garden when his mother gave him a rundown on the curate's house. Now retired from teaching, Tom Senior had plenty of time on his hands to indulge his favourite hobby, gardening. Father Mark smiled, 'As sure as night follows day, he will be over on Monday with all his gardening accoutrements', he spoke knowingly to himself. How predictable his father was: solid and dependable, strict but caring. Mark would like to think that he had inherited some of these traits from the man he always admired: his father.

He was stirred out of these thoughts by a gentle knock at the door – Canon Mullen, the parish priest. A tall thin man with patrician features, Canon Edward Mullen, known affectionately as Ned, had come to welcome him to the parish of Rathmore. Father Mark was touched by this kind gesture, as normally a new curate would present himself to the parish priest for inspection and possibly immediate orders. Canon Mullen was not like that – he didn't stand on ceremony – to him it was a normal courtesy. They took an immediate liking to each other and later on the Canon would become like a second father to him. For his part, Canon Mullen liked what he saw: a fine specimen of manhood, clear in his mind and articulate in his aspiration to be of solid support to him and his youthful desire to keep the parish and community spirit to the forefront of his key objectives. Already the Canon could feel the load lifting. As the Bishop had said to Mark, the fall of his previous curate had affected him deeply. He smiled at Father Mark's enthusiasm, the first time he had smiled for a long time. Mark saw the smile and was glad: the bond between the ageing parish priest and his new curate had started to grow. They talked for about two hours, with the Canon giving him a general overview of the parish and outlining the various duties he would like Father Mark to undertake. Then he left as darkness was falling. There was a lightness in his step as he walked home.
'Fine young priest. I must remember to thank Bishop Leo,' he said to himself prophetically, 'I hope Father Mark's good looks don't draw improper attention to him or that he is not tempted by a temptress.'

Laura smiled at Rita's letter. It was full of all the local news and there was an inordinate amount in it concerning the handsome new curate who had come to their parish. Obviously he had made a big impression on her younger sister. Laura would caution her when next writing regarding her feelings for this handsome cleric. The heat and humidity in Calcutta was intense, as was the terrible human misery and poverty she encountered every day. She had qualified as a doctor, following in her father's footsteps, three years ago. She had spent a year in Sligo General Hospital and had come to Calcutta two years ago in response to a plea for volunteer medical people from the famous Mother Teresa. Originally it was for a one-year stint, but she had remained on for another year, as she was so badly needed. Now that her second year was up she felt that she had done her share for the Third World and planned to leave for home within the next six months.

'Home,' she thought, and it brought pleasure to her senses. She could feel the cool breeze on her face, see the billowing clouds pass over Rathmore and hear her parents chatting as they weeded the garden or tended the lawn. All the familiar smells of home were in her nostrils as she thought of it. However it was short-lived, as the pungent odours of Calcutta soon cancelled out the fresh smells of home.

'C'est la vie,' she said and returned to the makeshift hospital to attend to a long line of afflicted men, women and children. 'I wonder how this new curate would like to sweat it out here for a few years?' she muttered. 'That was unfair!' she chided herself. 'I don't even know the man, and he is probably doing a good job in Rathmore,' she concluded and concentrated on her patients. Sallow-skinned, dark-haired with brown eyes, she blended in well with the people she ministered to. She was an extremely attractive young woman, just coming up on thirty. She had told her parents and anybody else that dropped hints that she was in no hurry to settle down. That night she wrote to Rita telling her of her decision to return, giving an outline of the progress Mother Teresa was making in getting much needed medical supplies and warning Rita to tread carefully as far as this handsome young curate was concerned – but maybe she was over-reacting. Perhaps she was too cautious where a handsome man was concerned.

'He is a priest after all,' she murmured. 'He too would probably be cautious as far as women were concerned and he has his vow of celibacy.' A voice whispered, 'What about his predecessor, Father Oliver and Mary Long?' Laura shrugged. It was unjust to be stereotyping and judging the new curate until she met him and that would be within the next six months.

Mark soon settled into the routine of a parish curate's life. He was already glad that he had swapped it for the academic one. He found the people friendly, if a bit reserved.

'This is only natural,' he explained to himself. 'After all, they had an unusual and, to many, a hurtful experience with my predecessor, who seduced a young married woman whose husband and three young children were liked in the community. The people have every right to be cautious,' he reasoned. He ploughed on, starting his day with 8.30am Mass and Canon Mullen said Mass at 10.00 am. He became involved in local organisations, getting to meet the parishioners on their own ground and steadily gaining their confidence and respect, never forcing his view, but still making his contribution to debates. He had found that Irish society expected its clergy to lead in community affairs. Sometimes this could be good, and other times it could be counterproductive, depending on the temperament of the clergyman. Mark himself felt that in the past it might have been a good system, where the priest was thought to be omnipotent, but now every community had well-educated parishioners in its midst, well capable of running various organisations very successfully. There were also some active retired people who were well able to make a contribution to the well being of the parish and Father Mark made a special effort to get them involved.

Slowly but surely he made steady progress in establishing himself in the community. Probably the best barrier breakdown occurred when he played an important role in helping Rathmore Gaelic Football club to become County Champions after a long period in the doldrums. His connection with and contribution to the Club opened many doors for him as Gaelic football still held a strong place in rural Ireland. For his part, Canon Mullen was delighted to have a curate so in touch with the community.

'So what if he shows an odd flash of steel on the field and forgets to count to ten, he is only human after all.' The Canon spoke softly to him. 'Only human,' he repeated to himself, conscious that Mark was a physically attractive man according to the confession of a few lustful women in the parish. The confessional was sacrosanct. He wasn't unduly worried as he felt Mark would be able to handle any unsolicited attention!

'How the time has flown,' exclaimed Mark. 'Where have the last six months gone?' he asked himself, knowing full well that when one is happy in an environment time really flies. He was sitting by the fire on a cold February evening, looking at his diary for the coming week. Saturday 20, 9.00 pm – visit Burkes for a homecoming party. Doctor Laura Burke was returning from Calcutta to the bosom of her family. 'It should be interesting to talk to her.' Mark always had a curiosity about faraway places, their people and their customs. 'Maybe Laura will prove to be an interesting conversationalist.' He continued to browse through his diary.

'Not too onerous – two christenings and a wedding this coming week, and maybe a funeral. Old John Styles told me that he had his bags packed when I visited him on Monday. Wouldn't it be great if everybody got that opportunity,' he mused to himself.

As usual the days sped by, and suddenly it was Saturday evening. Mass over, he returned home, had a shower and prepared for his visit to Burkes. As such, he wasn't really a party person, but the Burkes had gone out of their way to make him feel welcome and he enjoyed their company. If Laura was anything like them he felt that they would get on well too. From what he heard, she was around his age and a stunning looking woman! 'Less of the stunning,' he chided himself as he closed the front door and made his way to Burkes. Laura happened to be in the hallway when Mark rang the doorbell and she answered it. They were face to face. Not having been introduced, she studied him for a minute and then she knew.

'Father Mark, I presume?'

'Yes. Laura, I presume'.

They both laughed at this introduction to themselves. He entered the hallway, taking off his overcoat. She studied him. Yes, Rita's description of him in her letter was accurate. He was handsome, too handsome to be a priest. What a waste! Father Mark was far too discreet to pass any comment on the appearance of this beautiful woman who had admitted him. 'Stunning does appear to be appropriate,' he thought.

She brought him into the large sitting room where he shook hands with her parents who greeted him warmly, and Doctor Burke handed him a well-diluted tumbler of whiskey. Mark mingled with the other guests, but found it a bit disconcerting to find Laura's eyes on him whenever he glanced around the room. He thought of one of his mother's favourite songs, 'Some enchanted evening, you may see a stranger.' He hummed it quietly to himself. When he came to the bit 'and somehow you know,' he stopped abruptly, chiding himself.

'Tu es sacerdos in aeternum – thou art a priest forever, so pull yourself together and remember your vows.' Nobody noticed his temporary discomfort and he regained his composure. Whether it was telepathy or not, Laura felt that Mark had reacted as most men reacted in her company for the first time, and gave a secret smile.

'Priest or no priest – I want him,' she whispered secretly. Then she was utterly shocked at her desire for this man. He was a priest and she felt like a heretic. Thus the thoughts of both Laura and Mark went from sanity to insanity at their first meeting. They all moved into the drawing room, lined up to have their plates filled by Mary, the Burkes' longstanding housekeeper, and returned to the sitting room to consume their chosen dish. Mark was partial to fish, especially salmon, while Laura liked cold turkey. They were standing close, eating their meal, making small conversation, while at the same time studying each other. Mark, always self-assured and confident, was to say the least, uncomfortable, although he kept up a façade that didn't' show it. Laura was different: she could 'feel' Mark's discomfort and took pleasure in it.

After the meal they all sat around chatting, starting with the weather, moving on to politics and then religion.

'What do you think of priestly celibacy, Father Mark?' asked John Lang in a loud voice. There was total silence for a minute, then Mark launched into a ten minute dissertation on the subject, defending it and explaining it in great detail with compassion and eloquence. Another silence as they ingested his speech. Delighted with this exposition, Canon Mullen blurted,

'Well said, Mark, but what else would we expect, and you with your Doctorate in Divinity!'

'So you are a doctor, too?' murmured Laura, teasing him.

He smiled – an enigmatic smile. If only she could read his thoughts, they were in direct contradiction with what he had said about celibacy. Laura went to powder her nose and Mark was called to the front door with a message that John Styles was looking for the Last Rites. Putting on his coat, he walked quickly to his house, collected the Holy Oils and headed for John Styles' house. Two hours later John died. Mark had stayed with him to the end. It was too late to return to Burkes. He would probably see Laura soon and apologise for his quick departure.

Normally Sunday would be an easygoing day for Mark, but this Sunday was not a tranquil one for him: it was a day of turmoil and questioning his vocation. His thoughts turned to the night before, and his first meeting with Laura. The immediate whiff of cordite between them, their eyes hungrily searching the room for each other, the unspoken body language sending illicit messages to each other. Waves of desire swept over him as he conjured up her image. Was he going mad? Was his vocation being tested? He shook himself as if to banish these unbecoming thoughts from his person. He would go for his favourite walk through the nearby woods. That should help. Half a mile away, Laura was also in turmoil. She was appalled at her thoughts of Mark. A priest. What was wrong with her? She felt like Eve in the Garden of Eden, coveting the forbidden fruit, and Father Mark is surely the 'forbidden fruit', even if his body language at last night's party signalled that he was ripe for picking.

'I must be wanton,' she whispered to herself. Falling for a priest, knowing that it will cause untold pain and going against all that she believed in over the years. A priest was a 'No Go Area' in her makeup; hadn't she castigated Rita in correspondence for what had seemed like a crush on this handsome curate. Yet the more she tried to dismiss him from her mind, the more she was filled with a strong glow of desire at the thought of him. As if in telepathic communication with Mark, she stirred herself to shake off these overpowering thoughts of him. 'A walk in the woods might help,' she thought and changed into something suitable.

At the same time Mark was changing into his tracksuit, warm jumper and runners, and making his way to the wood, not knowing that Laura was entering it two miles away. It was late spring, but the days were still short. He loved this walk and found it very invigorating. He pushed Laura to the back of his mind. He was determined that he would resolve the problem. After all Mother Church came first, no matter what obstacles were put in his way. He was startled to see a woman running towards him along the woodland path. She was obviously in panic and ran straight into his arms, holding on to him tightly, trembling. Then her would-be assailant appeared, saw Mark and turned to run back. Mark made to go after him, but Laura clung tight to him.

'Don't leave me, Mark,' she whispered. It was Laura. His arms tightened around, her head rested on his shoulder. He could smell her perfume and feel the firm contours of her body pressing against him. He was filled with a warm glow of desire; his earlier thoughts of resolving the problem evaporated. She lifted her head, her lips slightly parted, smiling, inviting him. He bent his head in response; his lips found hers. She responded to his tight embrace, murmuring, 'Mark, Mark', in a muffled voice. A man and a woman going down the normal path that led to physical union, exploring, touching, feeling, murmuring sweet words to each other. Hand in hand, they walked back the way Laura had come. Dusk had fallen. They were oblivious to everything except themselves. They chatted and laughed like any young lovers out on a date, with Mark escorting her home. As they approached Laura's house they lingered, not wanting to part. He took her in his arms, kissing her tenderly at first, but again the fire of their hunger consumed them. Finally, they drew apart, both breathing deeply.

'How wonderful, Mark!'

'How wonderful indeed!' he replied.

Nearing Laura's house, she said,

'I will call to your house at nine tonight and we can resume our deliberations there.'

He laughed at her choice of words, implying a tryst.

'I look forward to it,' he replied, all reservations evaporating. He turned for home walking on air, not thinking that the actions of the last two hours would haunt him for the rest of his life as they would Laura.

Mark was surprised to see a note pinned to the door with a telephone number on it. Quickly he opened the door, went to the telephone and dialled the number. Sergeant Kennedy answered it. Puzzled, Mark identified himself.

'I am afraid there has been a fatal accident involving both your parents,' said the sergeant in a hushed voice. He continued, 'It appears that a young joy rider, who was also killed, crashed into them at traffic lights just outside Sligo town. I am truly sorry to have to break this sad news to you.'

'Thank you,' Mark replied tonelessly, putting down the phone.

Both his beloved parents dead in one fell swoop. Numbed by the sorrow of their death, he stood by the phone in complete shock for about five minutes and then went on his knees to say a prayer for them, tears streaming down his pallid face. He pulled himself together, picked up the phone and phoned his brother Tom in Dublin to break the sad news to him. After that he changed into his clerical suit, packed a bag and set out for Sligo, calling on the Canon to tell him the bad news. Canon Mullen was the soul of discretion and kindness and told him to take as long as he needed away from parish duties. Nell was surprised to see him. 'Mum and Dad were here for a few hours and so if you had come earlier, you would have met them,' she said.

At the mention of his parents he turned even paler. She was startled at his appearance.

'Let's go inside,' he whispered hoarsely. She led him into the living room where he broke the terrible news to her. She too was devastated. He stayed with her that night and they made the funeral arrangements for their parents. Tom and his family would be in Sligo in the morning and they could finalise their plans then.

'Isn't it a bit late to be going for a stroll Laura?'

'It's only quarter to nine and I told Lucy Brennan that I might call as she asked me if I would go to a dance in Sligo,' Laura replied.

Her mother's voice softened.

'It will do you good. Maybe you will meet Mister Right!'

'Maybe I will,' replied Laura. 'If only you knew,' she whispered to herself. As she walked gaily down the road to Mark's house, she was surprised to find it in total darkness and to see that his car was not there.

'Strange, but maybe he wants to play safe,' she mused. She rang the doorbell, but there was no response. She rang it again, still no response. She was in a state of panic. How could she go home now after misleading her mother? She went around to the back and tried the door. Luckily it was unlocked. 'He must have been called away urgently,' she surmised, letting herself in. At least she could wait until he returned. She poured herself a whiskey and water, went to his bedroom and sipped her drink. 'What a surprise Mark will get when he finds me in his bed waiting for him.' Tremors of desire swept over her at the delicious thought that they would consummate what they had started earlier that evening. She was so wrapped up with these fantasies that she fell asleep on the bed with a smile on her face. That smile was wiped off when she awoke at two o'clock, cold and shivering. There was no sign of Mark. 'How dare he stand me up,' she continued scolding to herself. She sat on the side of the bed, taking stock of the situation. Here she was in the curate's house, thinking that by now they would have sated their hunger for each other, and be planning their future together. She whispered, 'in the curate's house!' She was appalled at her boldness at suggesting this in the first place. 'No wonder he took fright,' she incorrectly thought and left for home, somewhat dejected.

Monday was a busy day for Mark, starting with Mass in the hospital oratory, then a tearful meeting with his older brother Tom and his family and firming up the arrangements. After lunch he travelled to his home parish to make the church arrangements with a most cooperative parish priest. He decided to remain in Milltown and receive the remains of his parents at the church. Tom and Nell could look after any details in Sligo. Looking back, his worst memory was of entering his old home that evening on his own. The sight of all the comforting, familiar things that had always been there, but now the deafening silence, only broken by the steady beat of the clock in the hall. He gathered himself together again, sitting in the gloom of the evening in his favourite chair at the kitchen table, his mood matching the gloom. Laura briefly entered his thoughts, sending a shooting pain of remorse through his body.

'I will have to sort that problem out after all this,' he promised himself.

As arranged, he met the funeral cortege on the church steps and led both coffins to the sanctuary, followed by Tom, Nell, relatives, numerous friends and a large congregation. Finishing the ritual prayers, he thanked them all for their presence and then joined Tom and Nell to receive the sympathisers, as was and is the custom. At about nine o'clock that night they made their way to the family home, had a light meal and retired early to bed, each one with their memories. At the funeral Mass he was joined by the parish priest and Canon Ned, who had travelled from Rathmore. He was touched by this gesture, as the Canon was getting on in years, but still had made the effort. Mark was surprised to see Bishop Brown ready to preside at the Mass and thanked him. The congregation marvelled at his steady celebration of the Mass.

The façade only fell once during the homily, when speaking endearingly of his dead parents.

'How ghastly he looks,' Laura whispered to her father as the funeral procession made its way down the aisle. Laura was deeply moved to see the man she loved, and would always love, a pale shadow of himself. 'The shock is taking its toll,' her medical knowledge told her. Alice Burke saw the tears in her daughter's eyes, which were following Mark. Her womanly intuition gave her a message that alarmed her. She kept her thoughts to herself, too concerned to voice them. She watched Laura closely as she sympathised with Mark. She felt that Laura wanted to embrace him.

'My God! Is my imagination running wild?' Alice thought to herself.

For his part, Mark showed little emotion and politely thanked Laura, her parents and Rita, as he greeted the numerous parishioners who had travelled from Rathmore for the funeral. After the interment Mark, Tom and Nell hosted a meal for all who wished to avail of it in the Milltown Hotel, and then they returned to the house.

The Burkes did not stay for the meal. They made a sombre return to Rathmore and dined at home. Alice continued to watch Laura covertly. For her part, Laura appeared out of sorts and morose. Alice knew her daughter too well.

'Now that you have had the time to think and make plans, Laura, have you decided on what you'd like to do?' Alice began.

'I thought she would like to join me in the practice,' interjected her father.

'No, thank you, Dad. I would like to return to Sligo General and specialise in respiratory illnesses,' said Laura.

'I thought you might want to travel abroad again,' said her mother hopefully.

'I love Ireland, and particularly Sligo,' replied Laura.

'Maybe you will meet a good Irishman and settle down,' Alice ventured. With a sigh, Laura said, 'Maybe I will.'

There was lack of conviction there, thought Alice as she became more concerned.

'Why was Laura staying in the area?' She thought she knew the answer – for Mark, but she kept it to herself.

That evening Laura wrote to the hospital's programme manager advising him of her wish to rejoin Sligo General and specialise in respiratory diseases. Her thoughts turned to Mark. Had he been a bit reserved at the funeral? Was there something in the vibes between them to show that his ardour was cooling?

'Given the circumstances, I suppose he was drained of emotion,' she reasoned. 'Come hell or high water, priest or no priest, I am going to have his child,' she vowed to herself. It was most unusual for a highly articulate, educated young woman to think like this, and yet, 'I want to taste the forbidden fruit, and Mark wants to taste it and me too,' she reasoned. Her reasoning was tainted by her lust for him. 'I admit it,' she told herself.

'What about all the people it would hurt? What about Mother Church?' a voice whispered in her ear. Her conscience began to work on her. She chose to deafen her ears and banish her conscience. Nothing would come between her and the man she had chosen as a mate, and that was that!

Laura's mother, Alice, had gone to her room to try and come to grips with and to resolve the problem as she saw it. Laura had rejected her suggestion of going abroad but would only be about twenty-five miles from home, and Mark, in Sligo General Hospital. Alice was a natural worrier and the more she thought about the situation, the more worried she became. She resorted to prayer and decided to play a waiting game. Perhaps Laura and Mark would come to their senses and realise their obligations lay elsewhere. Particularly Mark, as she knew Laura could be very stubborn and possessive. Clutching at straws, Alice tried to convince herself that no daughter of hers would set out to seduce a priest.

'The trouble is that Mark is a very handsome man,' she admitted.

The next day Father Mark, Nell and Tom discussed family affairs and decided that they would make no firm decisions regarding the family home or any other matters pertaining to their deceased parents until the next month. In all probability there was a will in place that would pre-empt any decisions they might make. It was a healing time for the three of them back in the family home, which held wonderful memories for them all, individually and collectively. The following day, Tom and his family returned to Dublin. Nell went back to Sligo on the

Thursday, leaving Mark on his own. Inevitably, his thoughts turned back to the previous Sunday and his encounter in the wood with Laura. Instead of a glow of yearning for her, a deep shame filled him at the memory. Perhaps it was the sudden shock of losing his parents that caused this remorse, particularly as they had been so happy to have a priest in the family and he had been on the brink of betraying them.

'Laura is a beautiful woman and will make some lucky man very happy,' he spoke to himself. 'I am in love with her, but it can never, will never come to anything,' he vowed.

'Are you so sure?' It was the same little whisper as Laura had heard earlier on during her hours of agonising on her dilemma, except the response was different. Mark had his vocation to think about.

'I have the title of "Father" and I will not add the title of "Natural Father" to my accomplishments,' he resolutely said. The next problem was how to explain this to Laura without causing an unholy scene. He kept turning this around and around in his mind not knowing how to address the problem.

He slept fitfully that night and returned to Rathmore the following morning none the wiser. It was now Friday evening and after a light lunch, he settled down to a sermon for Sunday Mass. He decided he would preach against divorce as the pro-divorce lobby appeared to be getting a lot of coverage, and so far the Church seemed to be unusually mute, or so it seemed to him. It was a well-reasoned sermon, carefully researched and thought provoking to the listening congregation, many of whom silently applauded Father Mark for tackling the issue and rebutting many of the pro-divorce lobby arguments. By one of those many flukes in life, there happened to be a journalist in the congregation, Mary O'Malley, visiting her uncle Joe for the weekend. Although sympathetic to the pro-divorce group, she was impressed with Mark's sermon. On Tuesday morning, the Bishop phoned Mark.

'I see you have appeared in print on one of our daily papers.'

'Have I really,' blurted Mark, thinking that he and Laura had been seen in a passionate embrace in the wood and that all hell was about to break loose.

'Yes,' continued the Bishop, 'it appears that you made a vigorous attack on divorce in your sermon last Sunday.'

'Oh that!' said a very relieved Mark.

'You can expect more publicity and probably a mixed reaction, some of it very negative and scurrilous, but rest assured, you have my support. I will be issuing a pastoral letter echoing your views within the next two weeks.'

'Thank you for your support,' replied Mark.

After that Mark picked up the newspaper, found the article, read it and considered it fair and accurate.

However, it was only the beginning of being cast in the public eye for Mark. Later that day he received a telephone call from the TC Centre asking him to join a panel debate on TV the following Thursday night. He accepted the invitation. The next two days were spent in further research and marshalling his thoughts and arguments against divorce. He was absent from the parish most of that time and hadn't seen Laura by the time he travelled to Dublin for the TC debate on Thursday afternoon. Both the Bishop and Canon Mullen were pleased that Mark had been invited to join the TC panel as both felt that he would give a good account of himself. He justified their confidence although there was one difficult period during the TV debate. This arose when an exasperated opponent said,

'Father, how could you feel for a woman in a divorce situation, never having experienced the love of a woman?'

'Oh, but I have!' replied Mark.

There followed a shocked silence, which not only happened in the studio, but permeated right across the country to the viewing audience, who now sat up in their seats. One and all jumped to the obvious question, could this handsome priest be admitting to a love affair? With bated breath everybody hung on to his every word.

Mark continued,

'Of course, a priest is as human as anybody else.'

His opponent pressed home the question everybody else wanted to ask.

'Did you sleep with her?'

'No,' whispered Laura at home listening to the discussion, her heart going out to Mark with this irrelevant questioning.

'Fortunately for me and perhaps the woman in question, I did not, as I realised that my vocation to be a priest and adherence to my vow of celibacy is of paramount importance and nothing will deviate me from it, no matter how difficult it may seem.'

His adversary continued,

'Have you told, or are you going to tell this to the woman who is obviously in love with you?' His tormentor was determined to score. Mark was annoyed,

'I will handle this in the best way I see fit; let's stick to the subject matter of this discussion.'

The colour drained from Laura's face. 'So he is determined to remain a priest,' she reluctantly admitted to herself and found it hard to accept. There was little point in pursuing matters. She would leave Rathmore and move to an apartment in Sligo where she would be starting in the respiratory department of Sligo General Hospital in two weeks. 'There is nothing to keep me here now and commute to Sligo. I must resign myself to it,' she said reluctantly to herself.

The reaction to Mark's admission on TV to being in love with a woman but unwilling to quit the priesthood was as expected. Instead of the forthcoming divorce referendum, the public and media commentators focused on the thorny question of priestly celibacy. Bishop Brown was angry. Later he was to admit that he commended Mark's candour, even if he could have been a bit more discreet. The following morning he phoned Mark and told him that he wanted him to go on an immediate ten-day retreat and call to him when it was over. Mark was hurt, but his Bishop had spoken. He packed his bags and set out immediately for the venue the Bishop had arranged for the retreat. In retrospect, this action by the Bishop was wrong as it created the public perception that Mark had been 'silenced' by the Church. This perception increased as the media indicated that Mark was not in his parish and nobody there knew where he was.

The hasty action of the Bishop rebounded on him and he was forced to issue a statement confirming that he had more or less ordered Mark to go on retreat. This only caused further resentment and Bishop Brown was now put on the defensive. It was strange then that Mark should be the one who would defuse the situation. At the end of the retreat Mark was astonished to see a crowd of reporters and photographers outside the gates of the monastery as he drove down the drive.

'What's going on?' he asked himself. 'Something must have happened while I was on retreat.' Letting down the window of his car he soon found out. Immediately he defended the Bishop, stating that it was good to have been on retreat as it gave him space to reflect and renew his vocation. Furthermore he would have done the very same had he been Bishop. This deflated the assembled reporters who had been licking their lips in anticipation of another Church embarrassment. Mark then made his way towards home and the meeting with Bishop Brown. The Bishop was in a very good mood.

'I must say you handled the media very well and diffused all the speculation in a very forthright manner for which I am grateful,' he said. He was quite happy that Mark was back on track again and nothing was said regarding the woman who had tempted him. They spoke generally about diocesan affairs and, of course, Mark's parish. There was no question of Mark being moved, in the Bishop's mind. Mark's temptation was over and done with, and he felt that Mark might even be the better of it. After an affable half-hour conversation, Mark made for Rathmore and called on Canon Mullen, who was overjoyed to see him as he feared Mark would be transferred or forsake his vocation. If he suspected the woman involved was Laura, he never mentioned her, although he remembered the glances between them at the party in Burkes some weeks ago.

After all the turmoil of the last two weeks, Mark was glad to settle back to his normal parish routine. For their part, the parishioners welcomed him back without any reservations. When he heard that Laura had left the parish he was somewhat relieved, although he would have preferred to have met her face-to-face and given her his reasons for remaining in the priesthood. As was normal, he called periodically to see the Burkes. Laura's mother, Alice, was particularly friendly and he wondered if she knew what could have happened between her daughter and himself. Anyway, he had plenty to keep him occupied and this thought evaporated from his mind. He continued to campaign against divorce and was asked to contribute articles to the local weekly newspaper on this subject, which he did. Naturally this continued to keep him in the public eye as dissenters took issue with his views and sought similar publicity from the weekly paper. In any event, the pro-divorce lobby won by the narrowest of margins in the ensuing referendum. Mark took this defeat philosophically.

'The people have spoken,' he said in a subsequent sermon. He was asked by the same newspaper to contribute a weekly article of his choice, which he did, and so he became a well-known and often-read contributor in County Sligo and neighbouring counties. This of course added to his workload, but he seemed happy to be kept busy. One might well ask, was this an antidote to keep Laura out of his thoughts? Perhaps, perhaps, perhaps!

Laura settled into her new duties at Sligo General Hospital very quickly. After all she was no stranger to the hospital and would have known most of the staff. It was rather strange then that Nell Somers was one of the few staff nurses she did not know. When they met she could see some resemblances in appearance and mannerisms that told her she was Mark's sister. This shook her resolve to banish Mark from her mind. Who could blame her? Working in such proximity to his sister was bound to trigger her feelings for Mark. No matter how hard she tried to extinguish the fire, it just would not quench. 'Such is unrequited love,' she murmured. Rather than sit moping in her apartment, Laura enjoyed a good social life. She played tennis, went to the leisure centre frequently and went socialising at the weekends with her friends. She met many eligible men, but always seemed to end up comparing them to Mark, which she knew was a mistake, but she just couldn't help it.

Laura was a dutiful daughter and travelled home to visit her parents and sister Rita at least once every month. In making these visits home, she felt that at some stage she would bump into Mark. As it was, she had seen him once or twice in the distance and had to restrain herself from going after him.

'This only happens in the movies, not to people like Mark and me,' she groaned as she saw him fade in the distance. She consoled herself. 'Eventually, he will be moved to another parish and coming home will be easier as he will be gone.' She repeated, 'gone, gone,' as she had done many times before. She steeled herself rather than give in to thoughts of herself and Mark in rapturous embrace.

Apart from her social activities, Laura loved to walk on the long promenade to the beach at Rosses Point, a small seaside village five miles north of Sligo in a most scenic area. She did this regularly. On one of these walks, she noticed a tall, well-built man walking in front of her. As she drew closer, she was disconcerted to see that it appeared to be Mark. The same gait, the same black coat and the same dark hair.

'Oh Mark,' she cried, rushing up to him, clasping him from behind. The man turned, and talk about embarrassment, her face turned beetroot. There was a twinkle in his eye.

'He's a lucky fellow, whoever this Mark is,' he laughed and all she could do was to laugh too. He continued, 'the only Mark I know is Father Mark Somers. He was a colleague of mine in Summerhill College where I still teach. Actually, he is my cousin, so I don't think it's this Mark you had in mind when you grabbed me from behind.'

'Of course not,' lied Laura. They walked together along the promenade towards the beach. He wasn't Mark, but she was attracted to him. He introduced himself as Tony Somers and told her that he lived in Sligo town with his widowed mother. She also introduced herself and told him of her work in Sligo General Hospital. They found that they had many similar interests, particularly this walk in Rosses Point.

On their return, 'Same time, same place, tomorrow evening?' he asked. She agreed, her first date since parting from Mark.

'Maybe there is life after Mark,' she mused as she drove back to Sligo.

Tony could not believe his luck. Imagine running into such an attractive woman. Whoever Mark was, he seemed to be out of the picture. Maybe he was meeting her on the rebound.

'Better be careful,' he told himself.

They met the following evening as arranged and this became a regular pattern. They became comfortable with each other. Laura was grateful that Tony did not try to rush things. He just seemed to plod along steadily, gaining her confidence. He never mentioned the Mark she had alluded to at their first meeting. He did talk about his cousin Father Mark briefly on a few occasions, which made Laura bite her lip.

'You know,' he once told her, 'in our family circle we always believed that Mark would go far in the Church, but events last year have probably put paid to that.' He went on to tell her of Mark's TV appearance when he told the country that he was in love with a woman, and Tony said that he reckoned that this revelation would be hard for the Church to swallow.

'The one peculiar part of all this is that he has started collecting Indian music discs, and we think that he must have met this woman from that part of the world.' Laura was utterly flabbergasted. So this was Mark's way of remembering her. He knew she had worked in Calcutta.

'Peculiar indeed,' agreed Laura.

That night was a sleepless one for her.

'Mark doesn't seem to be able to get me out of his system, no matter what he said. How wonderful.' There was a smile on her face as she slept. Tony was pushed into the background for tonight at least.

The next morning she decided she would travel home for the weekend and confront Mark with this new information. Nine o'clock on Saturday evening saw her on his doorstep. He ushered her into the living room. She came straight to the point, prompted by the Indian music playing on the CD player.

'I believe you have developed a taste for this music, how come?' she asked.

The reply from Mark was what she expected.

'It reminds me of the time you came back from Calcutta and how I fell head over heals in love with you at our first meeting despite my being a priest. And I don't seem to be able to get you out of my system no matter how hard I try, and believe me, I have tried hard!'

Laura was utterly gobsmacked at his lengthy reply. With tears in her eyes, and shaking uncontrollably, she looked at him.

'I can fight it no longer.'

With that, he took her in his arms and repeated that kiss of kisses in the woods so long ago. This time it went further: he led her to the bedroom. Still standing by the bed, he gently undressed her. She moaned at the soft touch of his hand on her bare skin. She heard the sharp intake of his breath. She saw his muscular torso as he rapidly undressed. He gasped at the light touch of her fingers running along his back. Fully aroused, they fell on the bed, their pent-up desires volcanically sated. It was a rapturous night for both of them, exploring, tasting, touching, totally immersed in each other, meeting their carnal desires. Exhausted, they both fell asleep in the early hours of the morning. Fortunately Laura had gone directly to Mark's house, so her family did not know she was in the town.

Mark awoke utterly drained. He stared at the ceiling. No rush, he was to say evening Mass that Sunday. Strangely calm, recalling the events of the past night, savouring every blissful moment with Laura. Laura? He turned his head at the thought of her, to find that she had slipped away. All that remained was the indentation of her head on the pillow and the faint scent of her perfume. He continued to stare at the ceiling. Slowly but surely, the horror of his transgression seeped into his conscience. He spoke softly to himself.

'Father Mark Somers, the paragon of priesthood has slept with a woman!' He kept repeating this and it sounded worse every time. In fact, he became drowned in remorse and self-flagellation. He spent a long time like this, but eventually arose and mooched morosely through the bungalow with tortured thoughts. Later that day he analysed the situation in the context of remaining a priest, no matter how much Laura meant to him, no matter what the cost. Stubbornly he clung on to remaining a priest. 'Albeit a tainted one,' he murmured.

That morning Laura had awoken early to find Mark asleep, an angelic smile on his lips.

'What a way to induce sleep!' She was flippant in her triumph. Noiselessly she slipped out of the bed, dressed and made her exit.

Her mother was surprised to see Laura so early in the morning.

'Where are you coming from at nine o'clock in the morning?' she asked.

'From Sligo,' lied Laura.

'Well, you look as if you had been up all night.'

'It was a spur of the moment decision, I got up early,' Laura continued the deceit.

'Anyway, we are always glad to see you,' replied her mother, putting an end to the interrogation, much to Laura's relief. She went to the bathroom, tidied herself and regained her composure. They had breakfast together and swapped news. Her father and sister Rita soon joined them and then they prepared for Sunday Mass, which had been their custom for as long as Laura and Rita could remember. Much to Laura's relief, Canon Mullen read Mass. The very thought of Mark saying Mass caused her to shudder. It would be too much, remembering that they were locked in passionate embrace only twelve hours ago. She blushed crimson at the thought of it, particularly as she was in church and shouldn't be entertaining these thoughts in 'the holies of holies'.

Mark composed himself again.

'It was inevitable that it would happen,' he murmured, acknowledging that the urge of the flesh had taken precedence over his man-made resolve to retain his celibacy. He spoke to himself, 'I have tasted the fruit, but that does not mean that I have to eat it!' It was not Mark's style to deal in duplicity and yet he prevaricated. Should he go to the Bishop and confess, knowing that this would bring swift retribution, or should he wait and talk it over with Laura? He chose the latter course and bided his time. On Wednesday morning the post brought a letter from Laura. He read it twice to absorb its import. The message was clear. She loved him deeply, but knew that he would never give up the priesthood for her. She said she accepted that, but she wanted to have his child. He recoiled in horror at this request.

'Surely this would only make matters more complicated,' he muttered. His natural instinct was to reply immediately telling her that this suggestion was a complete non-runner. He paused, 'After all, I am a compliant party in this affair, even more at fault for encouraging her'. Think of her emotional state, a voice cautioned him.

When he wrote to her it was a tender caring letter, pointing out his desire to remain in the priesthood and thanking her for her acceptance of this premise. Gently he told her that he would have to make a stronger effort to remain celibate and voiced the hope that she would meet somebody who could realise her dream as husband and spouse. She realised that their relationship was not, and would not, go anywhere. It was the type of reply that Laura expected, so her disappointment was diluted by this response. A postcard from her to Mark read, 'I understand and accept the situation.' For his part, Mark settled back to his parish duties a wiser man, knowing that he had played a compliant, if not encouraging role in the affair.

'Fate can play a strange part in seeking retribution for wrongdoing, and I hope I am not on the receiving end when that time comes,' he spoke to himself ominously. He shrugged as he made his way down to the church to say an evening Mass.

Time moved on and both Mark and Laura pursued their individual interests. After three years in the parish, Mark was expected to move on, but Canon Mullen's advancing years made the Bishop decide to leave Mark alone. He knew that his old friend, the Canon, had come to rely heavily on Mark. This was not to last. Shortly after the Bishop had told Mark his reason for not transferring him, Canon Mullen died suddenly. Mark was devastated, as the Canon was like a second father to him. They had formed a very close bond; something like a father and son. After the Canon's obsequies, the Bishop appointed Mark the administrator of the parish pending the appointment of a new parish priest. He promised Mark that he would send him assistance at the weekends from the College in Sligo until a newly ordained priest was available. He also told Mark that he would not be remaining in Rathmore, as he had another post in mind for him.

Now on his own, Mark was too busy to give much thought to what this new post might be, and even Laura receded from his thoughts, although he felt an odd twinge when she crossed his mind. About three months after the death of Canon Mullen, Mark received a letter from a firm of solicitors in Sligo asking him to call in connection with the estate of the deceased Canon. He duly made an appointment and much to his surprise, discovered that the Canon had bequeathed a lovely bungalow to him in Rosses Point. The solicitors told Mark that the Canon's only sister and family member had gifted the bungalow to the Canon five years before and had died the following year. She had been a local schoolteacher who had never married. Mark was overwhelmed by the late Canon's generosity and went to see the lovely bungalow in Rosses Point overlooking the sea.

'What a lovely place to come to for rest and relaxation,' he whispered as he admired the beautiful vista all around him. Looking up at the sky he said earnestly, 'Thank you Canon for this wonderful gift!' Now Mark had a haven to come to and was grateful to have it. After that he became a regular visitor to the bungalow when parish duties did not occupy too much of this time.

About two months after inheriting the property, the Bishop asked him to call on a Thursday afternoon at three o'clock. As he drove down through the town, unconsciously naming every dwelling that he passed and indeed every house for five miles along the Sligo road, he was sad at the thought that this would be one of his last journeys as a priest resident in the parish. The place had grown on him and he in turn was immersed in the place, even though he knew he could not remain there for the remainder of his priestly life.

'Hopefully my departure will finally quench the flickering fire in my heart for Laura, now that I will be removed from reminders of her', he voiced his earnest wish. How was he to know that she loved to walk in Rosses Point and explore the beaches there!

'Is it five months since Mark and I were in flagrante?' Laura asked herself. She found that the time had gone by very quickly since that night of unbridled passion and their subsequent mutual resolve not to repeat it. Even the briefest of thoughts of their union sent delicious tremors through her. True to her word, she made no effort to resume the relationship, although she knew Mark would find it impossible to resist her. She also finished with Tony, realising that there was no point in continuing, as she would only be misleading him. Outside of her work, she continued to lead an active social life and to enjoy her walks in Rosses Point. About three months after she stopped going with Tony, she met him at a function in Sligo. He seemed to be quite happy with his new girlfriend, so Laura didn't feel too guilty at having broken off their relationship. Looking at Tony again reminded her of his cousin, Mark. As if reading her thoughts, Tony asked,

'Did you know that your former curate is now the Bishop's secretary and living in Rosses Point?'

'Rosses Point!' repeated Laura. 'I knew he had become the Bishop's secretary, but I did not know he lived in Rosses Point.'

'Apparently the deceased parish priest of Rathmore left a bungalow to him in his will and the Bishop agreed that Mark could commute to Sligo,' informed Tony.

'Did he indeed, how interesting.' Her eyes gleamed and she moved on.

Not for the first time did she lie awake in bed when Mark came into the equation again.

'All alone in a house in Rosses Point and me thinking that he would be closeted with other colleagues in a parochial house in Sligo,' she murmured to herself, then giggled. 'I wonder what would happen if I was to become a nocturnal visitor. What would Mark do or say?' Her firm resolve to keep away from Mark seemed to be shaking. From then on Laura kept an eye out for Mark on her walks at the Point. It was easy to find where he lived, as he helped out in the parish in addition to his main duties and was well known. The bungalow was in a quiet cul-de-sac overlooking the bay and she could see that fresh renovations and external decoration had recently been carried out. She assumed that internal refurbishment had also been done. She spoke to herself, 'Mark likes to leave his mark!' smiling at her pun.

'Does he indeed', came a voice from behind her, a voice she immediately recognised. Mark had tiptoed silently behind her like a predatory cat. She turned and they both stared, seeing the hurt in each other's eyes. Laura broke the silence.

'What a beautiful location for a house,' she said trying to keep the conversation impersonal.

'It is, isn't it?' he replied. 'Would you like to see the interior?'

'I'm afraid I'm caught for time.'

'Just a quick tour and a glass of wine,' he countered.

'Well, OK,' her resolve crumbled.

He opened the front door and they entered the bungalow. After the tour, they sat in the sitting room sipping their wine, all very proper and correct, outwardly anyway. Inwardly could be another story. She looked at the painting over the fireplace.

'Isn't that a pointing of the forest walk in Rathmore?' she asked.

'Indeed it is, one of the many gifts I got from the parishioners.'

She got up to have a closer look at the large framed painting.

'It is very accurate, I can identify the spot where I ran into your arms, Mark.' Her resolve crumbled, her voice was shaky. Mark was by her side in an instant, taking her in his arms and brushing the tears from her eyes. She responded to his embrace, which came to its natural fruition in his bedroom.

They lay quietly there for some time. Then he said,

'I shall hate leaving this place and also leaving you.'

'Leaving,' she aid, 'why are you talking of leaving when you have hardly settled into your new post?'

'It seems that a new rector for the Irish College in Rome is needed, and I have been appointed.'

'Rome,' she repeated, 'and you were going to go without saying goodbye to me. Do I not mean anything to you?'

'Put like that, it makes me feel totally irresponsible', he replied. Another silence. He looked at her; silent tears were streaming down her face. She returned his look.

'I feel so used, realising that you were prepared to disappear without telling me. I thought it was more than physical attraction,' she continued.

'It is, it is!' he remonstrated. 'In so far as a priest can love a woman, I love you.'

'But not enough to leave the priesthood,' she countered.

'We have been through all this before.'

'We have, haven't we?' she replied. Laura left the bed, got dressed and looking steadily at him said, 'Goodbye Mark', closed the door and left the house. He heard the front door close and he was filled with a terrible sadness.

'I have nothing to be proud of,' he said in despair. 'I knew that we would succumb if she came into the house and yet I persuaded her,' remembering her reticence and his insistence at the outset. 'Maybe this sojourn in Rome will finally sort matters out and by the time I return our ardour will have cooled.' He would miss her and his home in Rosses Point, to which he had become very attached. The next few weeks were spent in preparing for his departure to Rome. In the August of his thirty-eighth year, he travelled to take up his new post as rector of the Irish College.

'You seem to have mastered the Italian language very well,' complimented the Cardinal, 'but I suppose after six years amongst us, you would.'

Mark was sitting in Cardinal Rodini's office wondering as to the purpose of this meeting. He knew of the Cardinal's reputation as one of the most powerful men in the Curia and a man not to be trifled with. As if reading Mark's mind, he said,

'Well, Monsignor, I am sure you are wondering why I asked you to come here this morning?'

'Yes, I am,' replied Mark.

There was a minute's silence, broken only by the gentle swaying of the pendulum of a large clock behind Mark. The Cardinal was a typical Italian prelate with a patrician, aquiline face and dark eyes, which were now studying Mark. He gave a small cough and began.

'I have been requested by our Holy Father to talk to you about returning to Ireland as Auxiliary Bishop with right-of-succession to His Eminence,

Cardinal Joseph Lucas, Primate of all Ireland and Archbishop of Armagh, who has requested an auxiliary because of advancing age and growing ill-health. How would you feel about it, Monsignor?'

Mark was filled with utter incredulity. He blanched and was speechless. Trained diplomat that he was, Cardinal Rodini could see that Mark wasn't going to jump at the offer.

'With respect to his Holiness and your good self, I feel that there are many others older and more mature than myself who are more qualified for the post,' Mark eventually replied. The Cardinal was surprised.

'I feel that many others would have said *aceipe*, but you are different,' he commented. 'Do you still covet that woman you spoke of so eloquently on TV all those years ago?'

'The Vatican was always well informed,' thought Mark, who replied, 'No, that is a phase of my life that is dead and buried.' The Cardinal shrugged.

'These things happen, but I am afraid that the appointment will have to stand. It is the will of the Holy Father, not an offer as I indicated at the outset.'

'Rome has spoken and your reluctant servant obeys,' responded Mark.

'Graciously conceded,' replied the Cardinal, making a mental note to look out for this Irishman with a mind of his own. They spoke affably on a number of topics and Mark was surprised to find that he was so well informed on the Irish Church.

'I once worked as a secretary in the Irish Nunciature,' explained the Cardinal. As their meeting was closing, he told Mark that it would be about ten days before a public announcement would be made. This suited Mark as he could see that it would take him time to absorb and become used to his proposed new status.

For the six years that Mark was in Rome, Laura got on with her life in Sligo. Her friends and colleagues could not understand why she had not met somebody and settled down.

'It's easy for them to say that,' murmured Laura. At the age of forty-four years, she had retained her good looks and her athletic figure belied her age. As fate would have it, herself and Nell, Mark's sister, became very good friends. While Mark was abroad, Nell looked after the bungalow and Laura had been invited to stay on many occasions.

'The irony of it!' she mused as she lay in Mark's bed, recalling how Mark had insisted on her seeing the house and the inexorable finale on this very bed. She blushed at the memory.

'Now Mark is to be an Archbishop and eventually Cardinal Primate of All Ireland, according to today's news, what next?' Given her situation, her reaction to the news had been mixed, glad for his sake, if that's what he wanted, and sorry for the secret he was carrying. Despite all his protestations, she knew that he was still torn between her and the Church.

'He had an opportunity to say no to the appointment, as I am sure they asked him where he stood with the woman he publicly professed to love all those years ago.' Momentarily she became angry, recalling their parting in this very room. Then, shrugging her shoulders, she dismissed these thoughts from her mind.

In another bedroom in the bungalow Nell was also alone with her thoughts.

'Mark to be an Archbishop and eventually Cardinal Primate of All Ireland. If only Mum and Dad had lived to see this day.' There was pride in her voice. Her brother becoming the eventual leader of the Church in Ireland. Her thoughts turned to Laura. 'She had seemed a bit reserved when she heard the news,' remembered Nell, 'I thought she would be thrilled like me, as she seems very fond of him and loves coming to the bungalow. Strange how she knew which was Mark's bedroom and likes sleeping there!' Nell did not like the way her thoughts were going and started counting sheep.

Laura was also drifting off to sleep when there was a gentle sound of the knob in the bedroom door turning. Now fully awake, she jumped up and the light was switched on. It was Mark, making an unexpected visit to his haven. They looked at one another in total disbelief. She was conscious of her attire and she reached for the dressing gown.

'Don't,' he whispered and reached for her. Fate took a hand. Despite the lateness of the hour, the telephone rang in the hallway. Mark hastened to answer it. It was the local hotel asking him to come immediately. A man had suffered a massive heart attack and had pleaded for a priest. They explained that the parish priest was away and had phoned his house on the chance that he might be there.

'Of course I'll come', replied Mark and hurried out in response to the urgent request.

Carefully and reverently he administered the Last Rites to the dying man. He could see the relief and happiness in his face. Mark was moved by the transformation from terror to happy resignation in the hapless man, about to face his creator. He stayed with him for the hour before he expired. Then Mark left the room.

Instead of returning to the bungalow he headed for a long walk on the beach. His mind was in turmoil. Not for the first time since he had set eyes on Laura all those years ago. No wonder his mind was in turmoil. In two hours his world had been turned upside down. From trying to force himself on Laura to performing the Last Rites on a dying man not much older than himself. It was mind-boggling. He, the Archbishop-elect of Armagh and eventual Primate of All Ireland, still loving and wanting Laura. What a mess!

'Of your own making,' whispered his conscience. 'How can you lead a double life?' it insisted. He climbed the brow of the hill, completely immersed in the conflict raging within him. A near fatal mistake. The edge of the hill subsided; he fell twenty feet to the ground and was knocked unconscious.

At the bungalow, both Nell and Laura were becoming concerned that Mark had not returned from the hotel. Eventually, Nell phoned the hotel to discover that Mark had left two hours earlier, having performed the Last Rites and remained with the dying man for an hour. She looked at her watch. It was two o'clock.

'Where could he have gone at midnight?' a rhetorical question. Panic set in. Both herself and Laura walked to the hotel that was about fifteen minutes distant from the bungalow. To their consternation they were able to see Mark's car with the aid of a torch they had brought with them.

'Inexplicable', whispered Laura.

Nell, pale-faced, was strangely silent. A terrible foreboding came over her.

'Something terrible has happened to him,' she cried.

'Not Mark surely, he is indestructible,' responded Laura.

They entered the hotel deeply upset, one for her brother, the other for her lover. Contact was made with the Gardai and rescue services. Both swung into motion immediately, despite the lateness of the hour. The two women returned to the bungalow to await developments.

It was dawn the following morning before Mark was found, still unconscious. He was rushed to the intensive care unit in Sligo General Hospital. Nell was extremely upset, as was Laura, who struggled to maintain her composure, in public anyway. She was acutely aware that the media, now on the scene, were extremely adept at ferreting out a story. Hence her apparent calm. Behind this façade, she was in deep turmoil as she gazed at the inert body and pallid face of Mark, the man she adored to distraction. Given her status as a staff doctor, little attention was paid to her almost incessant attendance at his bedside. Any questions she was asked by the media were invariably of a medical nature. Naturally it was front-page news on the local and national newspapers. After all, it isn't every day that an Archbishop-elect and eventual Primate of all Ireland is found unconscious at the bottom of a cliff. Mark showed no signs of revival.

It was three days after the accident, and the medical bulletins took on a more sombre tone. His brother Tom had the unenviable task of travelling to the family graveyard plot to tidy it up and perhaps, he thought, to prepare it for another family occupant. Nell wondered at Laura's composure, castigating herself for her thoughts earlier that week linking Mark and Laura in a romantic setting.

'How could I even think the like?' she reproached herself. 'Mark is my brother the priest. He would not look at a woman, even a woman as attractive as Laura.' She quietly entered Mark's room as if to upend her recent thoughts. She saw Laura sitting by his bedside, his limp hand in hers, gently stroking it and speaking softly to him. Nell was struck by the tenderness in her voice. This wasn't the tone a doctor took with a patient; it was more like a woman speaking tenderly to her lover. Nell was shocked. Worse was to come. She distinctly heard Laura whisper urgently,

'Mark, please don't leave me and your little daughter Catherine!'

At this, Nell gasped audibly and fainted. Laura rushed to the stricken Nell and gently revived her.

'It's all the strain of Mark's accident,' thought Laura, not realising that she had been overheard. Eventually, Nell came around but gave no inkling of what had caused her to faint. Naturally, everybody thought it was the strain of looking after Mark as well as doing her work that was the problem. She hid her feelings from Laura, even though her earlier misgivings had come to fruition.

Just coming up on six years old, Catherine Burke was a bright light-hearted young girl. She was dark-haired, like her unknown father, and very bright. So bright in fact that she would occasionally ask questions of Laura as to the whereabouts of her father.

'After all,' she reasoned, 'most of the girls in my class have Daddies, so why shouldn't I?' Technically speaking, up to now, Laura could truthfully say to Catherine that her father was abroad, but now this did not apply, as he had been sent back from Rome to become Archbishop Designate of Armagh.

'My God' she thought, 'How do you tell your daughter that her father is the leader of the Irish Catholic Hierarchy?' Inevitably, she would be faced with this earth-shattering disclosure to Catherine, an innocent child. Maybe she should fabricate some story until Catherine was older.

'It is the coward's way,' she said, 'but perhaps it would be best.' Catherine was her pride and joy, conceived in that lovely August evening when she reluctantly succumbed to Mark's pressing invitation to see his renovated bungalow. They had parted on bitter terms six years ago, when she discovered that he intended to travel to Rome to take up his appointment without saying goodbye. Subsequently she discovered that this liaison in Rosses Point had made her pregnant and she remembered her resolution when she first met Mark. She also remembered that she had resolutely refused to divulge the name of Catherine's father at the time of her birth. At that time, she recalled, society had become more tolerant of unmarried mothers. The one person who had become distressed was her own mother Alice, now getting on in years. To her credit, Alice never mentioned Father Mark to Laura, although her intuition told her that he came into the equation. Indeed, as Catherine's years increased, Alice thought she could see resemblances to her father, but held her peace insofar as was possible. Catherine lived a normal childhood, although Laura was very protective of her and kept her in the background. Naturally, it impinged on her social life, but Laura did not seem to mind. Her whole life seemed to revolve around Catherine. Mark was totally unaware that he had a daughter and indeed that she was an occasional weekend visitor to his bungalow in Rosses Point. It was strange then that Aunty Nell her mother's friend, who looked after the bungalow, had never mentioned Catherine's presence to her brother. How was Catherine to know that early in her life Laura had specifically asked Nell never to mention her presence to Mark.

'He might think of me as a fallen woman and have no more to do with me!' Nell recalled these words as she slumped in a faint on the floor in Mark's hospital room.

On the fifth day Mark showed signs of returning to consciousness much to the relief of the medical team who had become a bit concerned. Naturally, Laura and Nell were overjoyed. They had watched over him with great solicitude. He opened his eyes, had trouble focusing them, but eventually saw Laura at the foot of his bed and smiled. He then saw Nell beside her and gave her a smile too. The doctor came close to him and said,

'Father Mark, can you hear me?'

Mark looked at him, his lips moving inaudibly.

'My God!' exclaimed Nell, 'he cannot speak.'

Signora Bellini watched her husband Marco as he strode down the avenue to the university where he lectured in mathematics, French and English.

'How well he looks,' she murmured, watching his tall erect form blending into the distance. Her daughter Katrina had already left for school, and Dottoressa Bellini, as she was known, would leave for the Ospedale where she worked, about half an hour after the Professore, her husband. Sipping her cappuccino, whilst looking up and down the tree-lined avenue, already dappled in the early morning sunshine, was a habit she had formed since coming to Ravenna five years ago with her husband and young daughter. All three of them had grown to love this beautiful cultured city where the Renaissance had left an indelible mark. Her thoughts flitted back to the beginning of their sojourn in Ravenna. She smiled as she remembered struggling to come to grips with the Italian language. But she persisted and was now almost as fluent as her husband Marco. Katrina picked it up very quickly from her school friends and coming on eleven years old, there was nothing in her speech or behaviour to distinguish her from her Italian friends. Signora Bellini knew that if she were to be assimilated into the local scene she would have to conform, and to her credit, she had succeeded. So much so that she was able to take on an appointment in Ospedale Ravenna and this really helped her to fit in. Finishing her cappuccino, she tidied herself and also walked to the hospital. Their apartment, supplied by the University, was centrally located in the city and was spacious and bright.

Marco was also deep in thought as he strode down the avenue to the University. Unconsciously, as if in communion with his wife, his thoughts turned back to five years ago and his coming to Ravenna. He had no problems with the Italian language, thanks to his previous experience. He smiled at his situation. His colleagues, students and friends thought of him as the Italian married to the lady doctor from Irlanda, with a daughter Katrina. He did not particularly like this deception, but it had all been part of a game plan hatched in the Vatican five years ago. The recently elected Paul VII, formerly Cardinal Enrico Rodini, was the third person whose thoughts were similarly occupied by events of five years ago concerning the Irish priest. He was troubled, but his inscrutable features, a result of his Vatican training, did not betray his inner turmoil. He paced up and down the Vatican Gardens, going back in time, which only seemed like yesterday, as the events replayed themselves before his very eyes.

He recalled the morning five years ago when he had picked up the phone with a sense of foreboding that it would trigger events that could come back to haunt him some day. It was the Papal Nuncio from Ireland, giving him the news of Mark's accident and its disastrous consequences. The Cardinal was taken aback. He told the Nuncio to keep him briefed daily and to issue a press release to the Irish media stating that Mark's elevation to the Episcopacy would be postponed until medical reports were studied. The Nuncio carried out this order and the Irish public was curious to know more. For a few days Mark was front-page news with people speculating as to whether he would ever become their spiritual leader. Rodini recalled that he had waited until the media spotlight had faded from Mark and then summoned him to Rome. Even now, five years later, the new Pope grimaced at his memory of the interview. He recalled his secretary's surprise at being told that he wished to see Mark on his own. He knew that his secretary was wondering how he could interview a priest who could not speak.

Never a man to make small talk, Rodini said to Mark, 'I see that we both seem to have read the same book called *The Escapist*'. Startled, Mark looked at him. Rodini was triumphant.

'As I recall it, the hero played dumb so as not to divulge a terrible secret he was carrying. Perhaps this is the cause of your loss of speech?' accused the Cardinal. There was an ominous silence in the room, both men staring at each other.

Finally, Mark bowed his head and whispered,

'Si.'

Rodini smiled and continued,

'Could it be that the woman you loved has re-ignited that flame?'

'Yes,' replied Mark in English this time.

'Finally,' the Cardinal went on, 'could it be that you did not wish to harm the Church by publicly proclaiming your love for this woman, given that you were to be consecrated a bishop?'

'Yes,' Mark responded. He continued, 'Your Eminence is correct when you stated that I deliberately played dumb. I needed time to come to a decision.'

'Have you decided?' asked the Cardinal.

'Yes, I wish to be laicised and marry Laura.'

It was the Cardinal's turn to be silent. He looked at Mark, silently admiring his candour. Finally he said,

'Arrangements will have to be made to mitigate any damage to the Church. Please return here in two days and maintain your silence.'

The Cardinal sent Mark to a nearby monastery and set his game plan in motion.

Two days later the Cardinal unveiled his plan to Mark. Commencing with a press release neatly typed, it stated that due to his unfortunate accident and resultant loss of speech, the Pope has had to revoke the appointment of Monsignor Somers as Archbishop-Designate of Armagh, which was a matter of profound regret. It went on to say that the Monsignor would remain in Rome for the present and undergo medical treatment for the loss of his voice. Mark read the proposed press release at least three times, assimilating every word with growing anger at the blatant misleading of the press and indeed the Irish people. His anger subsided quickly. His dealings with the Vatican should have warned him that they were masters in the art of politics.

The Cardinal interrupted his thoughts,

'There is more,' he said handing Mark an Italian passport. It had the name of Marco Bellini on it.

'All it needs is your photo. Remove your collar, the photographer is awaiting my summons.'

Ten minutes later, the passport was returned with Mark's photograph neatly inserted in it. Mark was astonished.

'What now?' he asked.

The Cardinal gave an enigmatic smile.

'Well Professor, how would you like to take up a teaching appointment in the University of Ravena in one month's time?'

Mark was totally gobsmacked. The Cardinal could almost see the working of his mind and the myriad of questions on Mark's lips.

'Let us just say that His Holiness and I feel that we owe you this new start with the woman you love.'

Thus events of five years ago simultaneously occupied the minds of three people, all coming from three different angles. Mark wondered if the University President knew of his background, or did he just respond favourably to a request from Cardinal Rodini, who was his cousin, as he later discovered.

Laura, for her part, was happy in Ravenna living with her husband and daughter. Probably the only person uneasy about the situation was the newly elected Pope, pacing up and down the Vatican gardens. Long experience in Vatican affairs had taught him that sometimes the best laid plans of mice and men had an uncanny knack of surfacing when least expected.

'What havoc my exposed game plan would wreak on the Church,' he sighed.

Two years slipped by and it was now ten years since Mark, Laura and Catherine had settled in Ravenna. The Pope, now in the fifth year of his pontificate, had become so engrossed in Church affairs that his role as Cardinal Rodini in Mark's departure from the Church, receded from his mind. Mark, Laura and Catherine were totally integrated into the Italian way of life, and to a certain extent, their native country had receded from their minds too. Although they kept in touch with their relations by mail, Mark and Laura felt that it was best to make a clean break with Ireland, whilst Catherine didn't seem to mind once she was with her parents. She was unaware that her father had once been a prominent churchman and indeed would have been Cardinal Primate of All Ireland had he remained in the Church, and abandoned her mother. Catherine looked at the two of them discussing something or other.

'How lucky I am to have such handsome caring parents – *La Dolce Vita!*' she murmured. She looked up at the azure blue sky, 'Not a cloud in sight, although when we get the rare thunderstorm it is horrific.' She was speaking to nobody in particular, little thinking that a storm of a different kind, a storm that would rock the Chair of Peter, was about to brew up in holy Ireland.

It started very simply when Mary Rigney, now the lady editor with *The Daily Journal* came up with a weekly series of 'Where are they now?' in the paper. This entailed going back many years on the old editions of the paper, picking out people who had featured prominently in the news at the time and following this up to the present time. The series had proved popular with the readers and had helped to increase circulation, which was of course, her main objective. Thumbing through the issues of ten years ago, lo and behold, the handsome face of the Archbishop-elect stared back at her. Immediately, her curiosity was kindled. She stared back at the picture, her mind turning back the leaves of past tense. Her visit to Rathmore all those years ago when she had been a young reporter, Mary O'Malley, visiting her now-deceased Uncle Joe, listening to Father Mark's famous sermon on divorce, which subsequently brought him to national prominence through her report in *The Daily Journal.* Then she recalled the TV panel discussion, particularly the bit where Mark revealed his love for a woman, which was doomed. Mary recalled doing her article on priestly celibacy and indeed the physical effect Mark had on her in Church that day. 'I wonder did he affect all women that way?' she murmured and then got on with reading various articles concerning Mark up to ten years ago.

Mary was puzzled. The trail had gone cold after she had read the Vatican press release announcing that due to his illness (loss of voice), Mark's appointment as Archbishop Designate of Armagh had been revoked and that he had gone to Rome for treatment. Rhetorically she asked herself, 'I wonder what became of him?' Her gut feeling was that there was something amiss. Those who knew Mary could testify that her gut feeling was rarely wrong and that she would not let go of something until her curiosity was satisfied. This is probably why she was regarded as such a good journalist by her peers and had been made editor of her paper. She picked up the phone and dialled the Vatican Nunciature, explaining the nature of her query regarding Monsignor Mark Somers, the one time Archbishop Designate of Armagh, who seemed to have vanished. There was an audible intake of breath at the other end. Mary's antennae were now highly tuned. She felt as if she had pressed a button and the red light had come on instead of the green one. The Italian accent was unmistakable.

'I will make some enquiries and revert to you within ten days,' it said. The phone went dead.

'I just know I am on to something!' Not a shadow of doubt crossed her mind.

At the other end of the line was Father Luigi Siri, First Secretary in the Nunciature. His composure was shattered and his body trembled uncontrollably as he recalled the events of ten years ago when he had acted as secretary to Cardinal Rodini, now the present Pope Paul VII. He recalled the silent Mark coming for the interview. He, Luigi, had been told to wait outside. The summoning of the photographer and how the Cardinal had addressed the Monsignor as 'Professore' when they had parted outside his private room in the Vatican. It all came back to him. Luigi continued to shake, even though he wasn't privy to Rodini's game plan. In the Monsignor Mark affair, he had a fair idea of it. He had never liked his former boss, now the Pope: he felt that the blood of Machiavelli coursed through Rodini's veins. For a brief moment he thought of revenge on this haughty Cardinal now occupying the Chair of Peter. Luigi calmed down, walking pensively up and down the long corridor. Eventually he made his way to his office, sat at his desk, took out his pen and started in flawless Italian, *Sanctissima Papa*, Most Holy Father. He had decided to write directly to the Pope, and to bypass the Papal Nuncio, given the delicacy of the matter. He felt that the former Cardinal Rodini would have done the same.

Receipt of this letter by the Pope had the effect that Luigi had anticipated and regretfully could not physically witness: Paul VII literally disintegrated in his private study. It was as if he had been hit by an avalanche of disasters instead of just one. His iron self-control crumpled and he was overcome by a paroxysm of uncontrollable shaking.

'The game is up. No divine assistance can come to my rescue,' he cried. Even in the brief few seconds it took to absorb the import of his former secretary's letter, a kaleidoscope of future events concerning Professore Bellini (aka Monsignor Mark Somers) flashed before his very eyes. Beads of sweat formed on his furrowed brow. Try as he might, he could not bring his mind to focus on the problem. A sense of dread and foreboding totally paralysed his normally active and devious brain. There was no thought of Mark, only of how he could save his skin and remain the Supreme Pontiff. He cancelled all his engagements for that day.

This, of course, was grist to the mill for the media, particularly the Italian press with whom he had a rather strained relationship, going back to long before he became Pope Paul VII. They were immediately suspicious, knowing his devious reputation. They wondered aloud in their banner headlines as to what had caused 'Il Papa' to cancel all his engagements so abruptly. One newspaper was unwittingly unerringly correct, with a heading, 'Have the chickens finally come home to roost?' Underneath this heading was a short litany of some questionable actions he had taken and decisions he had promulgated since his elevation to the papacy. The paper noted that he had been particularly harsh to priests and bishops who broke their vow of celibacy. Maybe it ventured, some or one of these disaffected men was the present cause of His Holiness' indisposition.

'How near to the bone!' muttered the Pope as he read the article.

Reading all this unfavourable newspaper comment only served to drive the Pope to further distraction and agitation. He would have to pull himself together and quickly, in order to resolve the problem. At long last his mind began to focus.

'I will not disappoint my detractors,' he whispered. 'This business of Monsignor Mark must be resolved once and for all.' In his desperation to survive, and to a certain degree, as a form of self-preservation, he had decided that the Professore would have to be eliminated. Of course this was a shocking decision he thought as he prepared to retire for the night. In his paranoia, which seemed to have mentally unbalanced him, he felt that he was justified in liquidating Mark to ensure that the Church was not rocked by this scandal.

Oblivious to all this, Mark also read some of the same newspapers, and was rather taken aback, but not surprised, at some of the unkind comments about Paul VII. He had personal experience of the cunning Pope. He had hoped that the strict rule on celibacy would be removed, if not relaxed, when the Pope ascended the throne. Instead, he was aware that Paul VII dealt harshly with anyone who transgressed on celibacy. Mark did not dwell too long on these thoughts. 'After all, matters turned out well for me and I have a very fulfilled life with Laura, Katrina and my work.' His thoughts continued, 'It's a wonder that nobody back home in Ireland ever wondered what became of me. Out of sight, out of mind, I suppose!' Little did he think that he was the root cause of the Pope's problems, and that this same Pope, who had provided such an excellent alias for him, was now plotting to have him eliminated.

The following morning as he prepared for college, Mark was listening to the radio as was his custom. All of a sudden there was a break in the programme with a newsflash that Il Papa had suffered a stroke and was seriously ill. The newscaster said that the station would issue regular bulletins on the Pope's condition during the day. Mark shrugged, '*Que cera-cera*' he whispered to himself as he turned off the radio and headed to his work.

As she was leaving Rome airport, Mary Rigney also heard the news bulletin. Her Italian was not great but she did gather that Il Papa was seriously ill.

'Damn, damn, damn!' she muttered. 'Just as I was about to solve the riddle of Father Mark's disappearance.' She was totally disappointed but decided to make her way to the Vatican for a private audience with the Pope, which would not now take place. As she travelled on the coach from the airport her disappointment heightened.

'It must be divine intervention that is stopping me from solving this riddle of Father Mark.' The bells of St. Peter's were tolling as she arrived in Vatican Square. People were crossing themselves.

'Il Papa! Il Papa is dead.'

Professore Marco and Dotteressa Laura's secret was safe. On a notepad beside the dead pontiff's bed was written the word 'Professore' and Vatican officials were mystified as to what that meant.

John Deasy

Home - Where the Heart Lies

The whine of brakes and clanking of couplings signalled the arrival of the Dublin train. Ballina railway station was resplendent in bright sunshine on this August afternoon. Cheerful salutations and warm embraces greeted travellers as they alighted. Friends and relatives embraced lovingly as they made their way slowly towards the exit carrying one another's suitcases and chatting excitedly. Children, agog at the prospect of sharing gifts from an array of shopping bags that displayed the names of city stores, trailed close behind.

Danny waited until more eager fellow occupants had left the carriage. He wanted to savour the atmosphere of a homecoming he had looked forward to for many years. This was the Ireland of his dreams, the place he had left forty years ago to seek a living in the United States of America. Due to the recession of the twenties it wasn't a good time for employment. After several abortive starts, he finally got work in the coalmines of West Virginia – hard labour, good wages, but what an unnatural existence! His fellow workers were a silent, introspective, unfriendly mixture of ethnic groups whose only goal seemed to be the amassing of wealth – there was no social interaction and little opportunity of meeting with compatible company. He had never married. He remembered now, with a mixture of nostalgia, the girl he left behind with a promise to return when he had earned enough for them to settle down together. He wondered what had become of her.

Irish people whom he had met since he came back were outgoing, smiling and friendly. On the downward train journey he had a lengthy conversation with a man of his own vintage who brought him up to date on conditions in Ireland and topical events. They shared many personal memories; by the time they reached Athlone, they were talking like old friends. As the steam train puffed its leisurely way through the stone-walled fields and white thorn hedges of County Roscommon he looked with nostalgia at verdant green pastures where cows lazed in shade out of range of the midsummer sun, chewing the cud and swishing long tails at the flies that preyed on them. Men, stripped to the waist, women in light colourful dresses, barefoot children at play, all waved gaily at the passing train while they saved hay in the fields. This was the Ireland he remembered from his youth – neighbours coming together to help one another at hay and harvest, barn dances and celebrations when crops had been gathered and secured against winter storms, fireside céilidhes and storytelling during long dark nights – that was real living, devoid of a passion to accumulate wealth. People, though poor, were honest and above all, they were content with their lot. He hoped his native homeland of Ballinagree had retained its old charm. Lifting his bags, he went outside to look for a trap or jaunting car to take him to a hotel; none was to be seen. A lone hackney man, sitting in a brand new 1956 Ford, offered his services.

'Is there any place where I can hire a car?' Danny asked. 'I want to get to Ballinagree while the evening is still young.'

'Car hire isn't catered for very much here,' the hackney man replied, 'but I'm sure Willie Dan won't see you stuck. He has a garage over the town. If you like I will drive you there?'

Willie wasn't in any hurry to oblige:

'Are you sure you can drive?' he asked. 'I think renting a car to an American would be risky. You drive on the wrong side of the road – see what that can lead to?'

Lengthy consultation and close questioning ensued. Eventually Willie conceded

'I have a car that might fit your requirements. She looks a bit shook but her heart is sound. You can have her for a tenner a day; if she comes back with extra scratches I'll charge for the damage.'

'I hope you accept dollars,' Danny remarked as he handed him fifty and took his place in the driver's seat.

'I must remember to drive on the left. I wouldn't want to disfigure this beauty any further; there's scarcely room for more scores on the bodywork. See you, anon,' he chided, as he drove smilingly away.

'What a jovial, unsophisticated guy – as Irish as they come!' he mused as he set out for Ballinagree.

In less than an hour Danny was standing on the site of his former home. Nobody lived there any more; he didn't expect they would. His parents had long since died and his siblings, like himself, had gone abroad. Contact had been lost – he didn't know where they were now or whether they were still alive. He gazed with emotion at the remnants of their former homestead. Roofless walls where the thatched roof had fallen in, gaunt gables and chimney-stacks standing sentinel over broken windows and doors, all enveloped in a canopy of overgrown bushes and trees – a scene of total desolation and decay. He climbed on the roadside wall to catch a glimpse inside. Floor and hearthstone were overgrown with nettles and weeds; in the ash pit an elder bush had grown half way into the chimney place where the hob was still visible, that coveted seat he had so often fought for with his older brother. As a child he sat there while his mother busied herself around the kitchen, cooking, washing, sweeping and putting food on the big deal table when the family sat around to eat. He recalled the kitchen as it was at that time – the dresser with its array of gleaming plates, coloured jugs and mugs, the wag-of-the-wall clock that his father regularly wound every Sunday after Mass, the mantelpiece with its motley collection of china dogs, vases and bric-a-brac. He thought of the revered picture of the Sacred Heart before which they knelt at night to say the rosary, its miniature red lamp glowing in the darkness. Not a vestige of these remained. Words of a familiar song came to mind:

> Lone is the house now and lonely the moorland,
> The children are scattered; the old folk are gone.
> Why stand I here like a ghost and a shadow?

He took a leisurely stroll around the vicinity in an effort to reconcile salient features of the place he had known so well. Nothing appeared to be as he had imagined. Sturdy stone-built walls that had enclosed the haggard were now an unwieldy mass overgrown with briars and nettles. The thorn hedge that enclosed the vegetable garden had disappeared. A few moss-covered stunted apple trees were all that remained of the once prolific orchard. The tall beech, in which he and his brothers once built a tree house, was no longer there. The narrow lane along which he had driven cows to water was now a broad roadway with tracks of rubber-shod wheels. He came to the road leading to the bog where, so often, he helped to harvest the yearly supply of turf – a minimum of fifty loads to tide them over until the new crop had been saved. He remembered that road, a mere path on the bog's surface. It had no foundation, the holes were so deep that it was necessary to manoeuvre the donkey and cart between ruts to avert overturning. All had changed – no ruts, no potholes, no cart tracks. The path had been replaced by a smooth gravel-surfaced road bearing the imprint of tractor wheels and heavy vehicles.

Across the same broad expanse of bog, in his young days, families had worked side by side at the turf face, cutting, fetching and wheeling heavy black sods outfield to drier spreading ground, the air filled with shouts of boys and girls calling to one another as they worked. The smell of turf fires again assailed his nostrils; this was a hungry place where, at meal times, tea was brewed on an open fire; swirling wind blew smoke into the kettle and tea attained that special flavour that one got only on the bog. Today no merry chatter of young voices reached his ears, no evidence existed of slanesmen, stripped to the waist as they dug the wet peat, no fetchers loading sods onto wide-wheeled wooden barrows. Only the chug-chug of a mechanical digger disturbed the silence as it disgorged the soft peat and laid it in long symmetrical lines on the spreading ground. The lonesome cry of a curlew, flying at a safe distance, gave him an uncomfortable eerie feeling as the evening sun began to sink in a blaze of red below the western horizon. A sense of emptiness and desolation filled his heart as he retraced his steps. In his leisurely rambling he hadn't met one solitary person with whom he could exchange greetings or engage in friendly conversation.

'The village inn,' he pondered to himself, ' surely it must be the place where local people socialise. There I will meet someone to whom I can relate, a person of my own vintage who remembers me or some distant relative who knew my family.'

As he ambled slowly towards the village he passed neat farmhouses with extensive farm buildings, stylish bungalows with ornate entrance gates and tarmacadam drives such as he had never envisaged in this rural countryside. Forty years had brought an unexpected air of prosperity that he was glad to see. It was good for those people who obviously enjoyed a way of life so different to that which he had left – good for those who, unlike himself, remained behind despite the poverty and want then prevailing. Their changed circumstances would make for lively conversation.

The Magpie was crowded despite the comparatively early night hour – thirsty workers had come in from the fields to slake their thirst after the toil of a warm day. They chatted animatedly with one another. There was a pronounced lull in conversation as Danny entered; eyes turned on him. Who was the stranger? A Yank by his appearance? Who might he be? Nobody volunteered an answer. Looking around the bar, he failed to recognise any of those present. Nobody saluted him or offered a welcoming gesture as he walked to the counter. Even the barman was stony faced as he mechanically said:

'What can I get you, sir?'

Danny was aware that he was the focus of attention. As he slowly sipped a pint of Guinness his eyes roamed around the bar, recalling the smoke-stained ceiling from which sides of bacon and leather tackle used to be suspended. Shelves with bags of tea, sugar, salt, pepper, tobacco and sundry culinary items; heavy jute sacks filled to the brim with washing soda and bluestone for spraying the potatoes; casks of porter with wooden taps set on trestles behind the counter, bottles of whiskey, brandy and gin on top shelves – how he remembered! These weren't to be seen any more. Such intrusions would be out of place in this modern bar with its mirrored backdrop, glass shelving and steel barrels from which beer and porter were dispensed through proprietary pumps fitted to the counter top.

'Would your name be Brennan?' a voice interrupted his reverie.

'Yes, that's me,' Danny replied as he turned to face his enquirer. 'To whom have I the honour to speak?'

'My name is Casey – you wouldn't know me. I came to live here a few years ago. Are you on holidays? Where have you come from? What sort of place is that? What do you work at? Will you be staying long?'

The questions were rapid and searching. Having satisfied his curiosity, without more ado, the questioner returned to his group where, amid nods and whispers, conversation resumed. Now everybody knew who he was; perhaps some others present might approach him. No joy – Danny sat alone and isolated on his high stool while he drank his pint. In silence he mused:

> I feel like one who treads alone, some banquet hall deserted,
> Whose lights are fled, whose garlands dead, and all but he departed.

'This,' he mused, 'is not the homecoming I have looked forward to so earnestly all those years. I am in the heart of my native place but nobody is interested in speaking to me. There is no opportunity of recounting childhood events, no one to relate stories about characters we once knew, no mention of my parents or siblings. In the minds of people here, it is like I never existed. They couldn't care less. I am like a leper in their midst. They don't give a damn about me'.

'Can I fill you another?' the barman asked as Danny drained his glass.

'No, thank you,' he replied.

'No, thank you,' he repeated aloud as, slowly, he made his way to the door.

'No, thank you,' he said to himself as he emerged into the cool night air.

'No, thank you, I've had enough.'

'Danny Brennan, it's yourself that's in it,' a female voice called to him as he was about to drive away. He looked around to find himself confronted by a woman of mature years.

'Don't you recognise me?' she added, seeing his look of bewilderment.

'I'm afraid, madam, you have the advantage,' he replied.

'Julia Donegan,' she volunteered; 'we were in the same class at school.'

Danny scratched his balding pate in search of inspiration:

'If we went to school together, I should remember – forgive me, it's been a long time.'

'Too long for some of us,' she teased. 'Don't you remember how we romped in the hay on a summer evening, all alone after older members had left the field. We had our first kiss that evening, the first of many before you went away.'

'Julia, Julia, forgive me – how could I forget? I had more serious things on my mind at that time, making arrangements for going to America. To me, our brief relationship was a spontaneous boy-girl first attraction – I thought no more about it.'

'It meant more than that to me. Danny; I was hopelessly in love with you. How could I tell you? Girls at that time didn't show their feelings; you left home very soon after; I had no means of contacting you? All of those years I kept thinking of you, hoping that we might meet again.'

'Well, Julia, it looks like it has happened. Lucky we met before I left. My homecoming, that I have looked forward to for years, has been a disaster. I know I shouldn't have expected that things would stand still but I wasn't prepared for how everything has changed. They say one should never go back, it serves only to create disillusionment. You saw what happened inside the pub. The shock of not being known, of not finding anybody who remembered me or showed any interest in talking to me, hit me hard. Before your greeting reached me I was already starting back to where I came from, a wiser and sadder man. Now that we have met I am pleased to postpone my departure until you and I have had some heart-to-heart conversation. What say, you come with me to Ballina where, in the privacy of my hotel, we can recap on events of our childhood and share some experiences of our respective lives. Sorry, Julia, I haven't asked if you are committed to a relationship; I wouldn't want to interfere. As for myself I have no attachments, in fact I've never had. What do you say then?'

'Danny, if that offer had been made to me anytime in the last forty years I would have gladly jumped at it, so great has been my desire to see you again. Now that it has become possible, I'm not so sure. None of us are children any more; we have become inured to our respective lifestyles. Although I had many offers of marriage when I was younger, I remained single. Maybe I was still living in hope. Can I suggest that, instead of accompanying you to Ballina, you come and share a meal with me in my humble retreat down the road. Having lived there so long I am reluctant to exchange it for any upmarket modern hostelry. I'm not a gourmet cook but, in a situation like this, I can rustle up something edible. Will you accept?'

Delaying only to purchase a bottle of Burgundy and a box of chocolates, Danny was on his way. Long into the night they talked and talked. On both their sides, it was as if a tap was turned on, so much was recounted. Julia recalled the names of their classmates and gave a running commentary on each. Some, like him, had emigrated, others, regretfully, had died; only a few who lived out their lives in the immediate neighbourhood were still around.

'There was one young girl – Sally McCormack – what became of her?' Danny asked.

'We had an understanding that I would come back and marry her; with the passage of time and the difficulty of getting a decent job in America, we lost contact. Over the years I felt guilty at having let her down'

'You needn't have worried,' Julia replied, 'you weren't gone very long when she took up with a shopkeeper in Kiltimagh. I haven't seen her for years but, from what I hear, she still lives there with her husband and some of their family.'

'Julia, you have been my saviour. If we hadn't met I would have returned to America sad and disillusioned. Tonight's conversation is only the beginning. If I come back tomorrow will you accompany me to the local cemetery? I would like to find my parents' burial place and offer a prayer over them. After that we might go for a run in the old jalopy that I hired in Ballina. For old times' sake I'd like to see the lake at Pontoon. How about lunch in the hotel there?'

As they strolled along the shore after a sumptuous meal, Julia stopped suddenly. Wrapped in a wave of melancholic emotion, she burst forth:

'Danny, do you believe in fate? Around the time you emigrated I came here on an excursion with a group of pioneers from Ballinagere. We were all very young and impressionable. I must have been talking a lot about you and my feelings for you at the time. A friend told me if I put your name and a message into a bottle and cast it into the lake it would bring you back to me. I wonder whatever happened to that bottle. By now it has probably been smashed against the rocks or swallowed by one of the giant pike that inhabit the lake and consume everything that comes their way. In any case I reckon the cork that kept it floating would long since have disintegrated. Isn't it funny though that you and I are together here after all those years? Do you think there's anything in the legend?'

'I don't know anything about that legend, Julia, but I reckon that whatever you apply your mind to will eventually come about to your advantage. Maybe fate has conspired to bring us together again. As for me, I'm mighty glad this has happened. You and I may have outgrown the age of romanticism but, by the grace of God, there's a lot of mileage left in us yet. What do you say, we give it a shot and see if the old spark that you felt for me is still alive?'

'Easy on, Danny. Heaping fuel on a smouldering fire is a sure recipe for quenching it. I don't know your plans for returning to America but if you stay around for a few months and we get to seeing a bit of each other, I'll respond to your proposition one way or the other.'

'That's settled, then, Julia. Until now I was hell bent on getting away from this place as quickly as I could. I planned to return to West Virginia without further ado. I have no particular reason for going back there but it seemed it was the only place I knew. Now that we've met my mind has changed. Tomorrow I am going to set to work to try to restore the old family homestead. It will take a few months but doing it will give me a lot of fulfilment. Meantime, I'll hire a boat and occupy myself in a spot of fishing on Pontoon Lake when time permits. Perhaps you'll come along with me on some of those occasions. Who knows, we might even locate that bottle? I'm dying to know what you said to me in your message.'

Six months later:

'Danny, the house is beautiful. I'm glad you decided to restore it. If you agree, I'll sew curtains for the windows. We can't have inquisitive people peeping in at us.'

Martin Gormally

Letter from Bonzo

Press notice:
In an American court a judge awarded compensation of $45,000 to a woman whose kitten was molested by the dog next door that climbed through a hole in their boundary fence. The dog's owner accepted responsibility.

The following is a letter from the dog to his owner:

Woof-woof, Master,

I am truly sorry for landing you in the soup. I admit I gave that kitten a bit of a going over to keep her from depositing her foul smelling faeces among your Arum lilies and despoiling your beautifully manicured lawn with her scratching and scraping. But what unhinged, biased, human being awarded her owner forty-five grand in compensation? What right had the kitten to come into my patch to perform her filthy functions? Was there not enough space within her own territory to perform her daily evacuation!

I suggest, Master, that this was a premeditated attempt on the part of her owner to tarnish your reputation for keeping your garden in such pristine condition. Well-bred cats do not act in such an unsociable manner. Coming from a long line of Alsatian ancestry, I know how animals of noble origin should behave. Despite her owner's claim to the kitten's superior breeding, I have evidence of her flawed pedigree. Persian, my foot! I have seen her mother cavorting with the Town Tom under the acacia tree in their garden. I assure you, Master, that seducer was no Persian, nor did he conform to any authentic feline breed that I know of – if indeed such blue-blood cat species exist.

Master, I beg of you, do not pay compensation to that jumped-up social tulip next door. If she pursues you for non-payment, I will go to prison in your place. After all, I am to blame for the misadventure. As I committed the crime, if guarding your property can be so termed,it is I who should bear the consequences. I think I might just go through that fence again and give the lady herself a nip or two. That would constitute a valid claim for compensation. Then I'd get a longer spell in the jug. I'm told there are lots of lecherous cats in there. The authorities might give me a job controlling some of the more unruly ones.

Wow, wouldn't I enjoy that!

Bonzo.

Martin Gormally

Myself

The one who mocks me in the long mirror
Is not myself,
But a frail shadow of myself exiled from
That teenager of seventy years ago.

Thoughts

Dreams are like a summer breeze
drifting past with gentle ease.
Memories are like fragrant flowers
nodding serenely in sunny bowers.
Friends are like the trees so tall
outstretched arms lest we should fall.

The Dead Wood

No wake was held, no prayers were said,
The chainsaws roared, the wood was dead.
The blooming flush of life has fled.
Day after day the blackbirds sit
With scarce a stir, with scarce a sound
Staring with bewildered eyes
At corners where the martyrs fell.

Brigid Gunnigle

Who Am I?

Who am I, where am I going, I feel a stranger
Yet I am not in a strange place, I am with my family.
My youth has passed
Age has crept up on me at a slow pace.
I have not noticed it coming,
Shrunken limbs, hair growing thin,
Eyes dim, a mind confused.

Am I going to a strange place?
Will there be a brightly-painted hall door?
Will I ring the bell
Or will automatic doors open wide as I approach?

Will there be thousands of people?
Music, laughter and song?
Or will thousands of ghostly faces seem as one,
And shout in a loud voice 'Come, you have no choice'.
Stranger. Strange place.

Brigid Gunnigle

Across the Hearth

How silent have you been through the long wilderness
Of winter and faded summer.
To see you step across the threshold was my dream
Now lost in the murky darkness of December.
The veil of night is falling and
I can no longer see the moon.
Its face hidden behind heavy cloud and
Me hidden behind the pink striped curtains.
Across the hearth your empty chair gazes at me.

Memories scatter and reform in my mind
Only to vanish in the shady stillness of the room.
The years go over my head and words are forgotten,
Like the wind that blew yesterday.
I strive on without any definite aim
Sometimes filled with doubt and puzzlement
Because I am wandering between two worlds
One dead and the other a dreamer's world.
Across the hearth your empty chair gazes at me.

Brigid Gunnigle

Fantasy

Dear Doctor, could you tell me what the mid-life crisis means,
Me man is acting funny, now he's started wearing jeans.
He's like a trussed-up turkey that's ready for the pot
I'm getting worried it's some quare disease he's got.
His belly's hanging over, his backside's sticking out,
He's started drinking gin instead of pints of stout.
You remember, Doctor, when you sent him for that scan,
Well he came home from hospital a very different man.
Oh the waterworks is better, he's stopped running to the loo,
He thinks he's Ronan Keating and him turned eighty-two.
That prescription you gave him – 'twas a waste of time,
He refused to take it, demanded gin and lime.
I always got his pension, now he's getting it himself
And I swear to God in heaven all that's left might be pence.

You should see the bathroom, hardly place to put my teeth,
There's deodorants and hair cream, Lynx and Listerine,
Add to that a new spa bath, just to soak his feet.
When I turn on the telly all he does is yawn
But you should see the antics when that Natalie comes on.
He's shaking like a jelly and foaming at the mouth
There she struts behind the bar, big boobs sticking out,
God, there's many a time I feel like giving him a clout.
He talks about Viagra, now what the devil's that?
Is it for arthritis or t'oul pain that's in his back?
If you think 'twill help him, do the best you can
And bring him back to what he was – a quiet, dacent man.

Brigid Gunnigle

85

The Alcoholic's Prayer

Lord, take from me this dreaded glass
That has stolen my life away.
Give me the strength to battle on
And face another day.
My body is on fire,
My mind is cracked in two
There's strangers all around me
I don't know what to do.
My middle name is alcohol
Since I was but a lad.
I tried to kick the habit
But the pain is just too bad.
I've come through a long dark tunnel
Now I can see a spark of light
Dear lord, help me to win this final fight.
Keep my hand from reaching out
Push the glass away.
I yearn for peace and contentment
And one endless sober day.

Brigid Gunnigle

Broken Dreams

The wide-brimmed hat from the palsy shop
Shaded the swollen eyes
But the aching heart within her breast
Cried: Why, why, why?

The refuge door was blue she knew
A kind voice had told her that.
She hurried along through the Saturday throng
Her mind fighting right from wrong.

What had she done to deserve this abuse?
But her question had no positive meaning.
Her dream was love, happiness and reace
Now shattered by thumps of a fist.

Brigid Gunnigle

Words

Words are lights upon my feet
On darkened paths they help me greet the saddest day
The lonely night, endless hours put to flight.
Words are stars with glorious eyes beaming down on me,
Surrounded by their beauty I rest contentedly.
Words are warm hands outstretched to comfort and to care,
They melt the ice around my heart when oft times I despair.

Words are hopes that we have cherished
They are adventures that we plan.
They are rhymes and songs and stories,
They take me to far distant lands
Where I meet a whole new people
With words held in my hands.

Brigid Gunnigle

The Homeless Going Home

'I'll give him a blessing', the young priest said
The patient lay still in the hospital bed.
A pretty nurse in starched white
Pulled the curtain all around,
From kith and family not a sound.
Was it years or was it days since
He was loved in the dark confines
Of his mother's womb and lay
On the warmth of her breast?

He had peered out from his cardboard bed
had reached for the soup handed out
By a faceless friend.
Death had drawn a grey veil over the gaunt face.
A doctor lifted the long arms
And crossed them gently on his breast.
Two winos stood in uneasy silence
On either side of the bed, eyes minions of tears,
The bearded one reached out, caressed the dead face,
'We'll miss you mate, you was one of us'.

Brigid Gunnigle

Castle Daire

Deep down the back stairs Sarah, the housekeeper, ruled the kitchen with a rod of iron. Upstairs everything was spick and span, sailing like the Queen Mary, bone china, crystal glasses, monogrammed table linen. The ladies sat in the big drawing room, its bay windows overlooking Lough Melvin. It was there they practised delicate needlework, chatted with the guests and arranged parties and hunting dates.

      The basement door was always open, allowing steam from the huge cauldrons to escape. Kettles whistled on the big crane crook. Sarah stood, arms akimbo: 'Where are you, girl?' The kitchen maid ran, face streaked with coal dust – fifteen years old, an orphan depending on the charity of the big house, her legs tired form climbing the big stairs with water for the ladies to wash. Her hands were chapped and raw from scrubbing the slop buckets in the rainwater tank behind the pigsty. Her little basement room was fireless even in winter. But it was still better than the one she had in the orphanage. She had to share that with three other girls. Her table was an upturned orange box covered with a little tablecloth she crocheted from threads the chambermaid got upstairs. Sometimes she would daydream and think of the future. But loneliness was her constant companion and when Sarah called she knew there was no dream to follow.

      The institution ward is empty and dispassionate.
'I see you now, dear child of mine, born of a love that rattled and cracked when you were just a seed. A love that I thought would always wear a forever badge. You lie down in your small white cot, your puckered face reposing in sleep. The nurses and doctors are kind enough but cold and they ask so many questions. I cannot answer. I know you and I could bond together and I think you know too. But I have to go, and you will go to a new life that I can never be a part of. I look in your eyes: they are pearly grey, like raindrops. Sometimes you blink and I wonder what

you can see or hear. The staff here in the hospital think that some neighbour left me full of child and went his way. They are so wrong. I am a bundle of lies and fears. Silence is my sin. They ask the father's name – none; baby's name, bastard? yes. There is no more. I touch your cheek and hand you over. Maybe some day I'll see you or speak to you in a crowd and recognise you'.

One day in the seventies I met Sue, my friend, in the supermarket.
'Hi Breege, did you hear about the millionaire couple that arrived in the hotel the other day?'
'No, what about them?'
'I hear they are rolling in dosh. You should see the car they have – a big silver Merc.'
'Coming for the fishing probably, the mayfly will soon be up.'
'Ah! Mayfly my granny! Those two wouldn't know a trout if it leapt out of the water and kissed them, and I can tell you the Merc.did not come in a lucky bag either.'
'Sure they could be after retiring and be having a touring holiday,' I said.
'Why are they asking so many questions about the big house, I'd like to know. Sure that place is in rubble for the past fifty years. If they know about that place they are no spring chickens.'
'What about going for a coffee tomorrow, we might see them. If they want news we can give them plenty of waffle.'
'They have never enquired about boat hire, Rob says, and the lake is ideal now.'
The following afternoon we went into the lounge and ordered a drink. Jean, the barmaid, pointed them out to us.
'Very nice couple', she said, 'they had one of the best bedrooms overlooking the lake.' They seemed friendly enough. Sue, of course, took the lead and invited them over to join us. The woman said nothing. The man declined politely. He said, in a bit of an English accent, that it was too near dinner but agreed to meet us again. I said they were welcome to drop in if they were walking and gave them directions to where I lived. On the way home I said to Sue; 'Something about that woman rings a bell with me but I can't put my finger on it.'
'Funny you should say that,' Sue said. 'I feel the same. So come hell or

high water we'll pursue it further.' Two days later they arrived on the doorstep and introduced themselves,

'Bob and Mrs Metcalfe.' Lucky enough I had a bit of ginger cake left over from Sunday. I gave Sue a quick buzz. 'Bloody hell! See you in a minute or two,' she said and hung up. Conversation was general at first. Then Mrs Metcalfe said in a quiet voice:

'I'm Ellie. I worked in the big house many years ago.' I thought Sue would have kittens. Shocked was a mild word to describe us; all hell had broken loose. Bob stretched his legs and lifted the paper. Then with mugs of coffee the reminiscing started. All our names rolled off her tongue: mine, Sue, Cottie, Jamie, Madeline, Rose. Our seventy years rolled away in a flash – memories of the fishing with sally rods and string for line; the boatmen packing us into their boats; trips across to McClancy's castle. Ellie said she'd like to see the place again and would we mind coming with her. She decided we'd walk but with my gammy leg Bob took the car.

The long avenue was well overgrown. The roofless house was a heap of rubble except for a few windows gaping in a gable end. I stood where the steps used to be and thought I saw Dick, the groom, in his grey uniform and white gloves, assisting Miss Bettina and Miss Lillian to alight from the carriage. We remembered the day we sneaked up to see Mr Nicholas and his bride return from their honeymoon.

'What happens if she sees the ghost', Cottie said. 'Sure she'd be too grand to go up yon dirty lane and the style of her,' Rumour had been rife for years about the ghost appearing on starless nights. Jamie and Willie, the gardener, had seen it once – a pig with two heads. The night Major Thomas was killed off his horse it was supposed to have appeared and caused the horse to shy. There was also the evening we had to go to devotions. Mother had returned from hospital a short time before. Me and my sister and brother were sent to the chapel. As usual I met my friends and climbed the wall. Jamie said he'd take us to where the Major's horse had seen the ghost. We were afraid of our lives and at the same time killed with curiosity. We thought we heard a grunt or two and Maddie was the first to run. Then we all made off. Rosie wet her knickers and I fell and cut my two knees and had to lie to my mother. I said Kate Lynch's dog ran at me. Bathed in Jeyes Fluid and bandaged they weren't so bad. Then we were afraid one of the neighbours wouldn't have seen us at prayers and would tell on us. For days we were on tenterhooks. Ellie never took part in any of our escapades. She'd only get out for an hour or so the odd time. She'd have to be back on the dot, otherwise she'd get no food for the rest of the day.

Getting in the car again we headed for the graveyard. I had taken a hedge clippers as I knew the place would be overgrown. It was even worse when we saw it. The laneway was choked with scrub of every kind. Fair play to Bob, he did his best to clear a wee pathway. Broken tombstones were everywhere and we had to find the burial place of the big house family. There was ash and holly and briars but we knew Ellie was determined to find it. Stepping as carefully as we could we searched around. We knew the big house tombs had been made of white marble and stood side by side. Sue was the first to spot them, a kind of dirty green, with cracks everywhere and nearly split open. Bob tried to clear away the grime with tufts of damp grass. He wiped them as well as he could. I was the first to spell it out:

Here lies Thomas Charles Cumberwell
Who died September 25, 1924
His wife Margaret
Died April 17 1928

We could not read any more. Ellie went pale and silent and stepped as close to the tomb as she could. Sue started to laugh. She said:
'I'm going to keep away. That bloody Major could rise from the dead any minute. I'll take a look at Mr Nicholas in case he has done a runner.'
Bob was holding Ellie's arm. Suddenly she screamed, slapping at the tomb with her bare hands, tears rolling down her face. 'Bastard, bastard,' she shouted. We just stood like idiots. For what seemed like hours she sobbed uncontrollably. Sue whispered: 'Is she bonkers or what?' No one said anything. Then turning towards us Ellie said in a choking voice:
'My silence is broken at last. The sin is mine no more.' and then we knew about the long lost baby.

Turning on her heel Ellie walked back unaided to the car. We followed in silence. Over seventy years had rolled away. Tears still falling she said: 'What about that poem we wrote years ago? I still remember it.' And for the first time ever we saw her smile.

On Melvin's Shore

By Lake Melvin's shore in days of yore
We fished with rod and line,
As we lay afloat on an idle boat
While the sun all day did shine.

We heard the lambs in the meadows bleat
We watched the scudding clouds
And fairy music drifted down
From the hills above the town.

We paddled in our bloomers
We saw the mayfly dip,
And Dartry's mountains dressed in blue,
Gazed calmly over all.

We viewed the vales, the hills and skies,
White cottages by the lake,
And vowed that day, come what may,
Though our choices might be few
We'd meet again by Melvin's shore
And chase the Gilaroo.

Brigid Gunnigle

J. J. & Malachy

J. J. was coming from the local shop and he was very tired. His friend Mal was out to meet him. J. J. said; 'I thought I'd never get here'. They were both bachelor farmers and life-long friends.

'I have a slow puncture on my back wheel and every now and again I had to get off, pull in to the side of the road and pump the wheel up again,' said J. J. ' There was a motorbike behind me and two young brats on it. Every time I had to get off to pump the wheel they slowed down and were blowing the horn at me. One of them shouted at me –"What's wrong, Granddad, you know you should always carry a spare". If I got my hands on them I'd warm their lugs for them'. Then he said to Mal: 'I could murder a mug of tea'.

'You won't have long to wait now, the kettle is singing,' said Malachy. 'Them young brats, there's no manners on them'. So they sat down to enjoy their tea and loaf bread and Mal was looking forward to a smoke of Mick McQuaid tobacco after his tea.

Three days later

J. J. and Malachy were going to the rambling house. They did not go there a lot but J. J. said they would have to go there an odd time to keep up with the news. Then J. J. said: 'Do you know who I met coming out of the fort last night? Me bould Jim!'

'What was he doing in your fort, and anyway what took you to the fort at night?' asked Mal.

'Well, it wasn't really dark and I went for a bit of *brusna*. Don't I want a few *cipins* for the morning fire?'

'You could buy a wee bundle of sticks in the shop and they'd do you for a few mornings', said Mal, 'and did Jim explain himself?'

'When I asked him what I he was doing there he just said "Curiousity" and Mal, don't tell the boys; they'd only be jeering. He told me a long time ago that his country is a satellite and that on their TV they see us and what we're doing. They used to see the cutters of trees dotted about the country and did not know what they were. But he said to me "It would take me too long to tell you about them". I don't know what kind of a thing he is. You never see him coming and he can just disappear then. But one thing he did say was that if any of us would like to visit his country he'd arrange it. So how about it Mal? I'd love to see it'. 'Right. I'm with you J.J. Let's go'.

Nora Oates

The Broken Looking Glass

'Ah, come on girls, we are going to be late for the hop', shouted Molly to her four colleagues. They all worked in a local hospital in the town. They shared a large bedroom in a convent that was attached to the hospital.

'I don't know why we have to cycle out four miles to that God-forsaken village', said Mary, 'we can't even see ourselves in that broken old looking glass out there'.

'Who cares', said Breda, 'I will be more interested in looking at the boys'.

'Well Mary', Nancy butted in, 'you seemed to be enjoying yourself last time we were out there, with that lanky drink of water of a man'.

'I did not', said May, 'only that he danced the reels, set and hornpipe with me. He had a nose like a dripping tap'.

'Ah', Peggy said, 'you know we want to go out there because of Ann. You know she is madly in love with her Tommy. Hasn't he a farm the other side of the village – a very down-to-earth fellow, if you'll pardon the pun'.

They started off on their bikes; two and three abreast. They left their bikes at Breda's sister's house. Breda was the youngest of the gang. She was a very timid, unassuming girl. They put on their dancing shoes.

'Will I wait up?' Breda's sister said. 'If you're not too late I want to hear all the gossip'.

When they got to the hall they made a beeline for the cloakroom. It was only a lean-to at the side of the hall. Ann got into such a flutter when she saw her Tommy; it was as if there was no other man in the hall. She ran to look at herself in the mirror.

'I look awful', she said in a trembling voice.

'It's that awful old broken looking glass', said Mary, 'you look great'.

She danced with Tommy most of the time. She wished that the night might go on forever. She listened to the song *Mary Lou*, and it seemed to be written just for her. She made a date with Tommy for the following week. He was coming to town. They went to the Plaza cinema to watch *Gone with the Wind* and she thought her Tommy was far better looking than Clark Gable, only his voice was very hoarse and she wondered why. They made a date for the village dance two weeks on but her Tommy was not there. A friend of Tommy's approached her and told her Tommy was in hospital and sent his love and he would see her soon. Tommy was sent to St. Luke's hospital in Dublin. He had throat cancer and he died three months later. Ann cried for days and days. The girls were worried about her. She thought: 'Why did I not go and visit him in Dublin?' But then she thought he would come home hale and hearty. Gradually after a year she began to accept that she would not see him again.

During that time Breda found herself a man. Mary went out steady with her lanky man from the village and Peggy fell in love and married a porter from the hospital. In time the girls got Ann to go out herself to the village hall in Tully. She looked into the broken mirror, that broken mirror that she saw as just like her broken heart.
'I look awful', she said. 'Awful'.

Mary O'Connor

Was I There?

We received a card from Buckingham Palace with the royal insignia on it: an invite to the royal wedding. I ran down to our bedroom where Frank was still sleeping and I nearly shook the guts out of him.

'Look here', I said, 'we have an invite to the royal wedding'.

'Go away', he said, 'you drank too much wine last night'.

'Well, look for yourself'.

'Ah! Well, I'm not too surprised', said he. 'You know our O'Connors are the true descendants of King Rory O'Connor'.

'Well, ye must be well watered down since then', said I.

We went to Dublin shopping. He bought a lovely grey suit, a blue shirt and a pink tie. I bought this beautiful blue suit and a straw hat with some kind of reeds sticking out of it. It reminds me of an unfinished thatch roof. But so what! It was so expensive it had to be good.

Came the big day. We landed at Heathrow airport. A big limousine awaited us; the chauffeur doffed his hat to us. I turned to nudge Frank but it was George Bush that was sitting beside me, with that horrible fixed smile on his face. When we got to Windsor I was glad to see that it was Frank that was with me. I could give out to him. But what could I say to George? We were ushered up to our seats, sixth row from the top. Oh my God, I was so proud. I glanced behind me and saw Bertie and Mary Harney two seats further back. Behind them was Sir Elton John and his partner and there were other Dáil indignitaries – sorry, I meant dignitaries. Oh my God, there is Gerry Adams at the back of the church and what has he done to his hair? It looks like two horns sprouting out of his head.

Then the music struck up *Here comes the Bride*. When they came to the altar I was so shocked to see it was not Charles and Camilla. It was Audrey and Fred Elliot out of Coronation Street. The best man was Ken Barlow and, horror of horrors, Gail Platt was the matron of honour. Oh my God, Emily Bishop is the Queen Mother. She is casting baleful eyes at Audrey or is it Camilla? I am getting a bit confused at this moment. We are walking out of the church and all my Active Retirement friends are shaking our hands. They are saying they are so proud of us that we received an invitation to the royal wedding and that I should talk about it at our next meeting. Then the real couple emerged CHARLES and CAMILLA and they hugged us. Tony Blair was behind us and he could not even get a word in. Then I saw THE bold Johnny Stamford, Lynn and my friends from Forthill.

'Move over to your own side', came a voice that I recognised. 'You are taking up all the bed'.

Mary O'Connor

Johnny Walker

She pummelled his shirt on the washboard
as if it was he who was there.
She looked at the clock in anger
Jimmy was late from the fair.
Has he sold the two cows and calves there
Or are they still in the pound?
Or has he sold them for a good price
And treated the town bums all around?
That is my soft-hearted Jimmy.
I hope he hasn't bought a silly hat for me
He is very sentimental, you see
As soon as he's introduced to Johnny Walker
There is no telling with he.

Now the pummelling and scrubbing gets a bit calmer
As she thinks of her Jimmy – so fair
When first they went a courting
Without a worry or a care.
Oh! But his dinner is a shrivelling in the oven
His chops need artificial care.
And oh! the spuds
Oh! the spuds
The spuds, they are in despair.

Mary O'Connor

I am Seventy – No Celebration

I have all those aches and pains.
Now if there was a guarantee on my life
With good health and all faculties intact
For thirty more years or so
Then, oh! then, I would celebrate.
I could watch the success of all my family
Grow and grow in unity with each other
In forgiveness, the cure and key for all ills.

I could watch my darling grandchildren
Grow, each and every one of them.
I love them so, even though
They look at me askance
Granny, can we see your false teeth?
I am one step ahead of them.
I know I was their age so long ago
I looked on my elders of fifty or more years
As if they were from another planet.
What could they possibly know?

Ah! But life is such a teaser
I try to cram in so much in every day –
Bowling, reading even painting
There isn't enough hours in night or day.
Like the words of a song we all may know –
Where do you go to, my lovely,
When you're alone in your bed.

Well, I think of all the friends I knew
So many still with me, but I cannot forget
All my dear friends that have passed on,
My school friends, my dancing partners, my boyfriends.

Age, what have you done to me?
Grey hair, a double chin, varicose veins,
Tired old feet. But hold on –
There's a few good things left of me,
A sense of humour and loads
And loads of imagination.

Mary O'Connor

Two Little Girls

They sat side by side in front of the Stanley cooker, watching the glow of the red-hot embers. Neither spoke, lost in their thoughts. The younger occasionally glanced at her older sister, as if for reassurance. Everything was so lovely tonight, the warmth of the fire giving a feeling of peace and she could imagine all kinds of wonderful scenes as she gazed at the hot coals piled against the rungs of the open firebox. She was the princess and her prince charming was right there in front of the massive lump of coal, which, of course, had now become his castle. He would come for her one day and would never leave her. Again she looked at her older sister; who called her a 'silly billy' when she heard her playing her games out loud. She was so wise and good; Mama never had to scold her and she always talked to her about grown-up things. She wondered when she would be grown-up enough to share such conversations with her mother.

But tonight everything was perfect, or almost perfect. It was Christmas Eve and the silence was laden with expectation. It was just the same as last year and every other year, as far back as she could remember. When they were washed and ready for bed the nicest thing happened. They were allowed to stay up late sitting at the fire, looking for signs of Santa. Even as she looked now she was sure she saw him smiling at her. That would be her secret.

She looked at her mother and just at that moment their eyes met. She wanted to tell her that she loved her and that she was going to be very good from now on. Mama got so upset at times and it always ended in tears. The day she had broken that big vase in the hall her mother had been very cross and told her that she could never replace it. She had made her a 'Sorry' card at school next day but Mama seemed to get even more upset when she gave it to her. Adults were very complicated!

Her mother, too, was deep in her own thoughts. She cherished this moment; the silence and peace of Christmas were all around. She was so lucky to have two beautiful little girls, who were healthy and happy, though Amy could be quite a handful at times. She would have to try to be more patient with her – she was such a little baby in every way and looked so like her Dad. She wanted this moment to last forever. When carol singers had called at their door she felt the tears coming as they sang 'Silent Night, Holy Night '. It was just the same as last year, and every other year, or almost. For just one moment she had forgotten! For these few days she would not allow any worries to spoil the celebration of Christmas .The turkey was ready in the pantry and tomorrow they would all enjoy opening their presents in the sitting room upstairs. These were the only few days in the year that the turf was carried up and the fire lit. She hoped there wouldn't be a blow down – it all depended on the direction of the wind.

Amy looked at her mother again. She was so beautiful that she wanted to hug her but she was afraid that if she moved the spell would be broken and the moment spoiled. If only tonight could go on forever! She wondered why her mother looked so sad most of the time but just now she was smiling. She didn't dare tell her that she was so afraid of everything, even of Santa Claus. But most of all she was afraid that she was never going to see her father again. But tonight, she was so happy. Mama, Breege and herself had something very special. Earlier in the evening the singers had come to their door, collecting for the poor people. They had sung 'Silent Night' so beautifully. The words 'Silent' and 'Holy' were special. Tomorrow was Christmas Day and Granny and Uncle Jim would arrive for dinner. There would be a lot of noise and laughter. She preferred the silence they now shared. Would Mama let her set the table on her own? She was five and a half years old now and well able to do it. But Breege always bossed her around the place. Sometimes she really hated her. It was all right to be mad with her at times because the teacher had told them that you must love your neighbour and Breege was her sister, not her neighbour. Last year when she had helped set the table she knew she had done a good job putting everything in place, with folded napkins sitting beautifully on the forks. All Breege had said was:

'Don't you know how to count Amy? There are only five of us.' She had made no reply but Mama had seen the tears in her eyes.

'Leave her alone, Breege. It's all right, Amy, you've done a great job.'

The embers began to fade and still Mama did not ask them to go to bed. She became sleepy and comfortable and snuggled closer to her sister. Maybe she wasn't so bad after all! She began to think about her letter to Santa. She prayed hard that he would have read it in time to bring her the only thing she wanted for Christmas. She stared and stared at the fire and then had a great idea. She hadn't thought of it before, even though when Teacher had told them about the neighbour thing she had also told them about the angel whose job it was to mind each one of them. Why hadn't she thought of it?

'Please, please, angels in Heaven give us back our Dada for Christmas', she whispered. She waited for an answer but all she heard was: 'Off to bed with you girls now or Santa won't come'. The two little ones scampered up the stairs and into bed. As Amy snuggled down into her blankets she wondered what the morning would bring.

Rena Gallogly.

Friends

What is it that makes us become friends? We can agonize and moralize over the definition, the meaning and the slide rule that varies with each one of them. In simple terms, we get on well together, but then we often don't. Is it because we like them? If so, why do they exasperate us? Is it because we have so much in common ? Yet I love the ones who bring a totally different dimension into my life because they are different. There's Caroline, the 'grand' one, who always spoke of spending 'quality time' with her daughter, long before anyone else used the term. When we'd meet for coffee she was usually a bit late but she appeared like a vision, an ice skater, floating along with a snow white scarf, all chiffon, just touching the ground. Then she'd confide in me that she'd had an awful rush to get out! She liked cashmere sweaters; Edinburgh was the best place to buy them! She opened new horizons to me and she brought colour and zest to my life.

Ann is next on the list. Quiet- spoken, with a soft Donegal accent, she wrote such lovely poetry. I think I fell in love with the way she spoke. We both loved reading. We even went off for a weekend together to Galway to hear a reading by Margaret Attwood, leaving husbands and children behind to fend for themselves. After the reading, when we returned to the B+B, we sat up in bed and told each other our life stories, like two teenagers. It did us a power of good and we came home refreshed, ready for anything.

They're young, they're old, they're of every nationality and color, but all of them are friends in very different ways. They're always there for me. This is my resource centre, to be used certainly, but never, I hope, abused. According to my needs or desires I know to whom I should go. It's a bit like changing one's clothes to suit the occasion! There are my music friends, my singing friends, my teaching friends, my holiday friends, my reading friends, my writing friends and my old school-friends. And then there are my real friends.

'Give me ten minutes and I'll be over!' Josephine is there in the crisis, ready to listen to the sob story; not offering any solutions, but sharing the burden, which already begins to ease. I know I can rely on her; not even her husband will ever hear a word of what I've confided in her. Yes, this is different – she's not just a friend, she's a kindred spirit who understands exactly how I'm feeling.

Take Mary! 'Don't wear that jacket again; it does nothing for you!'. She is honesty personified – a bit abrupt and moody some days but we understand each other. Perhaps that's the starting point. Friends must 'gel'.

What about Veronica who's as deaf as a doornail but neither of us has ever acknowledged the fact. 'You never told me such and such,' she'll say and I'll look her straight in the eye and tell her I did. When I told her I had a grandchild she was quite excited, I thought, with a 'How lovely!' thrown in. Two months later when I arrived on her doorstep with the prized child in my arms, I was greeted with 'In the name of God where did you get that?'

Some friends come and go, others stay, and we are better people for having met them. Along the path of life the pattern may change. Our lives are richer because of friends. We may have many; we may only have a few; but they are precious.

Rena Gallogly

Don't Judge the Book by the Cover

As she placed the two cakes of bread on the windowsill to cool she glanced down the laneway leading to the main road. What she saw sent her dashing back into the kitchen where her elderly brother was downing his second cup of after dinner tea.

'Paddy, Paddy', she shouted, 'hide the bloody dog. There's a car turning in off the road and I think it's the Guards. We'll be up in court if they see him and he with no licence'.

Grabbed by the scruff of the neck the dog woke up with a yelp of fright at the treatment being meted out to him, and while whining in protest he was dragged from his slumber and his stretched out position in front of the open fire, to be thrown unceremoniously into the shed in the backyard. Hurriedly Paddy dashed into the kitchen to finish his cup of tea. He was only just seated back at the table when there was a loud knock at the door.

His sister, who had already discarded her wraparound apron, smoothed down her dress and touched up her hair in the shaving mirror hanging on the kitchen wall.

'Arrah, look who's here, Paddy. It's that nice young feller from the District Office – John, isn't it? Come in, *a grá*. I bet you're here about the grey heifer's lost tag and you're surely welcome. You'll have a cup of tea and one of my scones while Paddy there is turning in the cattle'. Coming into the kitchen the tall, slim man shook Paddy's hand and enquired 'How are you all since I saw ye last?' as Paddy made for the door, donning his cap, his sister's soft tone changed to a growl as she shouted after him:

'Get along with you and don't be keeping the man waiting'. As the visitor sat at the table she blew the ashes off the teapot lid, and filled the large mug she placed before him with the now well-brewed dark brown tea.

'Eat up them scones I only baked today. Wouldn't you think I knew you were coming?'

With this she pulled a chair up close to him and enquired: 'What news have you for me now? Tell me did that good-looking wan in your office ever get married? She was sporting an engagement ring last time I was in'.

'Ah', he said, 'that all broke up'. Moving her chair closer she warmed to her topic asking

'And how is it with that woman you married this very month a year ago? Any family yet?'

'Oh indeed, yes,' he answered, 'two sturdy boys'.

'Two?' she exclaimed as she moved her chair suddenly back from him. 'Two' she repeated as she lapsed into a deadly silence. Then she said:

'Ah, sure you did the right thing by her and not like some other of the boyos going about. You married and made an honest woman of her, fair play to you'. At this her brother appeared at the kitchen door to announce,

'I have her tied in for you now and I suppose herself there plied you with lots of questions, but I'll not keep you too long'.

Driving out of the yard, John smiled to himself as he made his way home to his wife and their twin sons.

Gerry Butler

The Harley Davidson

Jean looked around her sitting-room, and then gave a flick of the jay cloth to the mantelpiece to make sure there was no speck of dust there. She gave a last look into the dinning-room; everything was in order. She still had doubts about not using her best tablecloth, but her daughter had told her no one used tablecloths anymore, just a runner down the centre. She had bought her a new runner in Brown Thomas; it did indeed look elegant. Her best wine glasses were glittering on the sideboard next to the finger food. Everything looked expensive.

She had made an all out effort to do her son proud. He was bringing home his girlfriend for the first time. She was the daughter of a solicitor from a well-known law firm and Jean had high hopes of her son joining the firm if Olivia and he got engaged. They had met in Trinity where they were both studying law. John had been out to her house in Malahide many times. Jean knew she couldn't come up to the grandeur John had described but she would do her best not to let him down.

She checked her hair in the mirror over the fireplace, then glanced out the window. Her husband was coming up the path with that look on his face he only wore when he had something unpleasant to tell her.

'I hope you have plenty of food cooked. We are having extra visitors,' he said as he came through the door.

'He has invited some of his drinking buddies from the pub,' thought Jean, 'and on this day of all days.

'You'll never guess who is down in the hotel.'

I'm in no mood for guessing games,' said Jean crossly

'Well, it's your mother and she is after winning the Lotto and she is standing drinks for every one. The whole village is there. And that's not all. She had her new boyfriend with her.'

'What is wrong with him?' said Jean fearing the worst.

'Well he's no more than half her age and he hasn't a word of English. She met him when she was doing her test for the Harley Davidson. He

111

was working at the testing track, I think he's from Poland.'
'I don't believe it,' said Jean but at that moment the sound of a motorbike could be heard. Jean opened the door just in time to see her mother being lifted down from a motorbike by a tall young man. She then took off her helmet, through her arms around him, kissed him, and hand-in-hand like two lovers they walked up to the door.
'This is Karl. Isn't he gorgeous? Couldn't you just eat him?'
'I'd rather shoot him,' thought Jean silently as she automatically extended her hand. She invited them in and offered them a drink and a plate of nibbles.

At that moment John and his girlfriend arrived.
'The evening is going to be a disaster. Of all the stunts my mother has pulled this must be the worst. Karl had obviously heard of her Lotto win. Why couldn't I have an ordinary mother like everyone else?' Jean fumed.

After the introductions were made and everyone was seated Jean took stock of her guests. Olivia was very good looking and had a figure like a model. Karl was a fine looking young man but certainly not a suitable companion for her mother. How could she make her see sense without hurting her feelings? As the evening wore on Olivia seemed to be taking a great interest in Karl. She was asking him about the Harley.
'He doesn't speak English. He's from Poland,' Jean's mother said sharply.
'Oh great! My maternal grandmother was from Poland. I'll see if he understands me.' Jean's mother glared as her companion started to speak excitedly in Polish and hold Olivia's hand.
'He is going to take me for a run on the bike. Could I borrow your helmet?'

Jean's mother handed over the helmet somewhat ungraciously and they all went out to see them off except Olivia's father. He had poured out another glass of wine and was tucking in to a large plate of the finger food.

As Jean stood on the steps watching Olivia wrap her arms around Karl and burrow her face into his jacket, she saw that the scowl on her mother's face mirrored the one John was wearing. The last hopes of a bright future for her son in Olivia's father's practice died as the sound of the Harley Davidson died away in the distance.

Maureen Connolly

Kate's Last Kick

It was a cold morning in February 1894. Mary Cullen and Lizzie Moore hoisted their baskets on their hips and tightened their shawls around them as they made their way from the Haymarket to the vegetable market in Mary's Lane. They were hoping to spend a few pence on the vegetables they needed to feed the children. If Oul' Maggie was in a good mood they might even get some oranges or grapes thrown in – 'goin' off, Maggie. Looka'. Hay had been laid on the ground to deaden the noise of the traffic in Queen Street. One of the twice-weekly markets was being held in nearby Haymarket, so farmers with their fifteen-feet-high cartloads of hay had been coming in from Meath, Kildare and County Dublin since early morning. They were met by the men from the hay factors and business was conducted in a leisurely fashion. Farmer and horse were both patient as queues formed at the six weigh- houses. Sales over, the horses were fed and watered in a nearby yard. The men adjourned to the 'aytin' houses in Church St. or Benburb St. for their plates of rashers and eggs, with doorsteps of bread and butter and good strong tay. Afterwards they might visit one of the forges, saddlers, wheelwrights, seed shops, butchers or shops selling farm implements. And then on to queue at the entrance to Duck Lane for the leftover wash from the Jameson distillery with its unpleasantly sour smell.

Mary and Lizzie looked up at the windows of Harrington's public house. No blinds drawn and it was business as usual in the bar. So Kate Harrington was still alive, though very low, judging by the hay on the setts.

'That poor woman', said Mary, 'crippled with the arthritis she is. She must be bed-ridden now for at least two years. No one to keep an eye on that Billy Saunders in the pub either'.

'Sure you know what people are saying, Mary. Isn't he supposed to be operating on the 'one for you, two for me' principle? And sure his father and his cronies never seem to be stuck for the price of a gargle even on a Monday'. A little girl with huge cornflower blue eyes and a tangle of blond curls sidled round the door of the bar. That would be Betty, the old lady's granddaughter, poor Sarah's child. Kate had insisted on taking the child when Sarah died in childbirth six years ago. There was no love lost between herself and Terry O'Dea, draughtsman and whiskey-swilling teacher of Irish to the Jesuits down in Clongowes Wood College. All talk and no substance. He had soon forgotten her sweet Sarah and found himself another wife with a dowry in record time.

On the way back Mary and Lizzie were so busy sifting the gossip of the marketplace and congratulating themselves on the fruits of Oul' Maggie's generosity, that they had almost passed Harrington's before they noticed the closed doors, the drawn blinds and the black crepe on the knocker.

'Ah God rest her, poor craytur'. They crossed themselves as they joined the few women gathering round Billy Saunders.

'She passed away an hour ago,' he said, 'she had the priest and all the trimmings. The family has been sent for.'

'Big changes now, Billy,' said Lizzie, 'new brooms sweep clean.'

'We'll see, we'll see,' answered Billy. 'I know all the customers and I can run this place blindfolded.'

Betty stayed in the kitchen with Polly, the cook, and Nancy, her helper. They took turns comforting the poor child as she tried to come to terms with the fact that Grandma would be taken away and she would never see her again. Soon the relatives began to fill the house. The Naughton cousins from Rathmines alighted from the No. 22 tram about the same time that Martin and Alice Feeney got off the No. 16 from Terenure, having arrived there by steam train. Alice was her usual unsmiling self but her husband was friendly and affable. Polly always said that the Feeneys were like the little weathervane figures on the kitchen mantelpiece. Mrs Feeney presaged bad weather while her husband brought the sunshine. Suddenly there was a commotion in Queen Street. With a flourish a cab drew up outside Harrington's. Out stepped Terence O'Dea, immaculate in a black cashmere coat and a top hat, accompanied by his stylishly dressed wife and little son. He nodded graciously to the gathering neighbours and called for Billy Saunders. Having greeted his late wife's relatives, a dowdy lot by his standards, he gave Billy instructions for the undertakers.

'You make sure my instructions are followed, Billy, and I will look after you, when the time comes. Now follow me up to the drawing room.' As he mounted the stairs Terry was rehearsing his opening words to the assembled relatives. God knows they needed leadership, a shower of stick-in-the-muds if ever he saw them.

Standing in front of the fire in the drawing room, his thumbs stuck in his waistcoat front, heels teetering on the fender, Terry addressed Kate's family.

'She was a good woman, God rest her. Not the easiest in the world to get on with but ... she did her best. I'm a man to give credit where it's due'. His wife, Rita, nodded in agreement

'So we must provide a funeral that will respect dear Kate's place in the community but will also reflect our own status in society. The finest hearse from Hanrahan's, plumes on all horses, of course, an oak coffin and ...er... six, no, eight of their cabs to follow. It will be a fine turnout. Three times round the block, of course. We must respect those old traditions, and then on to Glasnevin. The brewery people and the merchants should be served here, I think, as we have the liquor on the premises, so to speak. And perhaps later the local customers might be allowed into the bar for a couple of hours'.

Martin gave a slight cough and suggested mildly that perhaps a family consultation on these matters might be best. Or in fact, that a near relative should handle things. Unfazed, Terry's face beamed under his mop of unruly golden curls.

'My dear fellow, in other circumstances I could agree with you. But as my dearest daughter, Betty, was the person closest to the late owner of these premises, I know I would be failing her if I did not personally supervise the arrangements for her beloved grandmother's funeral. Besides, as a man of the world, I am eminently fitted for those duties'. And he bowed condescendingly to the party. Nobody was ever sure afterwards whether Alice's lips were stretched in a smile or a grimace. All protests were overruled as Terry asserted his determination to look after his daughter and her interests, and after a few futile arguments they all subsided. It would be unseemly and disrespectful to Kate to fight over her poor corpse.

True to his word Terry organised the removal to the church, the journey to the graveyard with great success so that everyone was impressed and satisfied that Kate had been given a great send off.

'Of course it's no skin off his nose,' sniffed Lizzie as she sipped her port and lemon in the snug afterwards. 'The poor corpse is paying for this, you know. But she was always a dacent woman. So drink up, Mary'.

'Still he's a lovely figure of a man', sighed Mary.

'That's what all the girls say,' laughed Lizzie as she poked Mary in the side. 'You never know how many wives that fella will have yet. So there's hope for you yet, Mary'.

Their glasses refilled they toasted the dead.

'Lovely funeral, Lizzie'

'The best, Mary'.

Upstairs in the drawing room all the over-stuffed chairs, figurines and bric-a-brac had been dusted and polished. Ladies with upswept hairstyles and bustles perched ramrod straight on the chairs, their cups or glasses held daintily, as they sipped and chewed noiselessly on the tiny sandwiches and cakes. They spoke in muted polite tones. The gentlemen stood round confidently, bravely outspoken in their opinions on business, stocks and shares and government policy, mellow with fine whiskey and old brandy. Slowly the evening wore on until all but the nearest relatives had taken their leave. A tall, thin, be-whiskered man moved over to the table, opened his bag and placed a rolled parchment on it. Everybody recognised Mr Halpenny, the family solicitor, as he signalled for silence. Terry O'Dea sat comfortably in the centre of the room. His arm encircled his elder daughter, Betty, as she snuggled closer and laid her head on his shoulder. She smiled shyly at him – her Papa, the only person whom she had dared to trust tentatively since her Grandma's death.

Slowly and carefully his well-manicured hands untied the red ribbon and unrolled the parchment. His long fingers stretched the document flat on the table. A hand slipped into his breast pocket and produced his glasses, which he settled on his nose. Mr Halpenny cleared his throat in a genteel manner and settled to his task.

'It is my sad duty to read to you the Last Will and Testament of the late Katherine Harrington.' He began to read:

'I, Katherine Harrington, being of sound mind and ...' Here he was interrupted.

'Get to the main bequests, man. Never mind the whereats and wherefores', quipped Terry O'Dea smartly. 'Very well', was the prim response.

'To my faithful cook and friend, Polly McGowan, for her devoted service to me, the sum of £500, and to Nancy Turnbull, for her loyalty and service, the sum of £200. Billy Saunders, in my estimation, is sufficiently provided for, one way or another. The public house, known as Harrington's, is to be sold. My neighbour, John Martin has been promised the right of first refusal, and I expect my promise to him to be honoured. Now to the subject of Terence O'Dea and my beloved granddaughter, Betty O'Dea'.

'Ah', thought Terry to himself, 'I'm to be left in charge of the money to be used as I think best for Betty. Couldn't have come at a better time and not a moment too soon'. And he sat up straighter.

'Terence has the option of exercising his parental rights to bring up his daughter in his own household. In these circumstances, Betty O'Dea shall receive the sum of £2000 for her sole use on her twenty-first birthday. However should he abrogate his rights, then I appoint Martin and Alice Feeney of Main Street, Greystones to be her legal guardians. And I will and bequeath the proceeds of the aforementioned sale and all the remainder of my assts, of whatsoever nature to Betty O'Dea to be held in trust for her and to be used for her education by the said Martin and Alice Feeney. The interest from the investments to accrue to the said Martin and Alice Feeney on condition that Betty O'Dea reside in their household and be reared with their children'. The solicitor went on to name a few small objects and knickknacks from the house that were willed to the cousins.

Letting the monotonous drone wash over him, Terry sat in stunned silence. Had his face been made of glass it must surely have shattered.

'Of all the deceitful, low-down, cunning, vindictive, vengeful bags of knotted bones, she was the worst. I knew there was some powerful reason why I always hated her. And here it is, proving how right I had been'. Releasing Betty abruptly he pushed her away from him.

'Take her', he snarled at Martin Feeney, and knocking over his chair in his fury, he stormed out of the room followed by Rita and his toddler son. As the relatives gasped in shock the last sound they heard before the final slam of the hall door was Rita's angry voice railing: 'You couldn't mind your business. You couldn't even manage a dying old woman. My hero!'

[Extract form work-in-progress]

Bernie Doyle

Flaithiúlacht agus Féile ar Inis Meáin

Ar an radio a chualas an scéal ar dtús – turas ar an eitleán, trí lá ar lóistín agus dinnéar *gourmet* gach tráthnóna – ar £99! Ba bhreá an tariscint é. Glaoch amháin ar an nguthán agus bhí sé socraithe – dul amach ar mhaidin an Luain, filleadh ar mhaidin Diardaoin. Níl fhios agam an é an chaoi ina mheánn lucht Aer Arainn an paisinéir in éineacht leis an bagáiste, nó bheith ag amhairc ar phaisinéir in a shuí taobh leis an pilot a chuireann crith anama ort. I gcionn deich nóimead bhí Inis Meain leagtha amach ós ár gcomhair.

Bhíomar ar lóistín i dtí Mháire Ní Mhaoilchíaráin, teach ina raibh lóistéirí leis na blianta anuas. Is ann, freisin, a bhíodh béile ag Árd-Easbog Thuama nuair a thagadh sé le Baistiú Easpaige a bhronnadh ar na páistí. Ins na dachadaí thug an tArd-Easbog Breathnach (nach maireann) pictiúr dí féin do bhean 'a tí (auntín Máire) agus tá sé ar crochadh ós cionn an matal. Pictiúr álainn is ea é, ach ní fios cérb é an péintéir. Ach cuimhnígh go raibh Keating, Paul Henry agus Jack Yeats ar an oileán ag an am sin.

Chuamar ag spaisteóireacht. Tá furmhór na tithe suite i líne fada ar chnámh droma an oileáin, mar a déarfá. Taobh linn bhí an séipéal a tógadh i 1939, í gléasta go deas le fuinneóga de ghloinne dhaite le Harry Clarke, le dathanna áilne, seódmhar – gorm, buí, glas agus dearg. Tháinig umar baiste agus umar uisce choisricthe atá in úsáid sa séipéal ó séipéal den chúigiú aois déag. Tamall beag uaidh tá Dún Chonchúbhar, dún mór le trí ballaí cosanta, dhá chlocháin árda istigh ann, agus cúig nó sé d'iarsmaí clochach ann. Tá taobh amháin de suite ar an aill a thiteann 200 troigh síos go farraige; an-chosúlacht idir é féin agus Dún Aonghusa ar Inis Mór, ach gan an *cheval-de-friese* thart air ar na taobhanna eile.

Cómgharach don Dún atá Siopa an Dúin, le Pádhraig Ó Carthaigh, a thóg an bialann úd mar a bhuil an chef Frank Moynihan, as Cill Áirne, Conntae Cíarraí. Bíonn an bialann ar siúil aige le linn an tsamhraidh le seacht bliana anuas. B'eiseann a chuimhnigh ar an seift úd chun turasóiri a mhealladh go hInis Meáin, agus a thug cuireadh do Joe Duffy, ón Gay Byrne Show, teacht annseo chun críoladh a dhéanadh ar an radio fé na ceachtanna cócaireachta. Ansin rinne muintir an oileáin an tairiscint sin agus tháinig na sluaite. Agus tá an bhia ar fheabhas agus tá Frank féin agus a chuideachta go deas láthach. B'furasta aithne a chur ar na daoine éagsúla a bhíodh chun boird leat agus bhí an chaint agus an gháire ar siúil agus muid ag baint tathneamh as na béilí bhreatha. Annsin, sa phub, lean an cháirdeachas. Bláthanna ioldaithe curtha sa gháirdín agus i mboscaí taobh amuigh den teach tábhairne ar a dtugtar 'An Phub'. Tagann daoine as gach áird chun na h-oileáin.

Casadh sagart orainn a tháinig go hInis Meáin chun Gaelige a fhóghlaim. Bhí sé ann le sé seachtaine ag an am sin. Bhí leabhra aige agus dfan sé thuas staighre ag staidéar ar feadh an lae; sa trathnóna bhíodh sé ag labhairt le bean a' tí agus na comharsana. Bhí an Gaeilge caosach maith aige agus bhí sé chun cúpla seachtaine a chaitheamh i gcoláiste sa Cheathrú Rua sul ar fhill sé ar na hoileáin arís. 'Meiriceánach de sliocht Ghaelach ab ea é: é ina shagart sa tSualann, agus thóg sé blian *sabbatical* chun an teanga a fhóghlaim agus an 'sean tír' a fheicsint. Chuir sé J.M. Synge i gcuimhne dhom. Tugtar 'Teach Synge' ar thígh Mhic Dhonnchadha in a mbíodh sé in a lóistéir ann. Mo bhrón! Is truamhéalach an crot atá air anois. Tá súil agam go ndéanfar é a dheisiú agus a chur in eagar in onóir don file úd. Chuas amach tríd na carraigreacha liatha, leathana go dtí an áit ar a dtugtar 'Cathaoir Synge' air. Ciorcal déanta de chlocha atá ann, é oscailte ar thaoibh na farraige de, a dhó nó a trí de 'shuíocháin chlochach' ann. Tugann sé cosaint dhuit ón ngrian agus ón ngaoith, agus tá radharc mhaith agat soir go na Cliffs of Moher ar chósta an Chláir. Thart air tá piléir mhóra clocha ar imeall na haille, a thóg muinntir Árainn fadó ins an ré inar thógadar 6000 míle de bhallaí clocha chun a gcuid goirt a chosaint – goirt a bhúadar ó na carraigreacha millteacha le cré a rinneadar ón feamain ón fharraige.

Ins an gCo-op. a cheannaigh mé an cárta poist, bunaithe ar sean griangraf, in a raibh fear ina shuí, a iníon cois leis, beirt cailíní agus buachaill óg. An lá arna mhárach chonaic mé an griangraf céanna ar crochadh ar an mballa sa teach. Siad na daoine a bhí ann ná athair céille bhean a'tí, a iníon, beirt colcheathair agus buachaill comharsanach.

120

D'imigh an chailín bheag sin ag obair go hInis Mór in aois a sé bliana déag. Casadh Gearmánach uirthi agus i gcionn trí bliana phós sí é. Chuadar go Los Angeles, áit a bhuil sí go fóill, í 88 bliana d'aois. Nuair a thug a neacht cuairt uirthí cúpla blian ó shin bhí an Ghaeilge aice go blasta líofa fós. D'fág a lán, lán daoine na hoileáin. I Hartford, Connecticut, a chuir a lán díobh fútha, agus d'éirigh go rí-mhaith leo, ach is beag díobh a tháinig arais. Labhraidís Gaeilge eatartha fhéin i Meiriocá agus iad ag obair le chéile, ionas nach raibh fhios ag na Meiriocánaí cad a bhí ar siúil acu.

Séard a thaithin liom ar fad ná bheith ag éisteach leis na daoine ag caint le chéile as Gaeilge. Tá siad sásta caint le daoine go bfuil a bheag nó a mhór den teanga acu, cé nach bhuil líofacht cainte acu, mar nach bhfuil seans acu an teanga a chleactadh. Is maith an rud é go bhfuil leictreachas, gas, telefón, bóithre maithe, uisce ins na tithe, eitleáin agus báid mhóra, agus fiú amháin, innil 'sna curracha acu! Daoine foighneach isea iad, agus cé go bhfuil níos mó turasóirí ag teacht anois tá an síothcháin agus an ciúineas ann freisin, agus go mba fada a bhéas siad ann.

Foclóir:
Baistiú Easpaige : confirmation
Umar baiste : baptismal font
Umar uisce coisricthe : holy water font
Gloine daithe : stained glass
Seódmhar : jewel-like
Turasóirí : tourists
Athair céille : father-in-law
Neacht : niece

Bernie Doyle

Cothú an Dúlra
Protection of the Environment

Nós geal dom chroí a bheith 'mo shuí ar thullach fhéir nó fraoigh,
Ag inniúchadh gan strua ná gruaim mór-iontaisí an tsaoil,
A practice close to my heart - to sit on a mound of grass or heather,
Without care or trouble, closely studying the wonders of nature,

Gach luibh 's los, gach planda glas go flúirseach mórthimpeall,
Éanlaí cheóil in árd a nglór ag cantain ar a ndícheall,
Every herb and green plant in abundance around me,
Songbirds loudly singing their best,

Feithidí de chuile gné, an chuileóg ghorm géar-glórach,
Míoltóga beaga go tiugh sa spéir, fáinnleóga ar a dtóir,
Insects of every kind, sharp-buzzing blue flies,
Hordes of little midges that fill the sky, all pursued by swallows,

Iorraí rua ag dreapadh suas in áirde fríd na crainnte,
Sionnach glic, coinín 'na bhéal, ag éaló leis cois foinnse,
Red squirrels climbing high through the trees,
The sly fox, a rabbit in his mouth, slinking along a fence,

Torann sruth ag gluais le fán, fuaim aoibhin binn dom chluasa,
Corp nocht fén ghréin, mo cheann fé scáth – boladh fhéir ghlas fúmsa.
The sound of a rippling stream, music to my ears,
Naked in the sun, my head in shade; scent of green grass beneath me.

Ba chóir don ógra teacht annseo, amuigh imeasc an dúlra
Chun aithne a fháil ar chuile bláth i gcúrsa léinn nádúrtha.
Young people should come here, to this out-of-doors environment
To get to know every wild flower in a course of nature study.

122

Is mór an béim a bheadh ar chách faoi iontaisí ár dtíre
Dá bfaighdís oiliúint cruinn beacht ar gach a bhuil 'nár dtimpeall.
Each would attain a deep appreciation of the wonders of our countryside
If they were to receive clear-cut instruction on everything around us.

Is mór an dochair 'tá ar siúil ar ábhair bí 'gus uisce
Tré ceimicí 's leithreas braon ag sileadh isteach sna díogracha.
Serious damage is being done to food and water supplies
From chemicals and sewage effluent seeping into the watercourses.

Tá laghdú géar ar líon éanlaí, ar luinnduibh agus smólaí
Gan tráct ar an uile, beag 's mór. Ní chloistar anois an traonach.
Numbers of wild birds are in sharp decline – blackbirds, thrushes,
not to mention all the other species, big and small. The corncrake is no
longer heard.

Is braon liom siúd a chaitheann trúail cois abhainn, locha 's bhóthair,
Páipéirí, buidéil, cannaí stán, buinn toitíní, pluid 'gus éadaí.
I can't abide those people who dump refuse alongside
rivers, lakes and roads -
Papers, bottles, tin cans, cigarette ends, mattresses and clothing.

Is mór an iacall atá ar chách ár noidhreacht ghlan a chothú,
Dualgas catharthach orainn uilig, faire a dhéanamh uirthi.
A major onus devolves on every person to protect
our clean environment,
Civic responsibility demands that all of us keep guard over it.

Is cóir don bhreitheaimh i dteach na cúirte, pianós géar a ghearradh,
Sé mhí, ar a laighead, ag bailú brúscair ar shráideanna na cathrach.
The judge, in court, should hand down a severe penalty -
Six months, at least, collecting litter from the city streets.

Máirtín Ó Gormghaile
Martin Gormally

Out of Aran

High waves buffeted the Aran ferry against the quay wall, straining every hawser as the crew prepared for sailing. The darkening waters of Galway Bay reflected the rain-laden sky overhead.

'Damn this bloody weather,' exclaimed Saureen as she came aboard at the last moment. Above the whistling wind the captain's voice came over the loud speaker;

'Passengers are warned that the crossing may be choppy. I recommend that everybody stay below. The usual precautions are being taken.'

'An understatement, if ever there was one,' Saureen scoffed, scarcely heeding his words. 'Come hell or high seas I must get to Aran tonight. What if Peadar and Eileen haven't reached there? Their boat may have been wrecked; they may be marooned somewhere along the island's exposed rocky shore; they may have been washed into a cave in the cliffs. Maybe they're alive and calling out for me.'

Her woven multicoloured cape drawn tightly across her shoulders, the astrakhan coat that reached to her ankles and the tight tasselled woollen cap that covered her head and ears, shielded her from the worst of the cold. Ignoring the captain's advice to go inside, she clung with difficulty to the rail and gazed with a blank expression towards the island, an outline of which she could barely discern. 'Why should I be worried about the storm?' she asked herself. 'What do I care if this tub goes down or if I'm swept overboard? I have nothing left to live for. I have destroyed the only decent person I met with in all my thirty-six years – if Eileen and he are dead, I must bear my cross alone. People I once thought were bosom friends, have deserted me. Nobody wants to be associated with me any more: not a single person that I encountered today gave a sign of recognition. Friends indeed! Not very long ago I would have counted them in that light, but not any more. I had one staunch friend – too late I realise it. Now he has left me, gone I know not where. I may never see him again. The fault is mine, mine entirely.'

Seven years ago Peadar first came into her life; she recalled that evening so well. Clad in the traditional garb of the islanders, blue-grey home-spun trousers, sleeveless jacket of the same material, chunky hand-knit gansey, tight-fitting woollen cap, pampooties of hide, laced with leather thongs, he looked forlorn as he searched for a place to eat on a wet October evening in 1932.

'The fair was bad,' he told a man whom he met on the fair green. 'Demand was poor. I couldn't get anywhere near the value of the cattle I brought in from Aran. I cannot send them back because of the cost. But I'm damned if I'm going to give them away to those 'daylin' men who hover like vultures around the fair-green waiting to cash in on my misfortune and buy the beasts at their own price. I've heard of Aran men being cheated by those fellows. I'd drive the cattle into the tide before I'd give in to their knavery. I'll bring them a few miles out the road, to Ballinfoyle or Castlegar; some landowner will give them pasture until the November fair. First, I must have something to eat; I didn't have time all day and I'm ravenous with hunger. Will you keep an eye on the bullocks for me until I get back?' Roping the animals together, he tied them to a telegraph pole, and set off in search of a place to eat.

The lights of Rhona's café loomed ahead; he went in. Divesting himself of his rain-laden gear, he found a table. A waitress approached to take his order. Accustomed as she was to dockside workers, islanders and crews from visiting boats, she took stock of this well-set island man. She hadn't seen him before. His unruly mop of raven black hair, his blue-green eyes, strong cheekbones and soft-spoken voice appealed to her.

'A fine specimen of native manhood,' she thought as she took his order for boiled potatoes, bacon, cabbage and strong tea. Peadar had an eyeful of her too as she hurried between tables carrying three plates of food at a time to waiting clients. Not many females like her remained in Aran after the age of twenty; he had little experience of women, least of all those on the mainland. He admired her short trimmed auburn hair, her slim body and shapely ankles. He marvelled at her free manner as she chatted with all and sundry. When she returned to clear the table she spoke to him in a friendly way, and inquired the purpose of his visit to the city. He told her of his plight and his desire to find somebody who would keep the cattle for him until the next fair. She showed an unexpected measure of understanding.

'There's a man in Bushy Park who might help you,' she said; 'his name is Carty; he's a decent sort. Tell him Saureen sent you.'

Peadar's animals had been reared with care and attention since they were calves. Two had come from his own cows, two matching calves he bought from a neighbour. He had an eye for a good calf, one that would respond to feeding and grow into a sizeable one-and-a-half-year-old for sale. The shorthorn cows produced more than enough milk for the domestic needs of his mother and himself. Both liked a mug of fresh milk with their dinner; his mother churned some to make butter and to have buttermilk for baking. Peadar used the remainder to feed the young calves. He liked a drink of buttermilk when he was working in the fields or going on a night's fishing for herring or mackerel with his nearest neighbour and partner, Máirtín. They fished together in the hooker that they shared and were well acquainted with the storms and high seas that occurred regularly around the islands. Although both were experienced boatmen, Peadar's mother never let them go to sea without shaking holy water over them; she was conscious of the dangers that lurked beneath those mountainous waves. All had known of tragic occurrences in which fishermen from Aran had been lost, when a storm blew up suddenly while they fished for herring far out at sea or tended their lobster pots close inshore. Peadar's father had drowned when he was only two years old.

There were no other children in the family and, for all of his forty years, Peadar was the sole support of his widowed mother. Apart from infrequent trips to Galway to buy supplies or sell livestock, his entire life had been spent on the island where he tended his rock-strewn fields. He raised crops of potatoes, covering the outcropping rock with a layer of seaweed that he carried on his back in a wicker creel, planting seed and raising the ridge with sea sand. In autumn he cut and saved hay from the little fields and harvested the oats crop that he grew as a follow-up to the potatoes. From this he saved straw to repair the thatched roof of the stone built cottage that he occupied with his mother, securing the thatch against storm by means of stout ropes fixed to iron pins inserted deep in the walls. Inside, the house was clean and neat. The kitchen, with its hearth fire of turf carried in a fishing trawler from Connemara, had a floor of limestone flags, a dresser filled with shining crockery, a mantelpiece laden with ornaments collected by several generations of his O'Flaherty ancestors, all overlooked by a picture of the Sacred Heart and its little red lamp. In its warm glow Peadar and his mother prayed the rosary every night before they retired, putting themselves and their cares in the hands of the mother of God.

Saureen grew up in Galway and lived in Sickeen for most of her early years. Her parents were long dead and she had no siblings to compare with. She loved the freedom of earning money that she squandered with abandon on high fashion and city resorts. As a waitress in Rhona's restaurant she was in the way of meeting many visitors to Galway from at home and abroad. Her overt welcome and genial smile made her a popular figure. She was always willing to impart information on entertainment venues and city hot spots. Her knowledge of hotels, guesthouses and bars was extensive. She was no stranger to The Hanger and other ballrooms whose floors she often graced. To most people Saureen was a night owl, a social butterfly – she rather liked the latter approbation. Those who knew her more intimately were less complimentary.

On the occasion of their first meeting, Peadar, anxious to get back to his mother as quickly as possible, stayed only one night in Galway. Saureen gave him directions to a house where he would get accommodation. He thanked her for her advice in placing the cattle and promised to come to the café in November when he was back for the next fair.

'Wasn't I lucky to have met you,' he said as they bade one another goodbye. Back home he thought a lot about her as he went about his work, digging the potatoes and gathering the hay and oats into the haggard, where he secured them against winter storms. His mother was pleased when he told her how he had met a young woman and how she had helped him.

'Only for her I don't know where I would have found a place for the cattle,' he said.

'Buíochas le Dia (thanks be to God),' his mother exclaimed as she looked up to the picture of the Sacred Heart. 'I prayed that everything would go well for you.'

Peadar told his story to Máirtín who looked after Peadar's mother, milked the cow and herded the other cattle while he was absent. As well as being partners in the fishing trawler they had been firm friends from their youth. Máirtín had spent some years working on the buildings in England. Listening carefully to what Peadar had to say about Saureen, he looked at the ground but made no comment.

At the November fair Peadar was more successful. He sold his cattle at a good price and decided to remain in Galway to celebrate with two men from the island who had come to town for the same purpose. All three had money to spend. They went to an adjacent public house where they spent the evening drinking and exchanging experiences. Night had fallen before they remembered they hadn't eaten all day. Peadar suggested Rhona's café. They headed in that direction only to find it closed.

'Where will we turn to now?' they asked one another. None of them knew the city very well. As they stumbled awkwardly along Shop Street, in the light of a street lamp Peadar saw a well-dressed lady in high heels, ankle-length fur coat and matching headgear, approaching on the footpath. He was about to accost her for directions when, looking more closely, he saw it was Saureen. She recognised him but she appeared detached and unwilling to linger. Looking anxiously over her shoulder she said curtly,

'I can't talk to you now. There's a café in Quay Street where you will get food at this late hour,' and continued on her way. Peadar was puzzled by her reaction but he put the thought out of his mind as they made their way to the restaurant. Later he brought his companions to the house where he had previously stayed and they all got accommodation for the night. Before departing for Aran the following day he paid a visit to Rhona's cafe where he found Saureen busy serving tables as usual. She said 'hello' to him briefly as she took his order but she made no comment on their previous night's meeting. Her usual frivolity with other customers appeared to have evaporated. Although he couldn't understand her attitude, Peadar didn't draw her into conversation. He paid his bill and left.

Try as he might, he couldn't put thoughts of Saureen out of his mind as he went about routine winter chores back home in Aran. His mother's deteriorating health was a source of concern to him. Following weeks of treatment by the island doctor, the stomach ailment from which she suffered had not abated and he recommended that she should be transferred to hospital in Galway for further investigation. Peadar consulted Máirtín. The longer voyage to Galway at that time of year did not appeal to either of them. They decided that, given a lull in weather conditions, they would take her in the hooker across the shorter route to Rossaveel and from there by road to the hospital. They arrived at their destination two weeks before Christmas. Máirtín returned to Aran while Peadar stayed on in Galway to be near his mother. After visiting her in the hospital every day, he still had a lot of time on his hands. He thought of making contact with Saureen. This proved more difficult than he had anticipated. Workers in Rhona's restaurant informed him that she had left there a few weeks earlier. Somebody suggested that she had an apartment at Long Walk – they didn't know which house but they were sure local people would be able to direct him.

The long line of houses fronting the Claddagh basin looked ramshackle and run-down as he sought to locate the one he wanted. 'Try the red door,' a woman in a black shawl advised him. As he raised his hand to the knocker, the door opened and a tall swarthy man immaculately clad in a long coat, white collar, silk waistcoat with silver watch chain across his breast and a tall black hat, emerged. He glanced furtively to left and right before walking briskly away in the direction of the Spanish Arch. Peadar took advantage of the open door to enter. He knocked timidly on an inner door down the hallway to his left. There was a pause during which he heard some commotion within. The door was partly opened by a woman in furry slippers, long dressing gown and multicoloured headpiece knotted beneath her chin. In the dim light Peadar had to look closely before he was sure it was Saureen. She looked surprised to see him. Blocking the doorway with her body she inquired the purpose of his visit to Galway. She listened to his story about his mother's illness and expressed sympathy.

'I'm afraid I can't ask you in,' she said. 'As you see, I am dressing for an appointment. Perhaps we can meet later – say ten-thirty, in the Arch bar – we'll talk some more then and, if you wish, I will accompany you to the hospital sometime to visit your mother.'

Looking urgently at her gold wrist-watch she continued,

'I'm afraid you'll have to leave now, I must get dressed.'

Grateful for her few short words, Peadar walked on air as he beat a hasty retreat from the complex. He had found her and would be seeing her again in a few hours. A high tide lapped the quay wall across the road. Studying the area he reckoned it wouldn't be a very safe place after dark and he wondered why Saureen chose to live there. He must remember to ask her that when they met.

The hospital doctor was not hopeful. Investigation revealed that Peadar's mother was suffering from an advanced form of leukaemia. There was no cure for the condition. All the hospital could do was to minimise her suffering and keep her as comfortable as possible in the circumstances.

'Is she going to die, doctor?' asked Peadar as he wiped tears from his eyes.

'I see no other outcome, unless of course, you believe in miracles.'

Peadar was inconsolable. His mother had always been there for him. He couldn't imagine what life would be like without her. Stunned by the news, he walked across the Salmon Weir bridge to the Franciscan church. As he knelt before the Blessed Sacrament he wept uncontrollably and prayed aloud:

'Please, God, don't take her from me – at least not yet.' A stranger put a hand on his shoulder and said,

'My poor man, what is it that causes you such distress?'

In a broken voice Peadar related the story of his mother's illness. The man listened until he had finished.

'Dry your tears,' he said. 'Come with me and we'll have a cup of tea. It will do you good to talk about it.'

In an adjacent tea shop Peadar revealed the story of life with his mother in Aran, how he had never been away from the island except for an occasional trip to Galway and how, apart from his neighbour, Máirtín, he had no close friends. If his mother died he couldn't bear to go back there.

'What will I do at all?' he sobbed. The man was sympathetic.

'Do you know anybody in Galway?' he asked. 'Have you a place to stay while your mother is here?'

Peadar mentioned that Saureen had directed him to a boarding house in Shantalla and told him he was meeting her later that evening. The man inquired about this woman, what was her name and where she lived. He frowned on hearing that she had a place on the Long Walk.

'Not the best district,' he said. 'There are many stories about it. You would be wise not to go there after dark. I live on my own in Wood Quay a short distance from here. You seem to be a decent man. If you wish I can offer you accommodation for a little while until you come to terms with your mother's illness. It isn't good for you to be on your own at a time like this.'

Peadar moved into the home of Festy in Wood Quay. It was convenient to the hospital and he visited his mother every day. He wrote to Mairtín, giving him the address and telling him the news of his mother. He asked him to look after things for him in Aran until he got back. He didn't reveal the doctor's pronouncement to his mother. He had a feeling that she herself knew she wasn't going to get better but was keeping up a brave face for his sake. Festy's companionship was a boon to him. They became very friendly and occasionally shared a pint in the local public house where Festy introduced him to his friends and spoke of his predicament. People were sympathetic; they told him not to lose hope.

'God never closes one door that he doesn't open another,' one man assured him. Peadar wondered what new door would be opened for him when his mother passed on. Thoughts of Saureen kept coming to his mind all the time. He met her as arranged at the Arch bar. She was friendly towards him, asking after his mother and who was looking after things for him in Aran. She had never been to the island.

'Perhaps I can accompany you there sometime?' she suggested as she sipped a gin and tonic while he lowered a pint of Guinness. When he pressed her she drank two more. Over the following weeks they met regularly but he thought it odd that she never invited him to her apartment. Nevertheless he was pleased to be in her company and he told her so. He would be glad to take her to Aran when an opportunity arose.

Christmas in Galway was a revelation to Peadar. He had never before experienced the spirited scene that prevailed during the days and nights leading up to the festival – crowds milling through the streets, decorated shop windows laden with fashion wear, toys, plum pudding, sweet cakes, Christmas stockings and giftware. Hams and turkeys hung from butchers' ceilings, mouth-watering beefsteaks, chickens, chops, rashers, sausages and black puddings were displayed in windows. Shoppers laden down with baskets and parcels greeted one another in festive tones as they carried their purchases home. Crowded bars and hotel lounges remained open long after Peadar had retired to bed. The shouts of revellers reached him as he drifted off to sleep. He had no heart for celebration. Apart from a hot whiskey with Festy as they sat beside the fire after midnight Mass on Christmas night and a fling with Saureen to welcome in the New Year, he remained abstemious. The days lengthened, soon it was the feast of Saint Brigid, a time when, back in Aran, his mother wove crosses from straw and placed them in the rafters to ward off evil for another year. He remembered the mummers who went from house to house, their faces concealed behind masks, twirling and twisting around the kitchen floor while his mother plied them with sweet cake. As he watched her face grow pallid and her hair falling out every time he smoothed it, he knew instinctively she would never again do those things.

'Not much longer,' the doctor said.

His prognosis proved correct. On the night of February 14, (Peadar couldn't forget the date because Saureen reminded him it was Saint Valentine's Day), his mother passed peacefully away. Festy and some of his friends rallied around. They carried her coffin to St. Joseph's church where High Mass was celebrated next morning. Afterwards they laid her to rest in Bohermore cemetery. Peadar would have liked to bring her remains back to Aran where their forbears were buried but as his father's body had never been found, he didn't see a need to incur the additional cost and inconvenience.

'A family grave in Galway might be more meaningful,' he thought to himself; 'maybe I will eventually make my home here'.

He made a return trip to Aran for St Patrick's Day bringing Saureen with him. In the cobbled street in front of the cottage hens crowded cautiously around her feet and rose in fright as she impatiently shooed them away. She admired the stone cottage that Peadar had shared with his late mother: the open hearth fire set by Máirtín in anticipation of their arrival, the overhead mantelpiece with its complement of china dogs and vases, the neat bedroom with its soft feather bed, and the small four-paned curtained windows that were never opened. Peadar related to her how the doors of houses in Aran were always left on the latch. Neighbours would drop in without ceremony at any time of the day or night when the family was in residence. A stout bolt shot home on the outside of the door was an indication that nobody was at home in which case people wouldn't intrude.

'Despite the dirty hen-litter and messy ashes from the turf fire, I could feel at home here,' she murmured under her breath. She looked at Máirtín, his workman's hands scarred from old cuts, nails gnarled and thick as he shook her hand. He greeted her as Peadar's friend but she sensed he wasn't overly impressed. He reminded Peadar that it was planting time and asked him if he was going to sow potatoes as he had done every year. Peadar was non-committal;

'I'll think about it,' he replied.

For the next two weeks Peadar took Saureen on trips around the island showing her the sandy beaches, the steep cliffs, the ancient fort of Dún Aengus and the ruined monastery of St Éanna. They walked the bare limestone plateau and looked across at Innisheer and the coastline of County Clare. She loved the open air and scenery but wondered if she could endure the isolation of island life – it would be so different from the freedom of living on the mainland. If Peadar would sell up and move to Galway there might be a possibility of them making a life together. He hadn't proposed to her yet but she was in no doubt that he would do so before long. In the meantime she would use her womanly wiles to lead him on. Peadar didn't return to Galway for several weeks. Saureen told him she had things to do there and assured him she would eagerly await his return.

'Don't leave it too long,' she whispered as they said goodbye at Kilronan pier.

She waved and blew him a kiss as the small boat took passengers out to the Dun Aengus where it was anchored in deep water. He returned to the cottage, lonesome and downcast – firstly because of his mother's absence and now that Saureen had departed.

'Cheer up,' Máirtín said. Concerned as ever for his friend, he had dropped in with a bottle of poitín.

'Have a shot of this, it will put new heart into you.' As they sat around the dying embers of the hearth fire, late into the night, and finished the bottle of spirits, Peadar poured out his feelings of loneliness.

'I'm going to leave Aran and live in Galway for a year or two. I'm sure I'll get a job in McDonagh's fertiliser factory – they're always looking for able-bodied workers. I've grown fond of Saureen and I think she might have similar feelings towards me. In Galway we'd be close to one another and, if she agrees, I'd like to marry her. Will you look after the house and keep it safe from the storm? And will you take charge of the bit of ground and the cattle until I get back? As for the hooker, I'm sure you'll get someone to work with you at the fishing. The rest I'll leave to your own discretion. I'll write to you from time to time and you have my address in Galway if you need me.'

Máirtín listened to all that Peadar told him.

'Of course I'll look after things for you as long as you want,' he answered as he gave him a firm handshake.

'I wish you the best of luck in Galway. I hope you find happiness there. It's only natural that you should want the company of another woman after losing your mother but I think you shouldn't rush into any hasty decision about marriage – there'll be lots of time for that.'

MacDonagh's foreman took stock of this well-built, brawny-armed man who approached him for a job in the fertiliser factory.

'Hm, I reckon he'll fit in well here. I need strong able-bodied workers who can lift two-hundred-weight bags of fertiliser and stack them high in the store. We have lots of townsmen who can use a shovel but we sure can do with some stronger men for the heavier work.'

'You're from Aran, aren't you,' he commented. 'We've had islanders working here in the past and we were sorry to lose them when they moved to other employment. You may start tomorrow on a month's trial. If you prove your worth we'll probably keep you on.' Peadar found a place to live in Shantalla within walking distance of the factory and he started work the following day. Two pounds ten a week wasn't a great wage but it was enough to keep him going for the present. If MacDonagh's found him suitable they might increase his pay in the course of time. He renewed his acquaintance with Saureen. They met in the evenings whenever her round of social engagements permitted. They went for long walks along the promenade to Blackrock and shared a drink in one or other of the hostelries en route before he left her back to her house on Long Walk. She never invited him beyond the front door but he hesitated to ask her why.

'All in good time,' he thought to himself.

Occasionally when he retraced his steps along the Long Walk he met a well-dressed gentleman in a flowing black coat and tall hat sauntering in the opposite direction, wielding a silver-mounted cane as he walked. At work some associates to whom he told his story remarked,

'You'd need to watch out for yourself on the Long Walk at night; some unsavoury characters are known to frequent that place.'

'And what would bring them down there?' asked Peadar. 'Surely they could as easily take the air in Claddagh Park or along Sea Road?'

'I don't think it's sea air those bucks are after,' one man said laughingly. The others hung their heads and didn't respond. Although he laughed with him, Peadar was puzzled by the man's remark but he didn't want to show his ignorance of what might attract men to the area. Saureen was dismissive when he told her what the man had said.

'Don't be listening to those fellows,' she said. 'They don't know their ear from their elbow. What would they know about people on the Long Walk or their business?'

She didn't allow Peadar's return to interfere with her routine. They met on a regular basis; sometimes they went to the Town Hall cinema. On one occasion she took him dancing to the Hanger. Peadar wasn't conversant with modern slow waltzes and foxtrots but whenever a céilidhe and old time dance was called he was able to hold his own in battering the floor. Saureen, proud to show him off, cut a dash as she paraded him before her acquaintances.

'An unusual association!' one woman was heard to comment.

'I wonder what she's up to – a city woman taking up with a man from the Aran Islands? There's more here than meets the eye.'

Tongues wagged. Oblivious to all that was whispered or said, Peadar was glad to be seen in her company. He was happy in his new environment. He was close to the love of his life. The more he saw of her the more he wanted to spend his life with her. On a Sunday in September, arm in arm, they climbed among tufts of blooming heather on the hills west of Barna and gazed in rapture across Galway Bay to Ballyvaughan and Black Head. Far out to sea the Aran Islands, shrouded in a delicate haze of blue, appeared to rise from the sea like scenes from a fairy tale.

'Somewhere out there is Hy-Brazil, the Isle of the Blest,' Peadar said as he related the legend to her.

'I'd like to search for that island some day,' he added with passion. 'My mother always claimed it was where my father went. He was so happy there that he never returned.'

In a spontaneous moment of well being he whispered,

'Saureen, will you come with me to Hy-Brasil? I'd like if we could find the place and be together on it. I love you very much. Will you marry me?'

'Of course I will, Peadar,' she replied. 'I thought you'd never ask me.'

For weeks afterwards Peadar floated on air. He hadn't used his lovely tenor voice since his mother died – now he sang quietly to himself as he carried bags of fertiliser in MacDonagh's factory and on his way to work. He improvised the words of his favourite song 'Eileen, my Eileen' to read 'Saureen, my Saureen.'

He sang it to her whenever they were alone:

> Saureen, my Saureen,
> Wait for me, Saureen.

Delighted with his patronage she even tried to join in – 'That song has a ring of sincerity,' she thought.

'When will we have the big day?' she asked when the traditional period of mourning for Peadar's mother was over. 'I'd like to be married in spring.'

'Will we go back to Aran then?' Peadar asked. 'I'd need to do a few things with the cottage and bring a fresh supply of turf from Connemara for there's no fuel on the island.'

'Peadar, love, that might be a problem. I need to be in Galway on account of my business. I could fix up my place on the Long Walk or, if you'd prefer, we could go back to the house in Sickeen where I was born. There's nobody living there now. Don't worry about turf, I'll keep you warm wherever we are.'

This was the first indication Peadar had that they might not be going back to Aran.

'What was this about business?' She had never before mentioned that she had a business. He was reluctant to inquire in case it upset their relationship – he wouldn't want anything to come between them at this stage.

'I suppose I'll have to settle for whatever you want,' he said, 'but I'll need to go back to Aran frequently and to stay there for a week or two at a time, planting and reaping. That's where my home is and that's where I want to settle. It holds many memories for me. It's where I want to bring up our family if we are blessed with children.'

'Don't worry, Peadar, I'll come to Aran in my own time when I get things settled in Galway.'

Peadar had to be satisfied. Their marriage on the twentieth of April, nineteen thirty-four was a quiet affair. Festy and a waitress friend of Saureen agreed to be their witnesses. After the ceremony in the parish church the group adjourned to the Globe Hotel where they drank glasses of whiskey and pints of porter to wash down a sumptuous meal of crubeens, cabbage and potatoes. In his best tenor voice Peadar entertained the company with renderings of *The Sally Gardens*, *The Mountains of Mourne*, and other Irish ballads.

'What could be better than this?' he exclaimed to Saureen when they boarded the evening bus to Clifden.

'Are you happy?' he asked as they divested in their bedroom in the Atlantic Hotel.

'Very happy,' she replied. 'I love you Peadar. I hope we'll be together always.'

Peadar broke into his improvised song :

> Saureen, my Saureen,
> I love you too, Saureen.

The weeks after they returned to Galway were like an extended honeymoon. Peadar's heart sang with joy as he resumed work at the fertiliser plant. His mates at work were openly friendly; they congratulated him on his marriage. But when they thought he was out of earshot their remarks about women of their acquaintance who lived on the Long Walk tended to be less than complimentary. Phrases such as 'fancy women' and 'bits on the side' were thrown around in conversation. Peadar didn't really understand their significance. Never for a moment did he think that they referred to his wife.

'Thank you, God,' he prayed every day, 'for sending Saureen my way.'

From their front door he loved to watch boats coming and going in the Claddagh Basin and he frequently talked with fishermen on their return from a day's fishing. With his knowledge of the sea around the Aran Islands they had much in common. He was able to discuss with them where the best fishing grounds were to be found and what species of fish were likely to be running at different seasons of the year. The Claddagh men respected his knowledge and invited him to join them on fishing trips whenever he was off work. He became familiar with the fishing boats that plied in and out of Galway docks and he was competent to take charge of any vessel when other hands were occupied pulling in nets or packing fish. He enjoyed this new found taste of his former life with Máirtín and wished they were fishing together again back home in Aran. A cargo ship named *The Sansander* arrived regularly in the deepwater with fertilisers for MacDonagh's. On those occasions Peadar and his mates helped with unloading the cargo. While the ship was in dock, they worked side by side with the dockers and crew. The latter were of mixed nationality. Most of them had a poor knowledge of English and couldn't talk about their origins or their travels. The captain, a tall, good-looking man spoke perfect English. He frequently left the ship to visit haunts downtown. Looking at him closely, Peadar thought to himself,

'Haven't I seen that fellow somewhere before?' Offhand, he couldn't recall the circumstances.

The outside of the two-storey house on Long Walk looked dilapidated, but inside it was comfortable. On the ground floor one large room doubled as a kitchen and living room while another was a bedroom. Basic washing and toilet facilities were provided in a small annex to the rear of the building. To Peadar's amazement two rooms upstairs were permanently locked. When questioned about these Saureen told him that these were her business premises. They had to be kept under lock and key as her work was confidential.

'You see the telescope by the window,' she said when one day she showed him into the front room. 'I use it to keep watch on ships and boats that come and go in the bay. A friend of mine in the Customs likes to have information on any suspicious activities such as boats transferring goods from one to the other. It has something to do with

138

smuggling and evading customs duties.'

'And what is in the other room. Can I look in there too?'

'I'm sorry, Peadar, that's where I keep confidential information; I can't let you see that.'

'How come his wife didn't trust him to see the information she compiled?' Peadar wondered. He shrugged his shoulders but didn't comment further. In Aran he was aware that goods were often washed ashore on the tide, bales of rubber, barrels of oil, planks of wood from vessels that had foundered or been wrecked at sea. Items found were supposed to be surrendered to the customs authorities but few finders bothered to do this. To compensate for salvaging the articles they reckoned that they were entitled to keep anything that came their way. It was a case of 'finders keepers.' Sometimes they sold their booty to visiting boats. The few pounds they received made life on the island more tolerable. Peadar was uneasy that his wife might be involved in giving information to the customs men about any of his friends' boats and they might get to know about it. He had heard stories of bodies being found in the docks with no evidence of how they got into the water. He recalled the man he had seen walking on Long Walk the first night he visited there.

'Was he a customs man?' he wondered.

Rhona was disappointed that Saureen hadn't come back to work in the café. She had been a willing worker and was popular with the patrons. While Peadar pursued his job in MacDonagh's she seemed preoccupied at home during the day. They went together to one of her favourite pubs a night or two each week. There she introduced him to her friends and liked to show him off as her conquest. Peadar felt embarrassed particularly when he observed some of the company passing covert winks to one another behind Saureen's back. He didn't understand this reaction among friends; back home in Aran people were more direct. There at least you know who your real friends are. On nights when Saureen went out on her own, Peadar occupied himself with meeting some of his workmates for a pint in a local pub. He visited Festy or chatted with his fishermen friends. Usually he was home before her and, quite often, she showed signs that she had been drinking. He never upbraided her for her behaviour – why should he? Wasn't it normal for women to drink in Galway? One particular night as he walked along the quay he observed a tall man linking her arm-in-arm. The man faded into a doorway as they neared the house. Was this the man he had seen leaving on the first night he visited her at the Long Walk? Peadar decided to say nothing.

'I'm sure she'll explain the occurrence in due course,' he thought. 'He might be the customs man friend she talked about. What transpired between them would be confidential.'

Three months into their marriage Saureen confided she had something to tell him.

'I think, Peadar love, I am going to have a baby,' she said.

'That's wonderful news,' Peadar exclaimed as he embraced her and held her close.

'I love you Saureen,' he said. 'You know I always wanted a child of our own. I only wish my poor mother was alive to hear the good news.'

'When is it due to arrive?' he asked.

'Around the end of January if all goes well,' she replied.

'That's wonderful, Saureen, I'll be a father by Saint Bridget's Day – wouldn't my mother be proud! Do you think it is wise for us to continue living on the Long Walk with the sea coming right up to the door? Accommodation in the house won't be suitable for a child on account of the stairs. Will we go back to Aran as soon as the baby is born?'

'It's a bit soon to talk about that,' she replied, 'can we leave it until after the event?'

Peadar was content to wait; there would be lots of time to work things out. He decided to go to Aran for a few weeks to fix up the house and to tend to some urgent work around the fields. He told Máirtín how happy he was with the good news. There was a run of herring at the same time. Together they hauled several nets and salted their catch in barrels to provide food for the table during the winter. They joined with other islanders in drawing supplies of turf from the mainland. It was heaven to be back among his own people; he savoured the fresh sea air and the sunshine; it was so different from life in Galway. He couldn't wait to return to his native homestead.

When Peadar returned to Galway he found his wife had changed. Her normal breezy mood had become more sombre. She appeared much quieter in herself. He couldn't help noticing that her step had become heavy and that she didn't show a desire to go out at night as much as was her wont. Although he showered devotion on her and tended her every need, he received little approbation for his efforts. Her response to entreaties about her welfare and comfort was often curt; her patience with him appeared to be wearing thin. Hurt at her reactions, he put it down to temperamental change brought on by her pregnancy. Festy, who had never married, was in no position to advise him. Work mates to whom he confided his problem expressed their sympathy and told him not to worry.

'We men don't understand women,' they said. 'Don't take too much notice. Things will sort themselves out in due course.'

As summer merged into autumn there was no appreciable change. Sunday outings to Spiddal and Oughterard for afternoon tea or occasional nights at their favourite hostelries did little to reverse Saureen's sullen mood. Sleepless nights and long periods of silence replaced moments of tender interaction. Peadar wondered to himself if, despite his best efforts, their marriage was falling apart. As they lay in bed one night in early October Saureen turned to him and said:

'Peadar, you mustn't think that I love you any the less because of my recent behaviour. I can't help how I am feeling, I can only put it down to the baby I am carrying. I hope when it arrives my mood will return to normal. I'm asking you to bear with me until then.' A month later Peadar got a message at work,

'Go home at once, your wife needs you.' It wasn't very far; he ran all the way to find Saureen in extreme pain and two neighbouring women tending to her.

'Peadar,' she shouted, 'get the midwife, the baby is coming.'

The women directed him where to go, he raced like a madman to her door shouting, 'Come quickly, my wife is having the baby. I think she's dying.' Pacing the corridor outside their bedroom he cried and prayed: 'Please God, don't let Saureen die.'

Before long he heard the cries of a newly born infant. His knees crumbled and he had to hold fast to the handrail to prevent himself from falling.

'You may go in for a brief moment only,' the midwife said.

'You are the father of a beautiful little girl but your wife requires hospital treatment due to excessive bleeding. I will call a doctor and have her transferred.'

'*Míle buíochos le Dia* (a thousand thanks to God),' he exclaimed as he dashed to Saureen's side and kissed her pallid cheek. Tenderly, she gave him the little wrapped bundle to hold. Peadar's elation was sober; his concern for Saureen's welfare was uppermost in his mind. He followed the ambulance to the Central Hospital where, for several hours, he anxiously awaited news of her condition. The gynaecologist, when he appeared, was reassuring.

'A close call, Mr O'Flaherty,' he announced, 'but everything is fine now. Your wife and baby will remain in hospital care for a week or two after which I will review her progress.'

'What name will we call her?' Saureen asked as, with the baby on her knee, they sat in the visitors' reception room some days later. 'Would you like if she was called Eileen after your mother?'

'I'd like that very much,' replied Peadar. 'Eileen, my Eileen. Won't that be a lovely name – the same as my favourite song?'

When his initial elation had subsided Peadar began to realise that the premature arrival of Saureen's baby was, to say the least, strange. He was uninitiated in human fertility but he was well acquainted with gestations in the animal kingdom.

'Seven months pregnancy – a well developed baby – was something amiss here?' His work mates congratulated him on the baby's birth but in discussion they agreed that it didn't add up. When he went to the local pub with some of them for a celebratory drink he could see that he was a focus of attention by other customers. He was conscious of knowing nods between patrons and raucous guffaws following a witticism from one or other in the company. He felt decidedly uncomfortable. Saureen was no help to him. 'Premature births are quite common,' she told him. 'I have known several instances here in Galway.' Peadar would have liked to accept her explanation but a nagging doubt remained in his mind.

'Could it be possible that Saureen was pregnant before we married? Am I the real father of baby Eileen? How am I going to find out?' Memories of strange men he had seen loitering on the Long Walk came to mind. Tormented by a raft of unexplained circumstances, he decided to accost Saureen. She was defensive.

'Do you not believe me?' she demanded. 'Am I not your wife? How can we sustain a proper married relationship if you won't accept my word?'

'I want to believe you,' replied Peadar. 'I hope you are telling me the truth. I love you dearly and I will defend your virtue to the death. I have heard stories circulating which cast a doubt in my mind. If there is any substance in these I would rather hear about it from yourself. I love baby Eileen and I hope I am her father. If this is not so, please tell me now. I promise I will look after her in any event. A child shouldn't have to suffer because of the circumstances into which it is born. I want us to be happy as a family. I hope nothing arises to prevent that.'

Saureen didn't counter his statement. He interpreted her silence as acceptance of what he had said. Baby Eileen's cooing and gurgling was music to his ears. He grew to love her dearly and looked forward to the time when they would all return to the lifestyle that he knew in Aran from his childhood. He continued to work in MacDonagh's factory by day. At night he helped Saureen with her added domestic chores. He enjoyed their renewed conjugal relationship and was happy to baby-sit whenever Saureen took a night out with her friends. He wondered how she managed for money on those outings. She didn't work outside the house any more yet she never asked him for money.

'Babies can be expensive to rear,' he said to her. 'It's as much as I can do to save the price of an odd pint in the local with my friends. The people you meet must be very generous.' Saureen didn't comment.

The *Sansander* plied its regular trips into the harbour with supplies of fertilisers, at which times MacDonagh's workers were delegated to help with the unloading. The captain took advantage of shore leave to do things around town where, by now, he had become a familiar figure in bars and restaurants. Dressed in a long flowing coat that bore the insignia of his rank, a silk scarf and a tall hat, he twirled a silver-knobbed walking cane as he sauntered down the gangway and with lengthening steps took off in the direction of the city centre. Peadar watched him as he went.

'I must keep an eye on that fellow,' he said to himself. His fellow workers, seeing him pause to watch, joked him saying,

'Are you thinking of going to sea, Peadar? You'd look good in an outfit like that. Wouldn't it be a better life than shovelling fertilisers down below in the factory?'

Peadar didn't reply; he resumed his work.

Three years went by. In the balmy air of a sunny afternoon Saureen took Eileen for a walk along the seafront at White Strand. It was quiet and peaceful there. There was none of the noisy clatter of carts and sidecars that plied along the main route to Salthill. With a child in tow, walking was leisurely and it provided ample opportunity to stop for a chat and to sit on one of the fixed wooden benches for a rest. A tall, foreign-looking gentleman stopped in front of them. Lifting his hat in salutation, he greeted Saureen and stooped to pat Eileen's cheek.

'What a beautiful young girl,' he exclaimed, 'she'll be a stunner in another few years. Where would she leave it, having a beauty queen for her mother?' Saureen stirred uneasily and rose as if to continue her walk. Glancing to left and right she said,

'Thank you, sir, for your kind compliments. It's good to see you. We can't talk here. Come and see me at Long Walk when next you are in port.'

What if Peadar were to witness their encounter? she thought to herself. But then, he was far away down by the docks; there was no way he could have seen them.

The following year Peadar suggested that they should take a trip to Aran at the end of April when the days were getting longer and the weather was more favourable.

'Aran is beautiful at this time of year,' he told Saureen. 'I haven't been there for several months. I'd like to talk with Máirtín, find out how the fishing is going, and check on the house and its surrounds. It's our wedding anniversary around that time too,' he added when Saureen murmured something by way of objection.

'We could celebrate that here in Galway,' she countered, 'it isn't as if we were still honeymooners.'

'If you don't want to come with us,' Peadar replied, 'I'll go in any event and take Eileen, I want to show her where I grew up.'

Saureen relented, although her response showed she didn't favour the idea. They left one Friday aboard the *Dun Aongus*, planning to return early the following week. Eileen was enraptured – she had never before been on a boat. The sea was smooth as glass. On deck she raced up and down chasing gulls that followed the ferry, dipping their wings in flight to pick remnants of food thrown overboard to them by the passengers. She waved to trippers in small crafts and shouted excitedly to fishermen as they passed them by.

'I think, Eileen, you're going to like the sea,' Peadar remarked with pride.

The other travellers made much of her, praising her raven dark curls and plying her with sweets and money. Overcome with shyness she clung to Peadar's knee. When he lifted her up she threw her arms around his neck and kissed him. Saureen remained aloof. Standing at the ship's rail she looked back as the ferry moved out through Galway bay, past Black Head and the Cliffs of Moher on one hand and the rocky headlands of Connemara on the other. Soon the outline of the city grew dim in the distance. A soft mist was falling as they reached Kilronan pier.

Saureen didn't attempt to hide her distaste. Despite the cottage having been prepared and the hearth fire already lighting, courtesy of Máirtín, she complained that the rooms were cold, the beds damp and the lamplight was dim. With bad grace she boiled a kettle and made them a meal from the foodstuffs they had taken along.

'Wouldn't it be nice,' she said, 'if there was a public house near at hand where we could socialise and meet some people?'

Peadar was content to be back in his old home. He walked through the fields admiring every blade of grass, cattle grazing among the rocks, sea birds that piped and chirped as they darted hither and thither to the sound of waves on the adjacent shore. This was the haven of peace and tranquillity he had longed for every day since he went away. Eileen was filled with wonder and delight as he showed her around. She chased hens that gathered at the door, searched among the fuchsia bushes and came back with two brown eggs in her hand.

'Look, Mammy, we can have an omelette for tea. Daddy is going to catch us fish for tomorrow's dinner and I'm going to help him.' Saureen wasn't impressed.

'I hope he knows how to gut them,' she said. 'I only know how to cook fish that have been filleted.'

The weekend passed quickly. They had a picnic in glorious sunshine at Fort Dún Aengus where, lying prostrate, they gazed over the steep cliff face at miniature fishermen hauling lobster pots far below. They walked the shoreline at low tide where Eileen filled her arms with shells and rounded stones. Peadar showed them where to gather dilisk and carrigeen that they dried and brought back with them to Galway. Eileen learned the names of some sea birds, terns, gulls and herons. She watched the seals bob their heads above water as they feasted on smaller marine species. She was delighted at all the things she could see and do in Aran.

'Can we stay here always, Daddy? Why do we have to go back?' she wailed.

Two more years elapsed. Eileen was six now and at school. 'We're moving house,' Saureen announced as Peadar returned from work one evening. 'We must leave here tonight.'

'What's this all about?' he asked, bewildered at the suddenness of her announcement. For long he had maintained that the Long Walk was an unsafe place for Eileen but until this moment Saureen saw no reason to move from there.

'Why the sudden change of heart?' he asked. 'And to where are we moving?'

'The house in Sickeen is vacant,' she answered, 'I went up there today to check that everything is in order. We'll go after dark so that nobody will know. We are in danger here; we can't stay another night. I'll tell you all about it later. Get a hand-cart. All we need to take is packed and ready.'

On one hand Peadar was glad to know that at last they were to leave the Long Walk. He searched his mind for a reason as he borrowed a barrow from the factory yard where he worked. Nobody would miss it and he would leave it back early in the morning. Pulling the door shut they left at midnight, Peadar carrying a sleepy Eileen on his shoulder while Saureen trundled the barrow. Sickeen was silent as a grave. Early-rising residents had already retired for the night.

Eileen continued school in the Claddagh close to Peadar's place of work. On their way there every morning she told him about her teacher and named some pals whose acquaintance she had made, 'Brídeen Cloherty, Sorcha Beatty, Noreen O'Conneela.'

'Salt of the earth,' Peadar said, 'their parents are decent Claddagh folk. They mightn't have a lot of money but they are people you could depend on in a crisis, fishermen mostly, who have boats tied up in the basin and trawl nets in the bay out as far as Aran when there is a run of mackerel or herring.'

'I'd love to go fishing some time, Daddy. Will you take me out with you when I am bigger?'

'Of course I will, love. Boats are second nature to me.'

'I'd love if I could be a fisher girl instead of having to go to school. When will we go to live in Aran, Daddy?'

'Soon, if I get my way. But you know your mother is not fond of Aran – she doesn't like the idea of having to live there.'

With Eileen at school, Saureen was free to resume work at Rhona's for a few hours every day. By arrangement she chose to serve in the early part of the day or late in the evening depending on when the café was busiest. She renewed acquaintance with clients who patronised the restaurant, boat crews, dockers and travellers who regularly used the ferry. Some nights she didn't come home, saying it wasn't worth while as she had to be there for work early next morning. Peadar looked after Eileen on those occasions and helped her with her homework. He wondered what Saureen did during the midday period – she didn't seem to spend very much time at home in Sickeen. He knew she retained possession of the house in Long Walk; maybe she spent time there on her role of noting the activities of vessels in the bay although, since the outbreak of war, the number of foreign ships calling at Galway had diminished considerably! One day he was called to Eileen's school when she didn't feel well and had to be taken home. He didn't want to absent himself from work for a whole afternoon to look after her so he decided to look for Saureen at Long Walk. Lifting the latch quietly, he entered the hallway and was surprised to hear voices coming from the inner room. A man spoke in an authoritative tone:

'No, my dear, I can't let this go on any longer, we must come to an arrangement. My next turn in port is likely to be the last for some time. I want you both to come away with me. The girl is old enough to learn a new language. I will arrange a tutor for her in Spain while you get to know my house servants and take over the running of the estate. You will like it there, the weather is warm and the flowers in bloom are something out of this world. Soon I will give up seafaring and settle down to domestic life. For too long my house has been empty. I want to raise children and bring some life into it.'

'But what about Eileen?' the woman answered. 'She and Peadar are inseparable, she won't want to be part of this. And what of Peadar? I can' t just walk away from him like that. He stood by me through thick and thin. I feel sure he has suspected me all along but he didn't cheat on me. He has such plans for our life together; I can't hurt him like this; I can't break up our marriage.'

'My good woman, you have no choice. You should have thought about those things before events took this turn. Eileen is our daughter – we both know that. I have first claim on her. I insist that you do as I say. The *Sansander* is due in port again in three weeks. I want you to be ready to leave with me as soon as the cargo is discharged. You will need some cash to prepare for the voyage. Here, take this moneybag; it contains five hundred pounds. A similar amount in Spanish currency will await you when we reach our destination.' Peadar couldn't believe what he was hearing:

'They are planning to take Eileen away! I'll see to it that they don't get away with that,' he said to himself as he slipped quietly out the door and went to collect Eileen from school.

'I'll take her home and look after her myself until she gets better. I'll hold on to her even if I have to spill blood in doing so.' He said nothing to Saureen. The following week he went to Aran where he spoke with Máirtín.

'I need the hooker for a while,' he told him. 'I'd like to have it beside me in Galway. I'm dying to go to sea again before I lose touch; maybe I'll do a bit of fishing with the Claddagh men in my spare time. In the meantime you can take the cattle and whatever crops are ready and count them as your own. If I don't come back you can have the cottage too and all that goes with it.'

Máirtín wondered what was going on but refrained from asking. On a calm sea Peadar sailed the boat back to Galway and berthed it in the Claddagh basin. He went back to work as if nothing untoward was intended.

The *Sansander* arrived in port on schedule. Peadar was there once again with his workmates to help with the unloading. He kept an eye on the comings and goings of the captain whose frequent trips uptown continued; these appeared to occur regularly each afternoon. During the intervening weeks Peadar had secretly prepared the hooker for sailing and he had stowed enough supplies to last a few days in case circumstances demanded. Having discharged its cargo of fertilisers the ship was scheduled to depart that night on the late tide. The crew were duly notified and they spent their last hours on shore socialising with their acquaintances and lady friends. This resulted in some late arrivals on board. The captain rounded on them, proclaiming angrily that their next shore leave would be curtailed by way of compensation.

'I never saw him so irate,' the mate remarked, 'something is itching him. I'll bet things haven't gone right for him this turn.' He had been meeting with Saureen that afternoon to finalise their arrangements.

'I want you and the girl to come on board at six o'clock, immediately before the gangplank is raised. We will depart right away. I don't want any complications.'

Saureen did not dissent.

'Eileen, how would you like to come with me to Aran?' asked Peadar. 'I am leaving this afternoon on the hooker. Your mother is taken up with other business and cannot come with us.'

'Oh, Daddy, I'd love that,' she answered, 'but what about school? Won't we need to tell the teacher that I am going to be absent?'

'Don't worry about the teacher. Bring your school bag and books. We'll get in a bit of reading while we are away. I want you to take all your warmest clothes; the sea gets cold at night. Don't forget to wear the knitted woollen cap that covers your ears. I can't have you getting cold.'

'Daddy, this is great. I always wanted to go to Aran with you – just the two of us. I'll set the fire in the cottage and do the cooking while you catch fish. And I'll come with you on the boat when you go after the herrings.'

'Right then, that's settled. Don't say a word to anybody, put your things into this bag and we'll go down to the boat. I'll buy some food on the way.'

As the evening closed in, the hooker edged slowly out of the Claddagh basin and headed for the open sea.

Promptly at six Saureen walked up the gangway and went straight to the captain's cabin. He greeted her lovingly, throwing his arms around her neck and smothered her neck with kisses.

'Good work,' he exclaimed, 'now we can be together without interruption. Two days from now we'll arrive at my villa near Salamanca and I'll show you the apple groves and the olives. A little cognac to celebrate!' Emptying his glass in one gulp he asked,

'The girl – did you put her in her cabin?'

'Carlos dear, I have something to tell you,' Saureen answered. 'When I went to collect her at our home in Sickeen she wasn't there. I can't for the life of me know where she has gone. It's most unlike her not to be at home this time of the evening. Her books are not there either, which leads me to think she may not have returned from school. I'll go back again and see if I can find her. Can you delay the ship's departure for an hour while I go and search.'

'All right,' he said, 'one hour but, remember, not a minute longer.'

The captain informed the crew of a delay in departure. Saureen disembarked. At the end of an hour she returned.

'I didn't find her,' she announced, ' but I found this note on the table:'

'*Saureen, deceitful woman, unfaithful wife, I never thought I'd be writing these words. At last I have proof of your infidelity. I know of your plans to leave me and to take Eileen with you. By the time you read this note she and I will be far away. Don't try to find us. I never want to see you again. Your seducer can have you but he cannot have Eileen. I will see to that. If you had been honest with me at the time of Eileen's birth I would have forgiven you for being pregnant before we married. I loved you enough to accept your predicament and I would have married you just the same. You deceived me then; you lied to me repeatedly ever since and now you have plotted to deceive me once again. That I cannot forgive: Peadar.'*

On hearing the outcome the captain flew into a vile rage. Crew members jumped to their tasks as his screaming was heard all over the ship. People on the dockside stopped to listen :

' Stop, stop, I have heard enough. I see now how you and your husband have conspired to trick me. It is not you I want but our daughter. If I need a concubine I can find a dozen of your type in any port of call. I want my natural offspring who will bear children of my family line and make me a proud grandfather in my old age. Get off this ship. Go back to your brothel and find another sucker to bleed.'

'Please, Carlos, take me with you.' Saureen pleaded. 'I haven't tried to deceive you. I have no husband now. I love you and you have told me that you love me too. I will make up to you for your loss. I will give you other children. I can have no life in this town after what we have done, please don't leave me behind.'

'Put this woman ashore and take the ship out of harbour,' the captain shouted angrily to the mate.

Crying bitterly, with all eyes centred on her, Saureen disembarked. The gangplank was raised and the *Sansander* pulled away from the wharf. Weeping uncontrollably, she watched the ship as it headed for the open sea. There was no last minute gesture from the bridge where Carlos stood defiantly erect and stone-faced. In a mixture of shock and deep despair she turned to the nearest tavern to get a stiff drink and collect her thoughts.

'What am I going to do now that my life has been torn asunder on all fronts? News of being deserted by both my husband and lover has already spread like wild fire. I can no longer face those who previously hosted me. I will be an outcast in my native town.

Where is Peadar now? Has he left Galway? If so, where can he and Eileen have gone?'

She had many questions but no answers. Knowing Peadar's affection for Aran, she reckoned he might go there. But had he not said in his note to her that he didn't want to see her ever again? He would sense that she might seek him there. She decided to ask around and find out if anybody knew of his movements over the previous twenty-four hours. At the factory his fellow workers told her that Peadar had not turned up for work that day. Some fishermen in the Claddagh told her he had a hooker berthed in the basin in past weeks. It was there yesterday but today it was gone.

'A clue,' she thought, ' Peadar has departed by sea! But how can he sail a hooker alone allowing for the handicap of a young girl who demanded all his attention? Perhaps he had an accomplice, Máirtín, or some of his fishermen friends?' There was only one way to find out. She must go to Aran by the first available transport.

The *Dun Aengus* departed every morning from Galway but that was the longer route. She could take the shorter journey from Rosaveel on a boat that left in the evening. She would travel by road to Rosaveal and go from there. Having consumed several vodkas she went back to Sickeen to sleep it off. Despite her intoxication she was awakened in the middle of the night by a howling wind that rattled the windows and put buckets and barrels flying all around outside.

'A storm at sea! What if Peadar and Eileen are out there, buffeted by wind and waves? What chance would a hooker have in such weather? I must get to the island as speedily as possible and be there to lend a helping hand if they are in trouble. Peadar didn't really mean it when he said he never wanted to see me again. I'll get him to forgive me.'

She threw some clothes into a bag and hastened down town in time to catch the afternoon bus to Rosaveel.

She took up residence in Peadar's cottage and lay in his bed. Tormented by guilt and sorrow for her own plight, she couldn't sleep. Listening to the sound of waves breaking on the rocky shore, she imagined the worst.

'Have Peadar and Eileen made land on one of the islands? Has the hooker gone down in the storm? Have they been washed into some of the sea caves around the islands?' Nothing was to be gained from lying in bed, she must go out and search for them.

At earliest light she walked the shore at low water examining every accumulation of debris left behind by the outgoing tide. She scanned the horizon in the hope of seeing the hooker approach. She searched every nook and cranny along the cliff face and peered into every opening. She found no evidence that might throw light on what had become of the missing ones. Overcome by fatigue and hunger, she pursued her search until the incoming tide made further investigation impossible. Returning to the cottage to rest, she resolved that at low tide with the light of the moon she would pursue her search around the other side of the island.

'There can be no let up,' she said to herself, 'somewhere out there my nearest and dearest are in trouble. I will find them or die. I cannot go on living without them.'

In an eerie stillness she stood at midnight on the deserted beach listening to the surge of waves rolling towards the shore. Backed by a rising westerly wind, the tide began to fill. She shuddered: 'Was that a human head that surfaced momentarily out at sea only to disappear again in a matter of seconds?' Closer observation revealed it was a seal but the initial shock stayed with her. Among the flotsam and jetsam washed ashore was a collection of bottles, cans, sacking and torn garments. None of these bore any resemblance to garments worn by

Peadar or Eileen. She waded knee-deep into the tide to grab a floating spar of timber; it didn't match any part of a hooker. The absence of evidence of a tragedy at sea consoled her. Nevertheless she continued to search with even greater intensity.

The west wind brought a drizzling rain that reduced visibility to a few hundred yards. Above the lapping of the tide, from beyond the mist there came a plaintive wail. Saureen stiffened; she couldn't reconcile this sound with any she had previously heard. Was it the cry of a seal or something more sinister? For several minutes she strained to listen. Although the sound was repeated she couldn't make up her mind as to its origin.

'Is it a human voice?' she asked herself as she bent low to listen above the swish of the wind. 'There it is again – it is somebody singing!'

The sound wafted and waned and started to recede. She froze. She tore at her hair.

'There is no mistaking it; that is Peadar's voice. That's the song he used to sing to me in our courting days. He was always singing about this place that he called Hy-Brasil.'

She listened again - faintly it reached her:

'. . . on the . . . of the . . . it lay
. . . it . . . like . . . away . . . away.'

'That surely is Peadar singing – Eileen and he are alive – they are out there.'

The wind dropped to a gentle whisper. The rain shower ceased. The light of a full moon breaking through drifting cloud was reflected in the dark waters of the sea. It gave a clear view to the far horizon. There was no sign of a boat. The sound she had heard came and went until it gradually faded and died.

'Peadar, Peadar, come back to me. I love you. I want you. I want to be with you,' she cried as, frantically, she waded deeper into the rising tide. 'Bring Eileen back to me. I know I've done wrong. I've been unfaithful. Please forgive me. I promise I'll never, never again deceive you. Come back to me and we'll live together here in Aran that you love so well. I'm pleading with you, Peadar. Listen to me. Please, please, don't go away. Wait for me, I'm coming to you,' she cried in panic.

'I'll be your loving wife. I'll be a good mother to Eileen. I'll give you other children that are ours, ours, ours, only, and we'll be together for evermo.o.o.o . . . r.' A long-drawn smothered cry followed. Silence prevailed. Only the soft swish of the waves encroached on the eerie stillness.

[Extract from work-in-progress]

Martin Gormally

She

Why is it 'she'
When all is mean,
When one covers up,
And even the birds take shelter
And the field mice stay inside.

Is it not 'she'
When one basks out there
And the warm whiff
Of honeysuckle fills the air
The birds chirp merrily
And the field mice play.

This morning the garden lay
In a pink kimono
As the cherry tree strove
To hold her blossoms
She had worked on all year
To prove she is a lady.

This morning the bonsai chestnut
Tried hard to hold
Some of her blooms
As she bent with each
Gust of fierce biting wind.
That thinks to call herself 'She' !

Céline O'Flynn

Slíabh Dhá Éin

Slíabh Dhá Éin is no beauty to behold to those who do not see
Her difference and her frenzied state, and her *daithscéim corca is buí*
It's hard to believe there is no life in her, but so the *scéil* is told
There's not enough food to feed two birds, or shelter from the cold.

She is positively bumpy unlike her neighbour across the way,
Méadbh on her throne in her gown of stone, and Ben all majesty.
Her beauty is in how she receives the sunlight eve' or dawn
The pink, the purple, and the blue, or the grey and black of storm

There is a lake up there somewhere between the peaks
That is so deep, who dares to enter is threatened, so to speak
Their loved ones they may never see again, who anxiously wait
To hear their stories and fables of Slíabh Dhá Éin.

She rolls along the edge of sky, a tail of mountain Ox
Her streams run into sweet Lough Gill she meets at Dooney Rock,
She looks over to Hazelwood, Slish and Inisfree
Is she happy with the change she sees? Alas *Ochón mo chroí*

She stands there six hundred million years, the oldest range we know,
She has seen so many changes and families come and go.
It was bad when her rocks were turned for poles for ESB,
But now it's *brónach atá sí mar gheall* of the Comharlach 'pleannaí'.

High rise flats and offices are coming; soon it will be only she
Will remember the times when she hoped another bird to see.
She did not think of aeroplanes or 'copters to and fro,
Bringing industry to a land that once was *go mall*, - just slow!

Once people had time to greet the day, and bid one another adieu
To sit and chat, to sing and dance and care for all the few
Who lived among the rushes and tended to their toil
Of turf, the cow, the hay in May, the sheep and then the fowl

The Holy Well at the Hazelwood gate, brings people out to pray
The spiritual fervour, the rosary, the peace, and bird-song they say
Is due to one man Fr Egan, (long gone before our time)
Because he saw the need to build this Heavenly Shrine.

Throngs came there through the night, and at the dawn of day,
Through rough pathways by Cleaveragh, the Cairns and the lake.
The pier, the locals knew as the white wall beside the gate
Brought neighbours safe to dock their boats and sacraments to take

East of the Slíabh to Lahanagh,and west to Drumiskabole,
Ballisadare,to Kellystown, Cregg to Cill Easpogbróne
All roads led one way to Mass beneath the trees
At Aughamore Near, that holy place, the silence and the peace.

Mass was said there in the woods, during troubled times of yore
The lanes were trodden from the town and some came by the shore
The bell rang quiet, the Host was raised, the priest spoke softly then
And blessed them all with heads bent low until a year again.

The mountain looking down that day, still there as ere before
Looked with joy and filled the sky with hope forever more.
Slíabh Dhá Éin we gaze at you and wonder at your beginning
Did Jesus say 'Thou shalt be barren'? and are you forgiving?

Céline O'Flynn

From the Window

I cannot see her in the rocks
Though she landed a second ago
Her beige and brown is lost
Until she turns
It's a thrush.
Her speckled breast
Her quick step
To the left, then to the soil
Her ear bent low
She listens to the grub
Move under her feet -
The thrush.

Céline O'Flynn

Seasons

The heleboris at Christmas

Is the light for us outdoors

And then the birds are waking us,

And Spring alas is o'er.

The heavy scent of Summer

The sound of the humming bee

The red and rust of the trees at Fall

Bring us to our knees

To promise that we will do

What has been done before

To mind this World and pass it on

As has been done before

Céline O'Flynn

Christmas Gift

The Winter evenings draw us close
To the glow and warmth of the fire
The toils of the day are over
It is time for us to share
The stories, the news and the people we've met
On our journey through the day

The room is warm, the scene is set
The light is focused where
Dan with the paper reads aloud
The bits for me to hear
And discusses with me his views
But listens with one ear

My fingers never seem to rest
My knitting's on my lap
Five cables across each row
Five cables coming back
The pattern is by my side to check as I go on
To know it's going right, and rip if I go wrong

At last the reading's over and the paper put away,
His finger flicks the zapper and on the TV goes
All's well until the weather-man
Tells what the morn will bring
A day of sun or storm.
And then he zaps away

My mind is addled, my cable gone astray
Each glance I give a new play brings to my dismay
'There is nothing on that you would like'
I'm told in voice so firm
It now is time to rip again and rip, and zap and rip

This sweater grows so very slow
But there's one thing I just know
It will be ready for Christmas
But which one
I don't know

Céline O'Flynn

Old Ireland

In every house in Ireland
They gathered round the fire
When friends and neighbours
Came to call, sit and stay awhile.
News of the day was spoken
Laughter was shared by all.
The bellews turned in rhythm
To the sounds of the cricket's call.
Tea with bread and jam was had
With water from the well.
Memories were recalled by many
And some had tears to shed.
The box was taken down
From the dresser by the door
And before you knew it
The dance was on the floor.
Songs were sung
And stories told
And soon the clock rang out
The lamp was lowered
And 'God Bless All'
Was the evening's parting word.

Céline O'Flynn

Footprints

In whose footprints
Do I walk today?
As I go my way
Along the beach.

Who will walk in mine?
When I am gone
Paddling in the surf,
Enjoying the sunshine?

The indifferent sea
Obliterates them all.

Bermie Gilbride

Last Times

As we go through life,
Last times are rife.
Unrecognised as such
Otherwise too much,

A last time to tie their shoes,
A last time mend their clothes.
A last time fasten their buttons
A last time check their pockets.

A last time walk them to school,
A last time walk them home.
A last time comb their hair
A last time tell them what to wear.

A last time the garden they'll keep
A last time their friends here meet.
A last time crowd into the car
A last time settle a little war.

A last time hear their prayers
Are any prayers said these years?

Bernie Gilbride

164

The Barbecue

Their last night to gather in Monica's room; today they finished their exams; hard to credit. For so long they had dreamt about tonight thinking it would never come and now each felt a reluctance to break up the evening on this their last night in school. Sitting on Monica's bed watching the sun set, a red orb in a cloudless golden sky, they were afraid of what the future might hold. This small cubicle in St. Phil's dormitory had been their refuge for the last year. For five years they had shared their lives. At the end of each term they had hugged each other with a, ' see you in the fall, after Christmas, after Easter'. Happily they had gone their separate ways, secure in the knowledge that they would all gather on someone's bed the first night back after the holiday. Tonight was different.

Monica had been head girl in their final year and looking round, sensing the sudden loneliness of her friends, she turned to Barbara.

' Well Babs is that offer still on or are you getting cold feet?'

'Of course its on, lets discuss what Biddy has suggested. We all gather at my home for midsummer night, have a barbecue in our orchard wearing the old costumes from our attic. It should be good fun. Mum and Dad are going on holiday. Only Uncle Jack with perhaps an old crony will be there, watching football on TV, and of course Gramps. I expect Gramps will enjoy it, if he's not asleep in his chair, barbecues not being his scene.'

The mood lightened and all said goodnight and made their way to their respective cubicles, happy that their next meeting was arranged.

A week later Barbara kissed her Mom and Dad as they left for their holidays, Mom admonishing her to be careful in the attic and to put back all the old clothes carefully when they had finished. She really must get round to sorting out the attic when she came home. She was anxious too about the barbecue, warning about the danger of open fires, but having left Uncle Jack in charge of the cooking felt it was safe enough. Just then Barbara's Dad called 'For goodness sake come on, we'll miss our plane if you give many more instructions'. Giving Barbara a last hug Mum headed for the car, to Barbara's relief; Mum was so fussy at times.

Barbara's house was an old Manse in the country, surrounded by large gardens. To the rear was an orchard, with all sorts of fruit trees: apple, pear, gooseberry, blackcurrant and redcurrant bushes with raspberry canes and strawberry beds. This was her fathers' pride and joy and the barbecue was being held on condition that no damage would occur to his precious garden. In the centre was a lawn and it was there they hoped to dance and picnic.

Next morning the girls began to arrive. Mary was first living only ten miles away. Mary was tall and elegant, blue-black shoulder length hair with blue eyes – model material they all agreed, except Mary herself, who just wanted to be a doctor. She was aiming for all A's in her exam. Then Brid, average height, nut-brown curly hair, hazel eyes, came along. Business Studies was her chosen degree. After lunch Morna and Monica came together. Morna – small, blonde, brown eyed - was waiting to see what her results would be, but would like teaching if her points were high enough. Monica, a brilliant all rounder, had applied to do Archaeology. After lunch they made their way to the attic. Barbara's mother had been involved in the local drama group, hence the gowns available in the attic. She had collected many period pieces for their use in plays from all over the neighbourhood, and had stored them for the group in the big old-fashioned attic.

None of them knew what to expect except Babs, and as she led the way they were looking forward to what they might find. They climbed to the third floor and with much giggling opened the first door they saw. An eerie feeling came over them as they stepped on the dusty floor. The skylight was so dirty not much daylight came through. Grabbing an old rag Monica began to clean away the cobwebs, some of which caught in her hair, making her give a little squeal and breaking the sudden tension that had gripped them, while letting in a shaft of sunlight that brightened the whole place. They laughed aloud in relief. Looking round they saw large chests under the eaves, an old wardrobe and old suitcases. All sizes of hatboxes were heaped on top of each other; an old bookcase was full of what looked like a complete set of Charles Dickens. They could not believe their eyes; it was an Aladdin's cave, just waiting to be explored.

Glad that they were wearing old jeans and tee shirts they set out to find something for each of them for the barbecue, which they knew Uncle Jack was starting up in the garden. Only last night Babs had invited some of her local friends telling them to be sure to bring whatever musical instruments they might have.

The wardrobe was the first to be opened. Inside they found frocks, button boots, lacy shawls, embroidered blouses that went out with the last century. Their laughter could be heard right down the house. Everything was pulled out and measured against who ever had first lifted it out. Mary found a long muslin dress, which slid down her slim body as if made for her, with a huge blue satin waistband tying in a big bow behind.

'All 1 need now is a bonnet and 1 am Miss Muffet', she cried in delight.Brid found a dark skirt and matched it with one of the embroidered blouses, buttoned to the throat and declared herself Jane Eyre. Morna asked if all the ladies in that family had been tall, and willowy, as nothing came anywhere near fitting her. She was small and a bit plump. By then Babs had opened one of the chests. Finding it full of bed linen she promptly closed it again. The next chest had velvet curtains, folded in tissue paper, promptly closed. Then the last chest, much more difficult to open, revealed tissue-wrapped dresses. These were something else. Of rich shantung they shimmered in the sunlight, and a shorter dress was found for Morna, in all the colours of the rainbow. Monica in a long back skirt with frilly blouse looked the real schoolmarm. That left Babs herself to be fitted out. Back at the wardrobe, she had found a red satin evening dress with a tiny bustle and Morna shouted: 'Here is the ideal hat for that, just a few tiny plumes of red matching feathers'. Bringing their loot with them they closed the wardrobe and Babs went back to close the chest. Babs was fascinated with that chest; she had never noticed it before. She would ask her Mum about the chests when she came home.

They returned to their rooms and in great glee donned the ancient styles, much to the amusement of all. Eventually, carefully lifting their skirts they came down the stairs. They could hear Uncle Jack announce that the sausages would be burned if they delayed much longer. Out they trooped in all their finery to be admired. Uncle Jack had invited some of his friends and their sons and some lads from the neighbourhood.

'Have 1 missed something or is it a fancy dress night too?' exclaimed Uncle Jack. ' Come forward Miss Muffet, lets hope there are no spiders to sit beside you this evening. It would be a pity not to enjoy my barbecue.'

Admiring all the costumes and enjoying the comments from their friends, some of whom came in fancy dress too, he handed them plates and told them to help themselves. The window to the living room was open and FM2 could be heard in the background. The barbecue went a bomb, and afterwards they sat around telling stories and singing to the music. They paraded to model their outfits to much applause and laughter, admitting they were not the most comfortable clothes to sit around in. As the music was just made for dancing they decided to change into their own gear. Just then Gramps decided to join them coming out of the living room as they made their way upstairs, Babs bringing up the rear.

'Well Gramps,' she called. 'What do you think?' and she twirled around that he might see her frock.

'Fanny! Oh, is it really you?' he cried, straightening himself with the help of his stick.

'Fanny!!! Oh Gramps don't you know me, Babs.'

Uncle Jack had come to help his father out and taking one look at his father's face, shooed Babs up the stairs. But Gramps called out to her to stay. Bewildered she came down the few steps, and Gramps was holding out his hand, which she saw was trembling.

'You are the picture of your Grandma in that dress. It is the one she wore to our last ball.'

Uncle Jack took his father's arm and led him out into the garden. Seating him on his favourite chair he handed him a glass of brandy ordering his father to drink a few sips, as he feared the shock of seeing Babs in that particular dress might bring on a heart attack, even after all those years. Babs had taken the stairs two at a time fearing she might have upset her Gramps, having no idea that that dress was the one her grandma had once worn. She remembered the story of how she had been killed when the car skidded in snow coming home from a ball. She hoped the party was not going to be upset because of her choice of dress. When she came back to the garden she went to sit beside her Gramps, not quite knowing what to say. He held his hand out to her and asked her to introduce all her friends, apologising for getting a bit upset, saying the dress was the one worn by her grandmother on that fateful night. He asked her to stay beside him for a few minutes and he would tell her about her grandmother and that dress.

'She was fair haired just like you,' he said. 'But she had green eyes and wasn't quite as tall as you. That night she was the belle of the ball. We had a marvellous night. It was New Year's Eve 1950 and we sang and danced to the small hours. As we came home the place was white with snow. It was magic. Turning to come through the gate the car skidded hitting the gatepost and slid into a tree. She died in my arms. l had not even a scratch.'

'Oh Gramps, l had no idea.'

Babs wanted to call the party off but he would not hear of it saying, 'You made me happy as well as sad tonight. She would not want to spoil this night were she with us now. I can assure you that she and I would give you young ones a lesson in proper dancing under the apple trees. Away with you to your friends and let me see how well you can dance. I will be watching you. Midsummer night is a magic night when the fairies come to watch.'

As Babs joined the dancers Jack came to sit by his father. 'Jack my boy, Babs startled me in that dress. Funny what sharpens the old memory. Sometimes Fanny is very close, especially in the garden. Many a night we sat listening to the whispering breeze and the rustle of the leaves. She loved the orchard at any time but especially in the afternoons: the hum of the bees, the fast beat of tiny wings as the bluetits flitted hither and thither. When I sit of an evening sometimes it's as if she is with me.'

Uncle Jack put on old records of the fifties and watched with pleasure his father's foot tap in time to the music. The youngsters danced their modern dances, but Gramps saw in his mind's eye elegant ladies waltz and foxtrot as of old, seeing again the kaleidoscope of colour that had once delighted his eyes in the old ballrooms long ago. All too soon the night was over and the friends said their goodbyes, promising to come next day to go swimming with Babs and her friends. Uncle Jack began clearing everything away, when Gramps asked him to leave it and refused to go indoors, saying he would spend another while in the night air. He would give him a shout when he was ready.

When Babs' Mum came home two weeks later, Babs told her all about the barbecue and the fun they had dressing up. She even had some very good photos taken by Uncle Jack. On coming to Babs in the red shantung dress she stared in dismay and asked if Gramps had seen it. She had intended to give it to the drama group with their own stuff but had been loath to part with it. Gramps, on hearing her, asked that that particular dress be kept. It held very special memories for him, sad but also happy. He said how much he had liked seeing Babs in it. He thought that Babs might like to keep it and hand it on as a souvenir of her Grandma and of a happy evening when she celebrated Midsummer Night with her friends.

[Extract from work-in-progress]

Bernie Gilbride

Grey Rock

Coming down in the lift Nora's thoughts were miles away, the usual banter of her fellow workers unintelligible. She smiled and nodded but made no comments. O'Connell Street would be chock-a-block as usual at 5 pm on a Friday evening; everybody rushing for a bus, to a car park, or looking for a taxi as they made their way home. She stood for a moment and crossed the road to Wynne's Hotel. She would sit with a pot of tea, and consider what Mr Kenny of Maguire & Browne, Solicitors, had told her at lunchtime; would read again the copy of the will of Patrick J. Casey, of Morehampton Road, her late neighbour since moving into her apartment there almost five years ago.

He had been a tall elderly gentleman, always courteous, well dressed and helpful, and he had taken her under his wing in a grandfatherly way down the years, advising her on maintenance and any little problem that had arisen about the apartment. She, in return, had often done a little shopping for him, or looked after his cat when he would be away. He apparently had no relatives, lived alone and enjoyed city life, being interested in music and drama. He would sometimes have tickets for a concert or play to which he would bring her, enjoying her company as much as she enjoyed the outings. But that was the sum total of the friendship until today when, from Mr Kenny, she learned that he had left her his apartment, car, a holiday home outside Sligo together with a large sum of money In the will he said he had enjoyed her company and kindness over the years and hoped she would enjoy this inheritance from him. To say that Nora was flabbergasted would be putting it mildly. She had no idea he had that kind of money, though she knew he spent most summers out of the city and travelled abroad quite a lot.

As she sat drinking her tea she felt she wanted to pinch herself. This morning she had wondered where her life was going: in a rather dead end job, her ex-fiancé married to someone else, she had felt stuck in a rut and wondered what her next move should be. Time to move on and to start to trust again. She would see for herself her new inheritance. Imagine having money in the bank, she who always had to be careful of her money and budget for any unusual expense. A place in the country! This was going to take getting used to. What an opportunity to do some of the things she had always promised herself she would do someday. That day was here. Mr Kenny suggested she might sell the holiday home, but as she sat there she decided to go first and see the cottage for herself. She would go tomorrow, nothing like striking out immediately.

The drive down had been very pleasant. She had stopped for lunch on the way. Turning left off the Bundoran road, just outside Drumcliffe, she was now nearing Raughly, her destination. The house was called Grey Rock and she had no difficulty finding it. It was the last gateway on her left. On turning in, after a short driveway, it came into view: a long white bungalow with bay windows on either side of the porch. As she got out of the car she heard the sea, a soft slushing sound, with a gentle crash as the wave hit the shore. Carefully she inserted the key. It turned easily and the heavy door swung silently on well-oiled hinges. The main door opened just as effortlessly into the house. A large hallway greeted her, with doors on either side. The first door on her left opened into what she assumed was the sitting room, with a bay window overlooking the avenue and front garden. The second door opened into the living room: a revelation. Almost two full walls of glass, with double doors opening into a conservatory. The sea was in full view at the end of a long garden which appeared to give way to a tiny beach, part of a long curved bay, full at that moment of sparkling sea, with sunlight catching the crest of its waves. Back in the hall she opened the door into the kitchen, which she guessed would be modern and it did not disappoint. The long kitchen was glass from floor to roof, again overlooking the beach, with all mod. cons.

The next door from the hall opened into a bedroom. She felt loath to enter as she knew this would be personal. 1t too overlooked the beach and was en suite, simple in its décor, masculine, one would say. Closing that door gently, she decided she would go through it later, as she was suddenly overcome with emotion, at what her friend had given to her. The house was built on a rocky promontory and from the conservatory one felt one was on an island. Bewitched, she was enchanted. How had her dear friend ever pulled himself away to a city?

Opening the double doors of the conservatory Nora walked to the bottom of the garden. The tide was lapping the rocks. There was a sheer drop to the beach of about twelve feet, with rocks sloping away for another twenty feet. To her right a gate opened onto steps cut out of the rock. She did not go through; that would be for another day. Looking back at the cottage she was again taken with its panoramic view, its mountain backdrop. With the sun glinting on the windows, she knew in her heart she would never part with it. Following the path back to the kitchen she decided to spend her first night in her new home. She sensed that this was where she would always feel secure. Today, she had found her first real home since selling her own old home in Dun Laoghaire after the death of her mother.

She had been in Trinity College, a first year student doing Arts, when her father had died suddenly of a heart attack. Her mother, always delicate, had appeared to weather that tragedy quite well only to be diagnosed with cancer a few months later. Nora, being an only child, had given up her studies to nurse her mother. After her death, she had to look for a job. She had been lucky enough to get one in the Post Office and had remained there ever since. Selling the family home, it being too large for one person, and needing money, she had invested much of the proceeds in the apartment at Morehampton Road, where she now lived and where she had met Patrick J. Casey. Tonight she would decide the direction of the new life, which had been opened up for her by the letter from Mr Kenny, Solicitor. Having told him that she was going to Sligo to see the cottage, he had arranged to have the electricity switched on. The place was ready to be lived in immediately. She knew she would be happy to spend her first night at Grey Rock.

Next morning she explored the area, walking the beach, and decided to see Mr Kenny on her return to Dublin.
'I must get him to arrange the sale of my apartment and move into the larger apartment. I'll keep my own personal things and the things I brought from my old home, which my parents loved down the years. I'll travel first and see a little of the world, as Mr Casey had always been encouraging me to do. Over the winter I will re-start my University studies, but I will always keep my weekends free for Grey Rock on its rocky promontory'. She had thought it all out by morning.

Three years flew past. She visited France, Spain, Italy, and Austria over the summers, making many new friends and acquaintances, and seeing for herself the architecture and the historical buildings in the cities; the way of life in the more rural areas and the beauty of the landscapes of the different countries. The towering mountains, the lakes and coastlines were so different from home, but it was her time in Trinity College she enjoyed most. She loved to study and was very successful in all her exams. As she was awarded her degree, specialising in history, she hoped Mr Casey was looking down with approval.

That night, after celebrating with her friends, she went to his writing desk, which she used constantly, to put her parchment with the other important papers in a special drawer she had found at the back of the desk. As she pulled the drawer towards her, it got stuck and she thought she must put a drop of oil on the runners and tiny lock. She gently freed the drawer but as she closed it, noticed it was not closing properly. Again she moved her hand to the rear, feeling for anything that might have become stuck and found something hard. With great care she eased the piece of paper forward, pulling it towards her, but it would not come. She emptied the drawer, piece by piece, until she could grasp the edges. Slowly she managed to ease the drawer out fully and was amazed to find a space under the drawer where some papers were lying. She withdrew the papers very gently as they appeared to be very faded and worn. She opened the first paper, a marriage certificate, enclosing a photograph of a very young couple. The man was in full military uniform, the woman in bridal attire. As she gazed she recognised a young Patrick Casey, as the handsome young groom. The marriage certificate was that of Patrick James Casey to Jane Fairchild. His occupation was given as pilot, his bride's as nurse. Next she found a letter to My *Beloved Jane*, written from a barracks somewhere in London and signed, *with all my love, Rick*. In it Rick said he was flying that night and would be in touch as soon as possible. The letter was dated August 10, 1943.

Nora sat transfixed. Who could imagine finding such a letter, almost forty years later? She knew that Rick was her friend Patrick. But he had never mentioned a wife or marriage, nor even that he had been a pilot in the British Airforce as he evidently had, as she saw from the uniform. Tomorrow she would visit Mr Kenny to see if he could throw any light on the matter. What an ending to her big day. As she prepared for bed she knew it would be hard to sleep; her mind was in turmoil. Early next morning as she sat in Mr Kenny's office, showing him what she had found, he was as much amazed as she was, but promised to put in motion any feelers he could. 'To begin with', he said, 'I'll write to the British Home Office for any information they might have, and to the Registrar of Marriages for the years 1940-4'. With this Nora had to be satisfied.

Over the following months a few details did come through. From the British Home Office it was confirmed that Patrick James Casey had been a pilot with the RAF from 1940, and had distinguished himself over the course of the war, flying many missions over enemy territory. He had risen through the ranks to become Lieutenant Colonel. He had always refused office work, preferring action. After the war he had retired to business and there the trail went cold. He had qualified as an engineer before the war and travelled the world in this capacity. The Registrar of Marriages brought even less information. Nora, in her career as an historian travelled many times to London, lecturing, and doing research. During these visits she combed the records in a variety of offices, talking to anyone she thought might have known Patrick or Jane during the war years; to her great sorrow she had no success.

The next few years flew past. Nora found herself in great demand both as a guest speaker and lecturer on military history, gradually becoming famous for the accuracy of her detail particularly in regard to World Wars I and II. Like her many contemporary friends she enjoyed the companionship of men, though only as friends or fellow travellers, not as lovers. There had never been anyone of particular interest to her. This she regretted. She would love to have had someone special with whom to share her triumphs, and from whom she could have received support in the ups and downs of life. This was not to be and she became resigned to being single. Grey Rock was still her favourite place and she found herself spending more time there, even into the harsh winter months, when the angry Atlantic hurled storm after storm at the rocks beneath her home. Then when the storm had abated, she would muffle up well, go down the steps to the shore, sometimes picking up unusual pieces of driftwood.

On one such occasion, as she tugged to free a log sticking out of the sand near the water's edge, she heard a deep voice right behind her, 'Here, let me help you.' She almost jumped out of her skin with fright, as at that time of year nobody came down to the beach. Turning round suddenly, her foot slipped on some wrack and she fell headlong into an oncoming wave. Immediately strong arms lifted her and, apologising profusely, he blamed himself for having spoken so loudly, frightening her. He had called out as he went to her assistance, but with the noise of the sea, she had not heard him. All Nora could do was laugh. She was dripping wet, her auburn hair stuck to her head. She knew she looked a sorry sight. All concerned he offered to bring her anywhere she wished to go. Nora pointed to her home on the cliff top saying she would be fine as it was just up the beach and accepting his apology, raced off making for the house.

When she had showered and changed she heard a thud out the back and was just in time to see her rescuer walking away, having dragged a very substantial log to her back door. Forgetting all the cautions to be careful and never allow a stranger into her house, she called after him to thank him and to offer him a cup of coffee. She could see he had got rather wet himself rescuing the log. Rather reluctantly he accepted, knowing she might be uneasy having made the offer, but being rather taken with her. Not many women would have laughed after having been soaked and all through his fault.

As they drank their coffee she learned that he had bought a property a few miles away, near Cloonagh. He had retired, having worked as an engineer in Hong Kong for many years. He had always wanted to try his hand at sculpture and had seen an advertisement for a property on ten acres in the west of Ireland. On viewing it, he realised it would be ideal for him as there were large out-offices suitable for use as sculpture workshops with a comfortable dwelling, not needing too much repair. By then he realised he had not introduced himself.

'James Costello at your service', he said holding out his hand. 'Nora Geraghty. Very glad to have been rescued by you'.

That cup of coffee was the first of many and over the winter months they enjoyed many outings together. Trips to Dublin to shows, including the Russian Ballet, which Nora loved and to which Patrick Casey had first introduced her.

Like herself James had no immediate family, just the odd cousin, so they spent Christmas together. It was a magic time for them both. James proposed on New Year's Eve, as they listened to the New Year bells being tolled all over the world. Nora happily accepted. They were not in the first flush of youth, and both knew in their hearts they had met their ideal partner. As James put it so succinctly, they had done the things they wanted to do, travelled, succeeded in their respective careers, so why waste any more precious time. They were married in February as the snowdrops pushed their heads out of the cold clay.

James came to live with Nora. He knew she would never agree to leave Grey Rock. As he moved in he brought a mound of books with him, mostly engineering and sculpture. One day, as Nora was helping him arrange them in the study, one slipped to the floor scattering some loose papers around. Nora stooped to pick them up, when something caught her eye. An old photo, much earmarked, had slipped from a worn envelope and once again she was looking at Patrick J. Casey on his wedding day. Sitting back on her heels she felt the breath leave her body as she exclaimed:

'Oh James, Oh James, where did this come from?'

James, who was examining another book before putting it on the shelf, glanced towards her answering

'Oh that photo, that's my father. It was given me by my Aunt Maggie who reared me. Remember I told you my Mum was killed in an air raid in London during the war'.

Jumping to her feet Nora raced to the old writing desk. Pulling out the secret drawer she took out again the letter, certificate and wedding photo she had found all those years ago, identical to the one now in James' s hand. Could this be really happening? They sat for hours as Nora explained all the searches both she and Mr Kenny had made and how in the end they agreed they would never solve the puzzle of Patrick J. Casey.

Now it was indeed being solved before their eyes. James had been brought to Dublin by his aunt, following the death of his mother in the air raid on her way home from the hospital where she worked. His aunt had not heard from her for some time. She had run away from home to become a nurse at the outbreak of the war, much to her parents chagrin as they considered England to be very dangerous. After making enquiries about the Patrick J. Casey of the marriage certificate and drawing a blank everywhere, she had not bothered further, being only too happy to have her only sister's baby boy to care for, she herself being childless. She adopted him, giving him her husband's name. She had collected what few papers they had in the hospital where Jane had worked and in Jane's flat, and these had come to James on her death. They could only assume that Patrick never knew he had a baby son for whatever reason. Nora knowing him so well knew he too must have searched everywhere all those years ago for his beloved Jane. The realisation that fate had brought them together under such strange circumstances filled them with awe and a sense of the unreal. From heaven, Patrick, his father, had organised that he meet and marry Nora, whom he too had loved.

They talked long into the night, coming to all sorts of conclusions but knew in their hearts, all trails had long been exhausted. By morning they had decided to leave it the mystery it was and celebrate the life of Patrick in anyway they could. They travelled to Dublin to Glasnevin Cemetery. Nora brought James to his father's grave, outlining the reasons she had chosen that particular headstone with its simple inscription. Now, at least she had someone to discuss any addition to the simple wording she had chosen. James would not hear of any change, saying what was written on the headstone was sufficient. Nora had chosen a dark grey marble headstone and surround for his grave. Patrick had named his cottage Grey Rock so she chose grey marble to protect his mortal remains. The grave had been sealed and covered with marble chippings. With the morning sun glinting on the marble, it looked as simple and as elegant as she felt Patrick would have wished. Kneeling, they said a prayer: Nora, for the privilege of having known Patrick, James for the father he had never known but whom he believed, had guided him to Nora. On their return to Grey Rock, their lives settled into a regular pattern. Nora was finishing the paper she was writing for the War Memorials Commission; James was preparing for a small exhibition of his work later on in the autumn.

Secure in their love for each other, they enjoyed the companionship, exploring the complexity of their relationship. Their first summer together flew past. Walking the beach in the dusk, they watched the sun, sinking in a crimson orb below the horizon, make a shimmering pathway of gold across the waves to the shore filling their hearts with a sense of belonging, and a tranquillity they had never before known. Nora, who had never been so happy in her life, thought of how she might help James in his ambition to become a sculptor. He had taught her the finer details and qualities of rock and its importance in the modern world; to appreciate the dimension and character it can add to architecture. He had done a lot of study in his spare time when abroad, attending many unveilings of both large and medium pieces, taking classes and workshops when his work allowed. Now he was very much on his own. She decided that, whenever possible, they would visit exhibitions by sculptors whose work he admired that might be of help to him.

Late in September while in London for the publication of her latest paper, Nora overheard her editor apologise to a well known author, for her absence the following evening when they had agreed to meet, owing to a commitment to attend an unveiling of a piece of sculpture at a new recreation hall near her home. Nora, on hearing this, asked the exact location of the hall that she and James might visit and see the new sculpture, before returning to Dublin. She explained that James was interested in sculpture and was indeed working on some pieces at home. Immediately, her editor invited them both to attend the unveiling. She would be delighted to have them with her. It was to be a very formal occasion as the new hall was replacing one destroyed during the war. The local dignitaries would be present, and Nora being a historian, specialising in World War history would surely find the ceremony interesting.

The following evening they were collected at their hotel by the editor and her husband at seven o'clock. The new hall was richly illuminated. A red carpet reached from the pavement, up the entrance steps and into the foyer. It was a large building and many people had gathered to watch the dignitaries arrive. Inside the foyer the sculpture lay covered awaiting its unveiling. This was Nora's first time at such a ceremony. They wandered around admiring the foyer, the architecture and the many paintings adorning the walls, some modern, some old prints of the area as it had been before the war, many of the different planes in use during the war, Lancaster bombers, Spitfires and others. As the dignitaries arrived they noticed one elderly man in full military uniform being escorted to a seat of honour near the sculpture. They evidently had been waiting for him as the ceremony began immediately he was seated. The Lord Mayor did the unveiling and proceeded to address the crowd now gathered, giving a brief account of the area and the importance of such a hall for all, both young and old. He hoped it would be used continuously over the coming years by the community. He spoke of he old hall that it was replacing. That hall had been missed down the years, he said. Luckily, the site had been kept for this beautiful structure that he now had the pleasure of opening. Then, unveiling the sculpture, which consisted of young men in military uniform with a model plane in the background, so reminiscent of the war a round of clapping broke out spontaneously. It was a fine piece of work and Nora could feel James's excitement as he appreciated the craftsmanship and expertise of the piece. It was indeed a fitting memorial to the young men who fought so successfully in the Battle of Britain all those years ago and who gave their lives that others might live in freedom.

Afterwards, James felt a hand on his shoulder, and a jovial voice offering heartiest congratulations on a lovely piece of work. Turning in amazement that anyone would know him there, and be offering him congratulations, he encountered the elderly gentleman whom he had seen being escorted to his seat earlier before the ceremony. James was at a loss, as he had never seen the man before.

'I always knew you would do it and I have watched your career with interest as you know. For me this is your finest piece to date, Rick.'

Just then, a man approached them with his hand outstretched to the elderly man.

'Sir Henry, how good of you to come. How proud I am to have you with me, on this auspicious occasion'.

Turning to James, he held out his hand to him, and both stood absolutely still in amazement. James felt he was looking in a mirror. The man was identical to himself: same height, same build, hair turning grey, with a snow-white stripe over the right ear, brown eyes. For the first time in his life, he thought he was going to faint. The elderly man was staring, looking from one to the other and shaking so much they both made to grasp his arms to steady him. Just then, Nora put her hand on James's arm as much to steady herself as to reassure James. Afterwards, she told him she actually began to feel sick. In evening dress for the occasion, they had not even the individuality afforded by ordinary dress.

The first to come to his senses was the elderly man, asking that they all come to his apartment in Knightsbridge, where in its privacy, they could talk, away from the prying eyes and cameras he sensed were about to descend on them. Feigning weakness, he had them escort him to his chauffeur-driven car, waiting outside.

Nobody spoke on that journey. On arriving at the apartment block in Knightsbridge, they took the lift to his apartment and were admitted by an elderly retainer. Sir Henry ordered coffee, pacing his long sitting- room, until it arrived. As soon as it was served, he asked that they be left uninterrupted and excused his valet for the rest of the evening. With shaking hands Nora accepted the coffee sitting quietly, wondering what was going to happen. James and Rick sat opposite each other, looking at each other. Then they both began to speak together as if, suddenly, their tongues had been freed. 'Who are you?' they both asked of each other in almost one voice, their voices almost identical. James was the first to speak. Giving his name and introducing Nora, his wife, he briefly outlined how they had come to be at the unveiling. Rick acknowledged that the sculpture was his saying that Sir Henry had been his mentor and guide from his earliest years. He again thanked Sir Henry for attending as it had involved a lot of travelling for him. All this time Sir Henry kept looking from one to the other as if he simply could not believe his eyes. Now that was something new. James gave a short history of his life to then. He told of his mother's death in London on her way home from Charring Cross Hospital, where she worked as a nurse and of his subsequent adoption by his Aunt Maggie, who gave him her married name Costello. He told of his qualifying as an engineer, his working abroad for many years, his interest in sculpture all that time, his early retirement, his home now in the west of Ireland.

It was then Sir Henry who spoke. He told how his father had advertised for a nurse to look after his wife, who had had an accident, and was then confined to a wheelchair. This advertisement was answered by a young London nurse. She was interviewed in London by his father and given the job. She had a young baby whose father, she said, had been killed in the war. She came to live with them in Scotland all those years ago, and had never left the Highlands since. She was Julia Keyes-Casey and Rick was her son. After the war, in which he was a pilot, Sir Henry had returned home, and after his father's death had run the family estate and business. Julia had stayed on as housekeeper after his mother's death. She still lived in her own apartment at his home. Rick had been brought up with his own children and he had watched him grow, seen his talent as a sculptor develop, culminating in the memorial piece in the new hall tonight. As this was a memorial to Sir Henry's comrades, wild horses could not have kept him away. He had flown from Southern France outside Nice, where he and his wife resided for health reasons, just to be with Rick.

Nora asked if he had any date for Julia taking up her nursing post with them? 'Of course, my mother's accident occurred in late 1943'. She then told them about her inheritance, her discovery of the hidden drawer and its contents. Mr Kenny's and her own search for anyone still alive who could throw some light on her find. The times she herself had searched the many archives, but to no avail, and how in the end, they had given up. She told them of her finding the twin photo in James's papers, after their marriage, and of their realisation that James was the son of her benefactor, Patrick James Casey.

'An extraordinary story indeed', exclaimed Sir Henry. 'It may be worth our while visiting my home in Scotland and talking to Julia. Something tells me she may have some light to cast on all this. Thank God she is still with us and very clear of mind. I suggest we go to-morrow.'

All this time James and Rick were watching each other closely, unsure of how to approach one another. Their similarity being so real and now, listening to the two sides regarding both their lives, they began to think there might be some explanation and connection between both stories. Neither of them was quite sure if they wanted to find out any more. Both were happy with their lives today. Not really wanting any change, but still interested in following it through to the end.

The following morning they flew to Edinburgh, arriving about ten o'clock. Sir Henry had his car waiting and they proceeded to Dunforway Castle on the north west coast. On turning in at the massive gates Nora felt her heart lurch, a sense of dread at what the outcome might be, nearly overwhelmed her. Sensing her anxiety, James held her hand, gently caressing the palm. Soon they had arrived and the door was being opened. Dogs came bounding out, whimpering with joy, around Sir Henry's and Rick's ankles, welcoming them home. Inside the great hall was filled with a warm glow from the huge fireplace. A wide staircase curved around to a balcony and down to the hall again. Nora had never been in such a lofty hallway before. It was just as she had read about in her research for some of her papers, and she had feared that they had ceased to exist today. Sir Henry had evidently rung through last night after their departure, as his manservant came to bring them to Julia's private apartment.

As they followed him upstairs, he led them down a long corridor. Knocking on a heavy studded door, he informed the person inside that Sir Henry had come to call. The door was opened immediately by a young girl, who brought them to an elderly woman, who was sitting in a large armchair by a fire. Her face broke into a wide welcoming smile on seeing Sir Henry and Rick. Stretching out both her arms, she called out 'Sir Henry, Rick, welcome, welcome!'

On the way from Edinburgh, Sir Henry had advised that they greet her first; he was afraid the shock of seeing James, so like Rick, might frighten her. Sir Henry called James and Nora in. As soon as she saw James standing beside Sir Henry with her Rick on his other side, her face became ashen and she began to tremble violently. Placing his hand gently on her shoulder, Sir Henry spoke to her:

'Have no fear, Julia. Just tell us what you know, if anything, that can explain the identical appearance of these two fine young men.' Looking at Sir Henry she told him of Jane, her very best friend, whom she had known and loved from childhood years.

She had known Rick Casey, whom Jane had married in 1942. 'Jane and Rick were madly in love and they married in October 1942. He spent every free minute with her. He was a pilot with the RAF and often would be away for weeks. During one of these absences Jane discovered she was pregnant. She was overjoyed, but decided to keep it from Rick as she knew it would worry him that she might be unwell when he was not in a position to look after her. She was afraid too that he might be shot down. She knew that then her pregnancy would be an almost impossible burden for him. So she decided not to tell him for as long as possible'. Julia paused, remembering that anxious time again. 'When she was six months pregnant he rang asking her to meet him at their favourite restaurant in Piccadilly as he was being sent abroad on a special mission. Jane kept the appointment but Rick never made it.'

The fear that he was in danger worried Jane and as her pregnancy progressed, her health deteriorated. She had moved in temporarily into Julia's flat at that time and in the seventh month of her pregnancy, had given birth to identical twins. The twins, being premature, were delicate and were kept in hospital for weeks. James, the stronger of the two, was allowed home first. By then Jane had gone back to nursing, and to her own flat. She was convinced that Rick had been taken prisoner while on his secret mission and would not be home for some time. She had enquired from the War Office but was given no information. They both visited baby Rick most days and he was making great progress.

'Jane had all arrangements made to take Rick home the day she was killed. I was to collect him for her and keep him in my flat until Jane would be off duty and could call for him. When I heard of Jane's death I assumed that she had picked up James and had him with her and that he had been killed too. I decided to keep Rick and rear him for Jane. I felt that this was what Jane would wish me to do. The advertisement for a nurse in faraway Scotland was a blessing and when I got the job, I decided it would be an ideal place to rear a baby. Claiming him as my son, and believing Rick Casey to be dead, I felt I was doing what was best for us both. I could not bear to live on in London after Jane's death. I never again heard of Rick Casey. Nobody had questioned me but had assumed that I was Patrick Casey's widow as I claimed. I had also kept my maiden name Keyes. I have loved Rick as my own son, taking pride in his achievements. On looking at James today I realised he too had survived.'

It had taken a long time to tell this story and the grief Julia was experiencing was evident to them all. Falling on his knees by her side, Rick hugged Julia calling her Mother, and kissing her cheek many times. Sir Henry beckoned James and Nora out and leaving mother and son together, they went downstairs. James hugged Nora, knowing she too was experiencing great trauma. Tea and scones were waiting in the hall and Sir Henry insisted they eat something. Then having his valet show them to their room he bade them rest awhile, explore his home if they so wished, especially the grounds or walk the beach at the end of the garden. 'At times of stress,' he said, 'and this is surely one such time, the sea, and its timelessness invariably bring me solace. Tonight we will sort everything out after dinner.'

Their room was lovely and cosy with a warm fire glowing in the hearth. They rested close to each other, afraid to talk, unsure of what to say. James assured Nora that none of this would in any way interfere with their lives. He and his newly found brother, would get to know each other gradually and hopefully find affection and respect for each other over the coming years. Nora assured James that nothing could shake her love for him. She felt glad the trauma of the last few days had been explained away so satisfactorily. Having an identical twin would surely prove at the least interesting. Getting to know him and comparing their respective likes and dislikes would be fascinating.

Tracing their careers and meeting Rick's wife, at present in America with her parents, was something to be looked forward to with interest. Would she be like Nora in appearance? Or was that one thing in which they would differ? All this was for the future. James was more cautious. He wanted to get to know his brother first, and was not inclined to speculate, fearing that only their appearances were similar.

After a long rest they decided to walk the beach. As they walked they thought of all the people who had walked that beach before them all down the centuries, with their problems and cares, now long gone and forgotten. Admiring its fine golden sand and its rocky promontories on either side, the sea worked its magic, as so often before, and returning to the castle they felt relaxed and confident that all their problems could be solved given time. When they reached the hall they found Rick waiting. Nora excused herself, leaving James and Rick to talk. It was time to change for dinner when James came up. He looked happy and Nora gave a sigh of relief. Admonishing him to hurry and not keep Sir Henry waiting for his dinner, she hugged him, whispering 'I know it's going to work out well.'

After dinner they adjourned to a beautiful sitting room, with long windows overlooking the gardens with the sea in the distance. Sir Henry, before taking his place by the fire, made sure they all had a drink. Settling himself comfortably he surprised them all by saying it was his turn now to fill in a few cracks in the story they had heard today. 'I am sure you must have heard me gasp when Nora mentioned Patrick J. Casey. I knew Patrick Casey well. We became great buddies on joining the RAF. We trained together, flew together on many missions, and Rick was my guest a few times in Knightsbridge. I knew about Jane, the love of Rick's life, and that he had married but somehow in those snatched, rushed leaves I never met either Jane or Julia. The night Rick was to meet Jane it was to tell her he was being sent on a secret mission to which we were both assigned. That mission was to help the underground resistance in France. We were to fly out the following day but the flight was brought forward, by twenty-four hours to accommodate the resistance leaders in France, then under extreme pressure. There we helped set up all sorts of resistance groups, with radio equipment, and monitoring surveillance, under very dangerous conditions. Going from place to place, this took many months and we had no chance of contacting our families as that would be too dangerous.'

Their expertise being recognised they were sent to Norway the following year in the same capacity. They risked their lives many times in the snowy wastes of the northern coast; monitoring the movements of German troops, submarines and air power, again helping the Norwegian under-ground movement with radio equipment and their own invaluable experience.

'In the last days of the war we became separated. I believed Rick had been captured, as I had been, on one mission that had gone badly wrong. My own health had been affected by this experience and I spent many months in hospital in Geneva, Switzerland after the war. I never met Patrick again, had almost forgotten him until Nora mentioned his name last evening. Here my story ends. I hope that Rick and James will find comfort and love in their relationship. I envy them the possibilities this relationship affords them. I am sorry that my son Edward and his family are in South Africa where the family has business but be assured it will be my pleasure to introduce them next time you visit. I know Edward will be as excited as I am about Rick's new twin brother.'

Before leaving Dunforway Castle, next morning James visited Julia, who welcomed him with open arms saying 'Anyone belonging to Jane is special to me'. She spoke to him of Jane and her joy at their birth; of how Jane and herself were looking forward to seeing the amazement and delight on Rick's face when he was introduced to his twin sons, never doubting he would soon be home for even a short leave. She told him how Jane had called them both after their father, Patrick (Rick) and James. Her eyes filled with tears as she remembered Jane, so full of life, such a good friend. James hugged her promising to keep in touch and to come to see her again soon. He assured her that both Rick and he had already formed a bond, to be worked on over the coming years.

Nora and James left Scotland that morning, promising to come back soon. All Nora wanted was the security of her home, Grey Rock, after all they had gone through. They were happy to have solved so many of the riddles of the past in just a few days. She would enjoy telling all this to Mr Kenny. She would visit him at his office in Dublin as soon as possible.

As they left, Rick and Sir Henry came to see them off. Rick hugged them both, promising to come to Grey Rock and bring his wife, Rebecca, at present in America with her parents who had been ill, as soon as she returned home. Nora and James looked forward to being members of a much extended family.

That Christmas was very different to their first one. This time there were many special Christmas cards to be sent and great excitement as their counterparts arrived. Again it was a wonderfully happy occasion for them both. Nora had filled Grey Rock with greenery: ivy, holly and the resin scent of pine filled the air. Warm turf fires added their own special scent and were much appreciated by them both on cold winter nights, and by their many friends and neighbours who came to call over the Christmas days as, is the custom in the West of Ireland.

Rick came to Ireland the following spring and was enchanted with Grey Rock with its own sheltered beach and the feeling of being on an island. The daffodils and bluebells were at their best in the woodlands of Lisadell. He loved the area and who better to tell him its history than Nora. She entertained him for hours with the stories of the Fianna especially those connected with the area: Diarmuid and Grainne, Queen Maedbh and Cuchullain.

After dinner one evening, while Rick and James had gone to Cloonagh to see James's workshop, Nora, who had been thinking much about the events of the past few months, decided that she would go back to see Julia in Dunforway Castle, by herself if possible. Just to chat her and try to find out anything further she might know about Jane and Patrick. She was her only connection with the past and it would be through her that she might learn something of the early life of Patrick J Casey, or of Jane, of whom, to date she actually knew very little. She felt certain Patrick would have spoken of his family to Jane, perhaps even introducing her to some of them or even to his friends. Jane would surely have told Julia, her special friend. Nora decided she would go the first time James was away. She would travel alone as she was afraid of raising his hopes and just a little apprehensive, not knowing what she might hear. It would be her own little secret just in case nothing came of it. Anyway, she felt it was worth a chance.

That opportunity was to come about much sooner than she expected, as when he returned home that evening Rick announced that he wanted to bring James on a short tour through England. He wanted to show him some more of his sculptures and to introduce him to some of his teachers especially the man with whom he served his apprenticeship and who had encouraged him most. As his wife was still with her parents in America, her mother being seriously ill, he was free to travel for as long as they both wished.

On hearing this Nora expressed her delight, assuring them that she would be happy to begin her next paper. This had been bothering her, for some time. She knew she should make a start and would now have no excuse to put it off any longer. Knowing that spring was an ideal time to visit Rome with its many wonderful sculptures she even suggested they might include it in their itinerary. Should they decide this it would give her lots of time to visit Julia. She felt this visit was an urgent matter, as one never knew with older people. Something was telling her it would be foolish to delay. The next day, having thought it over, James and Rick decided to go at once, taking in Rome as Nora had suggested. She happily waved them goodbye at Dublin airport the following week. They little knew that she simply had a coffee before boarding her own flight to Edinburgh that same evening.

[Extract from work-in-progress]

Bernie Gilbride

Scene Through a Window

I had often spotted him before. I didn't think he was all that handsome. Some of the others I had seen in that area would beat him hands-down as regards to looks, but he had that proud swagger – you knew that he felt he was 'Cock-of – the-walk'.

On this particular day as I looked through the window he was on his own, walking slowly, looking only in one direction. Out of the corner of my eye I spotted the focus of his attention. There she was sitting under a tree, pretty as a picture – 'drop dead gorgeous; to die for' as the gossip columnists would say. She was young. Too young to be dating, you would say: a picture in black and white complemented by a red choker. She was groomed to perfection, not a hair out of place. It was no wonder that my so-called 'Cock-of-the-walk' stopped in his tracks. Slowly he moved towards her. Cautiously he took up his position a little distance from her. I wondered if they had met before. Had they had a row or was this just a chance meeting? I could see that he was staring at her – with desire I thought. Soon she started ogling him with the most erotic gestures. Cheeky hussy, I thought, at her age: she's letting herself in for trouble. I felt I should be getting on with my business but I could not tear myself away from the window – and anyway the pair hadn't spotted me.

Soon it started to rain; that drizzling, wetting rain. 'This is it,' I thought, 'either he will make his move now or he will go home'. But no – he just sat there oblivious of the rain, still staring at her. She was in the shelter of the tree of course and went on posing with that 'come hither' look.

Suddenly she decided to move off. Just then he made his move and went to follow her. To my amazement she turned round and spat at him and would have hit him across the face had he not been agile enough to get out of her way. I couldn't understand her reaction – she had appeared so keen on getting his attention and she had looked so well bred. I could see that her admirer was stunned. I was glad that he didn't know that I had witnessed his rejection. After all even a Tom Cat has his pride!!!

Jo Butler

The Italian Saga

Well it's all over now, that long awaited and much talked about holiday. It got off to a good start. My two daughters and I, flying into Rome airport arrived safely but minus our three cases. They had been left in Dublin but after much explaining, complaining and form filling, we got compensation of £100 per case. I was sorry we hadn't brought four cases. The first day was spent sightseeing – the Coliseum, the Trevi fountain, the Spanish steps and the Irish College. We spent the next day in the Vatican. We didn't see the pope but we saw the underground tombs of the dead popes. We queued for the Sistine chapel; no seats and I expected it to be bigger.

That evening we flew to Turin, settled into our hotel and came down to our evening meal. There, sitting across the room from us, was Biddie Murphy the priest's housekeeper from home. As well as being the housekeeper she practically runs the parish, 'Father Pat does everything', she says. I sometimes think he is a bit afraid of her. I kept my head down hoping she wouldn't see us, no such luck. Over she came and sat herself down at our table. She told us all about her trip. She had seen the famous shroud of Turin and now the next thing on her agenda was to hear mass in a Salesian chapel. She had a cousin who was a member of that order. 'She would' I could hear Mary say, in an audible whisper. She then told us all about Saint John Bosco, the founder of the order, about his missionary work, and his work with homeless boys. 'And of course you know he was born in Piedmont,' she said. 'Of course we do,' said Mary 'we have great devotion to him'.

Martina was told to find out where the nearest Salesian church was situated and that was when we ran into our first problem. Nobody in the hotel spoke English and Martina had very little Italian. So an English/Italian dictionary was found. Mary wrote down the word Salesian, the hotel receptionist looked it up, and with a big grin on his face he wrote down the address. Biddy was pleased and a taxi was arranged for the following morning. It arrived on time and Martina handed him the address. In hindsight I should have realized that something wasn't quite right. The taxi driver looked at the address and he looked again slowly at the paper in his hand. Then with a broad smile he opened the door for us. My only thought was that it must be a long journey. I hoped I would have enough money, he might not take Visa and Biddy would tell everyone at home about it. It was quite a short ride through the narrow streets; not many people around, except a few men on the street corner with body piercing and tattoos and wearing heavy chains.

The taxi driver stopped suddenly at the end of a long street and he pointed to the door in a narrow house. It didn't look like a church. But before I could voice my uneasiness Biddy was halfway across the road. She looked a strange sight in her raincoat and walking stick; she looked more like someone going to herd sheep on a winter's day in Donegal than a woman going to church on a scorching hot day in Italy. We followed her and soon were inside the dark building.

Biddy headed straight for the end that was lit up. As my eyes began to adjust to the dim light, I could see there were no chairs or pews only large couches, and the people sitting on them weren't saying prayers. I tried to grab Biddy, my only thought being to get her out of there fast. She knelt down at the first vacant couch, closed her eyes, took out her rosary beads and started to pray. 'There is a strange smell off that incense', she muttered as the unmistakable smell of cannabis wafted towards us.

'It's Italian', said Mary quick as a flash.

Just then the background music grew louder. A strange figure like a priest came out carrying a karaoke machine and a microphone. Two scantily clad girls accompanied him. He was wearing a toga and a garland of ivy leaves around his head. He looked more like Nero on a bad day than a priest. Biddy peered short-sightedly through her thick glasses.

'They are strange vestments', she said.

'Designer gear,' said the irrepressible Mary. Biddy closed her eyes and continued to pray.

'How am I going to get her out of here?' I thought quickly and decided to pretend to faint, then I would have to be carried out and we could all make our escape.

Before I could put my plan into action the music grew to a loud crescendo. I recognised the tune, '*He's got the whole world in his hands*'. Just then a screen unrolled down on the back wall; figures danced across it. This gave a whole new meaning to the line '*He's got you and me brother in his hands*'. The lights went up. Biddy looked at the fellow on the stage, just as he was dropping his toga. There he stood stark naked with the two girls clinging to his legs. With a bellow like a badly gored bull charging a matador, Biddy rushed up to him yelling, 'You blasphemous idolater, I'll rearrange you'. She made as if to strike him down when all hell broke loose, screaming and shouting. No one screams quite like the Italians. I was sure we were going to be murdered on the spot. Just then we heard the sound of a siren; the room filled with police. It was a raid by the vice squad. We were all handcuffed and taken to the nearest police station. Martina demanded an interpreter. The sergeant looked at Biddy in her long coat and acceded to our request. Luckily for us it was an Irish girl who came. Martina told her the whole story from the time we asked directions from our hotel receptionist. She promptly rang the hotel and the man told her he had looked up Salesian and couldn't find it. The nearest word to it was salacious and he thought the senoras were looking for some erotic entertainment.

When the sergeant heard the whole story he kissed Biddy on both cheeks. He said if there were more people like her it would make his job a lot easier. Biddy decided to picket the 'den of vice' as she called it, and when she got home she would write to the pope about it. The girls thought the whole episode was hilarious and couldn't wait to tell all their friends about it.

Every week when I collect the local paper I expect to see myself on the front page, with the headline: 'Irish Pensioner Arrested in Orgy by the Vice Squad.'

Maureen Connolly

The Big Job

I have got it made with the most prestigious job in Brussels. Who would ever have thought it – me, little Mickey Tom Patsy MacAvaddy, from the back of Rossinver mountain. But here I am: my own office, my own phone with a direct line to the Taoiseach, Bertie Ahern – I call him Bertie of course. I have another line to Hans, Hans Fischler that is. There's my name on the door and my title: Michael MacAvaddy, Administrator for Connaughht. Sometimes when Hans is in a jocular mood he calls me the Mickey for Connaught. When people speak of me in years to come, it will be with wonder and awe. My name will be up there with Daniel O'Connell and Brian Boru. You will wonder how all this came about, how I developed the master plan for Connaught.

It all started like this. My Auntie Maggie's cousin twice removed, is related to the EC commissioner. One day my mother asked her if the commissioner could find a job for me in Brussels. On the following Monday I was flying out from Dublin on the government jet. For the first six weeks I posted letters, took phone calls and made cups of coffee for hung-over ministers. One morning I accidentally read a memo intended for the commissioner. It was from Hans Fischler to say something would have to be done about the farmers of the north west of Ireland. He was at his wit's end: what with headege, area aid, suckler cow premium and all the other grants. It was all costing far too much. 'It will have to stop', he said.

'This is my big chance for fame and immortality', I said to myself. There and then I printed out my grand plan for Connaught and sent it off to Hans Fischler. This is a copy of the plan.

1. The province of Connaught, outside of the towns, to be turned into one large safari park with all kinds of wild animals: tigers, lions, giraffes, elephants, and monkeys. Rangers would be on horseback, wearing kilts and carrying spears to herd them.

2. Rows of two- and three-bedroom cottages to be built on the outskirts of every town with little factories of small cottage industries: spinning, weaving, kilt making to give employment to the ex-farmers and their families.

3. The demolition grant was to be paid to every farmer who demolished his house and relocated to the town houses. The amount of grant would be worked out in relation to the size of house, outhouses and hay barns.

4. Mud-walled cabins with thatched roofs and half-doors to be built in isolated places throughout the province as tourist attractions.

5. Some of the older farmers and their wives will be employed in those cabins during the tourist season. The men will be dressed in frieze breeches and *báinín gansies*, the women in red petticoats and shawls. As the tourist bus pulls up they will be seen feeding the pig at the cabin door and the chickens will be seen coming out from the kitchen. FAS wages will apply.

6. For the grade A tourist there will be special events organised: poteen making, leprechaun hunts with small children dressed as leprechauns. Wakes with singing, story telling with a plastic corpse provided, crossroads dancing and many other events to be worked out at a later date, will be the norm.

Well, there you have it! That is how I became the most important man in Brussels. Watch out, you people of Connaught, this plan will soon be up and running. And, if the money is right, I have some great plans for Donegal. For example we could cover it with ice with roaming polar bears, seals and penguins. But that's work for another day.

Maureen Connolly

The Goose

'I am going to invite your parents over for their Christmas dinner', said Mary. John and Mary had only been married for a few months and Mary was looking forward to showing off her new home and her culinary skills.

'We will keep one of the geese and fatten it,' she decided.

All went fine; the goose grew fatter. Mary had the Christmas cake and the pudding made and then disaster struck. One morning as John was making his way across the yard towards the byre, he noticed a trail of feathers leading from the fowl house, and when he looked in the goose was gone. The fox had come in the night. Mary was in despair. John tried to console her.

'Kill one of the hens', he said, 'they won't know the difference.' John had never seen her so angry.

'Your mother wouldn't know the difference between a hen and a goose!' She almost hit him.

'When you go to town to sell the potatoes on Big Market Saturday, you will go to the butchers and buy a goose,' Mary said. John wasn't too pleased at having to buy a goose. It would put a big hole in the money he would get for the potatoes, but because he didn't like seeing Mary so unhappy he agreed to get a goose.

Before the day dawned on the Saturday before Christmas, John set off for the market with a cart full of potatoes. Trade was brisk and early in the day he had all sold. He then went down to Leonard's in Holborn St. and stabled his horse. He was starting to get hungry and decided to go to Martin Heraghty's eating house on Bridge St. While he was there who should come in but his two cousins from Glencar. They were home on holidays from England and they had lots of stories to tell. So they all went back to Connolly's pub on the Line, where they spent a pleasant evening drinking and swapping stories. John forgot all about the goose.

It was getting dark when he set off on the journey home. As he was turning into Duck Street he was forcibly reminded of the goose, for there, crossing before him were three geese. Now if John had been sober he wouldn't think of stealing a goose, but he was very drunk. Without thinking of what he was going to do he jumped down from the cart, and threw the reins across the shaft. Leaving the horse standing unattended in the middle of the road, he made off in hot pursuit of the goose thinking he could catch her. The goose was having none of it. She turned, spread out her large wings, and ran at John with her long neck outstretched and took a bite from his leg. John turned and ran for the cart with the goose in hot pursuit. When the horse saw John running and the large bird chasing him, he gave a shake of his head and took off like the proverbial bat, with John trying in vain to catch up with him. The last John saw of his horse, he was galloping by the County Home gate with the cart hopping from side to side on the potholed road. John stood and looked back at the three large birds walking in single file across the road. As he watched them walk with their heads held high the awful truth dawned on him. These were not geese but swans and he had always heard it was unlucky to touch a swan.

'It must be true,' he said to himself. 'I have lost my horse and cart. How am I going to tell Mary?' Wearily he turned towards home.

An hour later as he was passing Drumcliff graveyard, he met two men going to play cards in a neighbour's house. He asked them if they had seen a horse and cart passing but no one had. They invited him to the house; someone there might have seen his horse. In the house four men were sitting at a table playing cards; an oil lamp hanging on the wall gave off a yellow light. A woman sat at a big open fire. He told them his story leaving out the bit about the swan. No one had seen his horse and cart but they promised if they heard anything they would send word to Leonard's pub in Grange. After a big mug of tea and two slices of home made bread, he was persuaded to play a few games of cards. Some hours later he realised the lateness of the hour and he started on the road for home again.

As he drew nearer his own lane his steps grew slower. He was very tired. He had walked twelve miles, and he didn't know how he was going to break the news to Mary about the horse running away on him. He turned in his own lane and saw there was light in every room and light streamed out from the open door. A crowd of men were standing outside talking to a strange priest.

'It must be the new curate,' he thought, 'I haven't met him'. He began to panic; something must have happened to Mary. He started to run in through the open door and through the crowd standing around in the kitchen, up to the room where the women were gathered saying the rosary around his bed. The bed had a new white bedspread and the blessed candle was burning on the table beside it. There was no sign of Mary.

'What's going on here, where is my wife?' he asked.

Then he noticed. Mary stood up at the back of the crowd. She took one look at John and fell down in a faint. By then the priest had come,

'Are you John Brady?' he said.

'I am.'

'Your wife thought you were killed when your horse came home without you. When she was a child, her grandfather went to the fair of Sligo and his horse came home without him. His body was found later on the road. He had fallen out of the cart. So when your horse came home on his own, she thought you were dead. All these people have come here for your wake.'

Mary had come round by this. She ran to her husband and kissed him. All John could say was, 'I forgot the goose'.

'I am glad you did, because I have so much food and drink and tobacco got in for your wake that I don't know what we'll do with it'.

'I know what we'll do: we'll have a party', said John and he took down his accordion, and such a night of singing and dancing and eating was never seen in the town land again.

The night of John Brady's wake was talked about for many a year in Gort Na Shí.

Maureen Connolly

ABOUT THE AUTHORS

BUTLER Gerry: Born in Cork city in the late twenties. Qualified as a veterinary surgeon and ran a practice in Co. Mayo for a number of years before joining the Department of Agriculture and Fisheries from which he has retired. His hobby is landscape painting and he is an ardent trout fisherman. He is a founder member of Sligo Active Retirement Association. Both he and his wife are members of SARA Writers' Group and live in Sligo.

BUTLER Jo: Born and reared in Co. Fermanagh. Lived in Mayo for thirteen years. She has been living in Sligo for more than thirty years. She has been a member of SARA Writers for five years. Previously published in *Evening Echoes, Autumn Leaves, Halcyon Days* and *Hearths and Homesteads*.

CONNOLLY Maureen: A native of Ballintrillick, Co. Sligo. She is a member of SARA and Benwiskin Writers and is interested in drama. She has contributed to *North West Extra, Random Memories* and *Comhain and the Flowering Oak*.

DEASY John: Grew up in Limerick. Retired from the bank, he and his wife came from Kilkenny to retire to Rosses Point, Co. Sligo. He has been published in *Evening Echoes, Autumn Leaves* and *Comhain and the Flowering Oak* and cited reading, community affairs and writing as his main interests.

DOYLE Bernie: Grew up in Mayo. Qualified as a teacher and taught for sixteen years in Kildare, Dublin and Mayo. Has lived in Sligo for twenty-five years. Trained as an editor, proofreader and translator. Her main interests are hill walking, reading and gardening. Contributed to *Evening Echoes*.

GALLOGLY Rena: Born in Manorhamilton, Co. Leitrim. Has lived in Co. Meath for some years. She returned to Sligo in 1975. She is now retired from secondary school teaching. This is her first publication with SARA Writers.

She has been published in *The Irish Times*, *The Leitrim Guardian* and other publications. Her main interests are reading and music.

GORMALLY Martin: A native of Tuam, Co. Galway, he has lived in Sligo for thirty-seven years. He has been writing on and off over a number of years and contributes regularly to a Nostalgia column in *The Sligo Weekender*. Published previously in *Evening Echoes*, *Autumn Leaves*, *Halcyon Days*, *Hearths and Homesteads*, *Dolly Mixtures* and *Comhain and the Flowering Oak*.

GILBRIDE Bernie: Born in Sligo and lived there all her life. She started writing in the summer of 2000 and has contributed to *Autumn Leaves*, *Halcyon Days*, *Hearths and Homesteads* and *Comhain and the Flowering Oak*. Her interests include painting, photography and history.

GUNNIGLE Brigid: Born in Kinlough, Co. Leitrim. Married and is living in Cashelgal, Co. Sligo since 1941. She joined SARA Writers in 1997. She was published in *Evening Echoes*, *Autumn Leaves*, *Halcyon Days*, *Hearths and Homesteads* and *Comhain and the Flowering Oak*. Her main interests are reading, writing and painting.

OATES Nora: A native of Grange, Co. Sligo, she lives at Teesan near Sligo town. She is a founder member of SARA Writers and has contributed to *Evening Echoes*, *Autumn Leaves*, *Halcyon Days*, *Hearths and Homesteads*.

O'CONNOR Mary: Born in Lixnaw district in Co. Kerry in the early thirties. In England met and married a Sligo man and came to live in Sligo in 1964. She joined SARA Writers in 1999. She has contributed to *Autumn Leaves*, *Halcyon Days*, *Hearths and Homesteads* and *Comhain and the Flowering Oak*. She loves knitting, reading, meeting people, dancing, playing cards and writing.

O'FLYNN Cèline: A native of Dungarvan, Co. Waterford. Moved to New York after college days in UCD and NCAD. Came with husband and family to Sligo in 1965. Retired from NWHB in 2004 and joined SARA Writers. Her hobbies are all the Arts from gardening to painting.